Sentimental Journey

A Christmas at Ruby's Place

Holly Schindler

Sentimental Journey

A Christmas at Ruby's Place

Published by InToto Books

Copyright © 2019 by Holly Schindler

Cover design by Holly Schindler

Cover images by Mira_Bavutti and LiliGraphie, courtesy of Shutterstock

Fonts: Sheila by Laura Worthington, Grandma by Hannes von Döhren, and Garamond by Robert Slimbach, courtesy of Adobe Fonts

Welcome

to

Ruby's

...where Christmas wishes come true.

1.

If you ask, Angela will tell you about the Christmas Eve of 1979.

It is the always story she relies on, the one she brings out when people want to talk to her about visiting Ruby's Place in times gone by. She was fourteen that year. Trying to figure out how to walk that awkward edge between girlhood and womanhood.

And it was the last year she'd come with her Aunt Elizabeth, the movie star of a woman she'd once hoped to be like someday—the designer dresses, the updos, the husky Lauren Bacall-style voice.

If you ask, Angela will tell you all about the winter white cashmere overcoat Elizabeth wore that year. She will also tell you about her own heels and silk stockings. Her silver clutch. The first time she'd worn any of it in public. And how, to her amazement, none of it seemed like a costume.

She will tell you about Elizabeth's banter with her best friend, her Ruby, the owner of the establishment that bore her own name: Ruby's Place, the sign always aglow in warm red neon. She'll be sure to mention the way Ruby called Elizabeth "kid," always with such affection. She will tell you Elizabeth's health was starting to fail, but she was ignoring it.

They all were. We're built to turn a blind eye to incoming hardships.

Angela will tell you about Scott Drummond, too. How they were schoolmates. How Scott always spent his own Christmas Eves at Ruby's Place with his dad, Walter—Vice President of the Bank of Sullivan, champion of women's businesses at a time when most grumbled and sneered at the idea. She will laugh about the way her heels and her updo and her makeup had made Scott squirm at the table with his father that year, 1979. But then, doesn't it always make boys that age uncomfortable? she might ask you. They can't seem to figure out if you look less or more like yourself. Or if they should admit that they like it.

She will describe it all—the snow, the night, the smell of pine, the embarrassment of not being able to order a glass of wine, and really still wanting a plate of marshmallows even though it was kid stuff. She will describe the stars and the icy smell in the air, the piano notes and the carols. She will tell you about the grand loveliness of it all.

She will say, quite simply, that she has often thought how wonderful it would be if there was a door somewhere in our memories. One that you could open and walk through. A place where you could not just recall but feel all of it again. Like watching a movie and living it wrapped up into one.

She would tell you that some people would probably choose never to return to the trials and uncertainties of real life. Just keep going back through the door of memories to relive old times. Even if it meant giving up on finding the joys of today.

She will sigh and push her flyaway gray strands from her face. And she will ask you if she can pour you another drink.

Scott, though, would tell you her story is not quite true.

Not that Angela is a liar, Scott would likely insist—and quickly. He would tell you that he simply knows it's not the last time she visited Ruby's Place.

Was it ten years later? Maybe? Late '80s, he would say. Rough guess. It seems to him that the infamous sweethearts' graffiti, the message that once had most of the town chattering, had already been carved into the sidewalk just outside the entrance—*Rob & Geena 4Ever 1987*. Helps to narrow down the date a bit.

Scott was seated in the back corner, sharing a quiet drink with a woman. He has been married so long, the girls who came before his wife are blurry, their edges smearing into each other. He does not remember her name, but he remembers Angela.

She came in wearing jeans. A long leather coat. Ankle boots.

She sat at the bar. She smiled at Ruby. They exchanged a few words.

Scott brought his date's empty glass to the bar for a refill. A fuzzy navel, which he found embarrassing to order.

Angela was wearing a ring then. He'd noticed it right off. He had to, the way she kept turning it around her finger, staring at the stone with a kind of sad, faraway look.

The thing about engagement rings, you can see all your dreams in them. That was what one of his girlfriends had said. But Angela looked like someone who was staring into something broken. Something unrescuable.

He hated it. But didn't know how to make her feel better—or if it was even his place.

He wanted to tell her he remembered her. That long white dress she'd worn years earlier. The fancy purse and her high heels, which had made her a good five inches taller than him. He wanted to tell her he remembered how she had sparkled so much it had almost frightened him. No—not just sparkle. She was like a spotlight that forced you to turn your head.

"How's Walter?" Angela'd asked.

"You remember my dad," Scott had responded, happily surprised.

"Scotch neats," she muttered. "Double-breasted suits. Sideburns. Lover of Lawrence Welk." She paused to roll her eyes. "And you," she finished, knocking back her whiskey shot. "Lover of you," she murmured, thunking her glass back down.

"Angela remembers *everybody*," Ruby announced, joining the conversation. "Go on. Try her."

"The piano player," Scott tried. "The one—"

"With the sequin jacket? Evie. Martini. Three olives. Former cruise ship entertainer."

"And the guy—the one—with the electronics shop…"

"…and the chip on his shoulder?" Angela finished. "Roy. Roy Weber. His brother-in-law worked for him. Hamm's Beer. Smoked Pall Malls. Really could get worked up about the sight of a woman in pants, though."

"You remember all of it?" Scott asked, impressed.

Angela shrugged. "People feel like they can talk in front of a little kid. They don't think they listen. I was here a lot. With—" Her voice trailed before she could say it: *Aunt Elizabeth.*

"People don't think kids understand," Ruby corrected.

"Angela would," Scott said softly, with not a hint of sarcasm. She was one of those naturally smart people, he'd always thought. Not a bookish sort. She'd done well in school, it seemed to him, but she wasn't a grade chaser. She was smart enough to know that it wasn't everything; it didn't make one person better than another; a GPA wasn't an identity.

And she was also smart enough to know what a person's identity really was. You felt sized up every single time she looked at you. Not in a harsh way, or even a permanent one. She could smell lies. And see your angle.

Scott remembered the way Angela could squint at you, grunt a "Huh." And how the tone of the *huh* proclaimed whether or not you were being straight with her.

She always knew.

And now?

Scott wanted her to look at him again. Wanted her to size him up, tell him with one look that he should be ashamed of himself for stringing Ms. Fuzzy Navel along.

But she was too far away to reach that evening, it seemed. Scott left her alone; she finished a second drink and Scott watched her leave while the woman at his table told him a story he was only halfway listening to.

That, according to Scott Drummond, was the last time Angela visited Ruby's Place.

* * *

And then—two years ago, right in time for Christmas—she returned.

Not for Ruby's Place, though. Nobody returned to town to go to Ruby's. Not by then. Ruby's Place had been closed for years.

But that didn't mean the old business was entirely dead, either. Or so Angela was about to find out.

The group who gathered in the evenings in the darkness of Ruby's Place knew it. "The regulars," they all called themselves.

They were usually a lively bunch. *Lively.* So many punch-lines and double-meanings to describe them. Ghosts. That was also a word. The easiest one. Not that any of the regulars liked it. The term made them sound two-dimensional. Cartoonish.

And they were anything but.

The chatter and voices and drinking ceased completely the night Angela returned, all of them tilting their heads and listening to the happy hum that hit the air the minute she crossed the city limit.

Angela greeted Officer Vargas as he patrolled the town square. She stood on the edge of the carved-up section of sidewalk, staring at the names that had long ago been written into wet cement: *Rob & Geena 4Ever.* Wondering what had happened to those kids.

The same way she sometimes wondered what had happened to her own youth.

She pressed her face closer to the foggy, dirty plate glass of Ruby's Place, thinking of everything that had brought her back home—the broken engagement, the apartment with lackluster furniture, the half-paid-for used car. She had acquired so little. In the season of the year that was all about acquisitions (gifts and feasts and abundance, *more, more, more*), everything about her felt especially empty: her pockets, her heart.

The future, it seemed, had played a trick on her. As far as gifts went, the future had turned out to be a fancy box with nothing inside.

It made her heart ache, staring through the old front window of Ruby's Place. By then, the glass was marked with a few cracks and a "For Sale or Lease" sign. All she could do was remember the way it had been. Remember the way she'd felt inside. How she had once assumed the world would be when she was finally fully grown—how she'd believed it would welcome her.

The snow was falling. She was cold.

And she could not just stand there forever, staring into the building, her solemn face reflecting back at her in the plate-glass window.

She started to turn away.

A cardinal flapped his wings, swooping toward her and

knocking her brown knit hat off her head—the ugly one she loved because her sister had made it.

She had only just picked it up when a man walking down the sidewalk crashed into her, slamming her shoulder and the side of her head against the door of Ruby's. So hard, her shoulder exploded in pain and she saw silver sparks of light. So hard, the rusty padlock fell and the entrance squeaked open.

Angela was inside the long-closed Ruby's Place.

Don't make the mistake of discounting this as sheer happenstance. Or luck.

Because the regulars knew that Angela had memorized all their stories. The same tales she had recited to Scott while sitting at the bar some thirty years earlier. So wouldn't it also be possible that they sent one of their own out onto the sidewalk to stop her from leaving, push her into the building?

Couldn't they have all been waiting—*with bated breath,* that would have been the saying, though it no longer applied to this crew—to find out what she would see once she was back inside the building?

Would she still be able to recall their stories?

For so long they had been wishing, unseen, for the right person to come along. Someone who would remember what the old place had been. Someone who had truly seen it. Someone who would restore it rather than reinvent it, someone who would never dare knock it down or gut it, turn it into something else.

Angela rubbed the side of her head, grumbling under her

breath. And she began to weave between the regulars, trying not to bump into anyone.

She saw them. Because she *did* remember. She still knew every single story that had lived inside Ruby's Place. Knew them all so well, in fact, that when she stumbled inside, the memories engulfed her all over again. Revelers were toasting. Music was playing. A scene ripped straight out of the past.

Only, it was so real, it didn't feel like memories. Not to Angela. She assumed some investor had come along and reopened the place. *Why haven't they taken down the For Sale sign yet?* she wondered. Maybe it didn't matter. The place was already packed. Surely, she thought, the people inside had to be current Sullivan residents. Obviously, they'd learned to ignore the For Sale sign.

As she settled onto a barstool, the regulars sent Elizabeth to sit beside her. To show Angela they were not so current at all.

You know us. You listened. You lived our stories, with each and every retelling.

With her long-lost Elizabeth beside her at the bar, it slowly started to sink in that Angela recognized all of them. Every single one of the regulars. Including Ruby, whom she realized was tending bar. Serving up her old favorites. Marshmallows and cocoa.

"To the ghosts of Christmases past!" Walter Drummond bellowed, relying on the joke that made most in the room groan.

Angela's eyes swelled as she realized what it all meant.

Elizabeth and Ruby shared a knowing look.

"You called it, kid," Ruby told Elizabeth.

They toasted Angela's return—and, they knew, what would soon be the long-awaited return of Ruby's Place.

2.

December 24, 2019
~Our Journey Begins~

Oh, am I glad I caught you. Got the car all packed, I see. Front door locks checked and double-checked. Mail put on hold. Presents wrapped and in the trunk. Kids all bundled in the backseat. Got your hot chocolate in a thermos and a tin of sugar cookies to pass around. The family dog is in his new traveling sweater, and the radio's tuned to a station playing classic carols.

You're on your way. Long-distance family is waiting for you at the end of a stretch of highway two states over.

But listen, before you go, I have to let you know: you should stop at Ruby's Place.

It's last-minute, but I can still make reservations for you. They're very important—if you want to have the full experience.

You've already heard of it? Doesn't surprise me. Great little place out there in Sullivan, Missouri. Besides, after so much time all cramped up in the car, you'll want to get off the highway. Stretch your legs. Sullivan's the perfect place to do just that this time of year.

But *Ruby's*. On the town square. Look, you didn't hear this from me, but something strange is happening in there.

Nothing bad, of course. Nothing dark and sinister. It's not a *dangerous* place.

Mysterious, you say? Yeah. That's a good word.

For the last couple of years, right in time for Christmas, things start to get even more puzzling. And *this* year, why, secrets have been spilling out all over town.

You should know—what's that? Sounds good, you say? Well, yes, I was already heading out that way myself. Still room in the car? Let me get my coat. And give me a minute to call Ruby's, add you to my own reservation.

Only makes sense for us all to head out there together. I do know the way by heart.

I can tell you all about Ruby's on the drive to Sullivan. It really is quite the story.

3.

~Sullivan~

It's best that you know, before you arrive, that Sullivan is a small Midwestern town built on memories.

Perhaps you already think that's true of most small towns. After all, they rarely have much to boast about: no giant industrial complexes or tourist attractions or even statewide championship sports teams (underdog tales are always prized because they are, in fact, quite rare). Small Midwestern towns are not often the places people choose to land. They are, instead, places where people are drop-kicked by marriage or proximity to a bigger city; they're places where people are born and simply remain.

What small towns have to set them apart are their stories. Memories. Told and retold by individuals regarded fondly as "old timers" holding court outside of flea markets or hardware stores or post offices. Handed down like heirlooms or hung out proudly like a flag on the Fourth of July.

Officer Vargas would agree to as much. Foot patrol means he has traveled the Sullivan square daily for the last twenty years, like a toy train rolling around a track. He has heard the same tales—about the old courthouse fire or the time Bonnie and Clyde drove through or the Black Christmas ice storm of '85—enough times to anticipate every detail, regardless of the teller. He knows them like he knows the streets he travels. At this point, he can recognize the people of Sullivan by their voices, the same way he knows that the *woosh* of an entrance has its own pitch, and can tell, without looking, if the door that has just been flung open belongs to the It Ain't Over Yet flea market or The Page Turner bookstore.

His own stories, his own yesterdays, also swirl around Officer Vargas as he travels the square, pausing as his toes hit the edge of an old stretch of sidewalk: *Rob & Geena 4Ever 1987*, carved more than thirty years ago, when the cement was still fresh. The date gets him every time—he graduated with the two high school sweethearts, which makes him feel like something of an artifact.

In some ways, Officer Vargas feels that Rob and Geena's story belongs to him, too. They're all tangled up together—and not just because of high school. He grew up admiring Geena's father and the legend of her grandfather, both police officers. Inheriting a parent's profession is also often the way of small towns, isn't it? Children of police officers and teachers and firemen want to grow up to wear the same titles their parents held—like the two Barister men. Officer Vargas is somewhat unusual because he is the first generation in his own family to wear a shield. As a young man, though, he'd looked up to Geena's dad with as much intensity as any son.

These days, when he sees Geena's name in the sidewalk, he recalls how, as a little boy still with his fruit punch mustache, he had learned that Charlie Barister, Geena's grandfather, had died in the line of duty. Back then, the tragedy had seemed so honorable to him. Heroic, even. Last year, it seemed to him that Officer Tom Barister, Geena's father, had the right idea, dying an old man with a grown daughter.

But rarely are Officer Vargas's thoughts only about himself, while patrolling. He is constantly on the lookout for new conversations he can get into or start up, often pulling new passersby into lively chats that end with smiles and *see you soons*.

Why's that, you might ask? It's not about passing the time. Think about it. Don't we all believe the quaint small town is somehow safer? But where did that idea come from? Isn't it that we believe it is harder to rob or hurt or inflict damage on people we know? If a person is not real to us, it is easier to take from them— the crime does not seem truly as horrendous. And because it is easier to know most people in town when the population is so small, why, then, a small town must be a safe place to live. Isn't that it?

Officer Vargas thinks so. He purposefully keeps the people of Sullivan talking to one another—directing them toward each other with questions: "Aren't you looking for a job?" he often asks. Or "Didn't you say your mom was trying to sell her car?" Or "Your son's getting ready to apply for college, isn't he?" And then he points out the store with a job to fill, or the guys looking to buy a car, or the parent who has navigated the application process. He deals in smiles and handshakes—pieces of candy for the kids.

Now that Ruby's Place is successful enough to be causing something of a renewal on the town square, bringing more visitors off the highway, sparking enough interest that "Grand Opening" signs have recently appeared in the windows of an ice cream parlor and a hair salon, it seems more important than ever to Officer Vargas that he make introductions. He acquaints all the new faces with Scott Drummond, general manager of the Bank of Sullivan (promoted up from the small business loans department), who steps from his office every single day for a noontime walk. Tina at the It Ain't Over Yet. Angela, constantly busy with Ruby's Place. Rob, the same Rob of sidewalk fame, who now owns Sullivan's only bookstore.

In a way, Officer Vargas is something of an adult crossing guard. Directing traffic. Or maybe it's more like a walking chamber of commerce. Telling newcomers how Angela bought Ruby's two years ago, after it seemed that there was no one left on the planet with enough capital or patience to repair the empty, aging building. "Yes," he proclaims, "we'd all just about thought that building's time had come and gone. Hard to believe only a handful of years ago, this square saw so little traffic, nobody around here even thought to repaint the faded lines of the parking spots."

He knows it probably seems, to the visitors, like empty chatter from an officer with nothing much to do. But it's a small price to pay for making sure the newest faces view Sullivan as a living creature and not backdrop. It's a small price to pay to keep the people of Sullivan safe.

He does not mind it when, on days like today, snowflakes circle through the air. Somehow, in Sullivan, the snow swirls rather than dumps, like the pieces in a snow globe. It collects softly and strategically—on window ledges or door wreaths. The alleyway behind the stores. Leaving behind a scene worthy of a post card.

He has noticed recently that snow does not seem to stick on the aluminum stars that hang from light poles—those old Christmas decorations dug up by City Council this year. Hard to date them, but most agree they look like something out of the 1950s. There's something chrome bumper or pointed tailfin about them.

Sometimes, as he walks, the square will grow quiet. Without the sounds of shoppers' chatter or the laughter of children that seems to him to mimic the peaceful coo of doves, Officer Vargas's mind will wander. Sometimes, a great deal. In the peace of a small town, any member of the police force often has time enough to become something of an amateur philosopher.

And Officer Vargas's own personal philosophical theory is this: Memory is a junk drawer.

Just as he has reached his own hands into the junk drawer in his kitchen and wondered what made him hang on to such odds and ends, he has often marveled at the tales that he has heard and memorized and retold—why some seemingly random, unimportant memories have stayed with the storytellers, while other details have grown faded and hard to recall.

In a town as small as Sullivan, he has also decided, the wads and scraps and odds and ends of *everyone's* memories are all jumbled together. He and Rob and Geena aren't the only people in Sullivan all twisted up in one another. How many times had he been listening to someone tell a story only to watch them frown and rub their forehead, struggling to come up with a detail they can't quite put their finger on? And how many times had someone else piped up, filling in the blank?

Yes, what one person accidentally loses hold of, another has inevitably kept in their own memory junk drawer—it only takes a little sifting through the strange bits and pieces, and eureka! There it is, the tidbit someone else had forgotten. The missing little slice that makes another's story complete.

This junk-drawer theory of Officer Vargas's is actually far more spot-on that he—or anyone else living in Sullivan—could have ever guessed.

At least, they would not have guessed it before their stories took an unexpected turn, during this year's Thanksgiving weekend.

4.

~*November 29, 2019*~

Angela loaded the boxes on her two-wheeler in the back of Ruby's Place. Ancient, wooden boxes. Fruit crates, with lovely (if faded or crumbling) lithographed company logos on each end: Del Monte, Jewel Pears.

"Not sure what you can do with this stuff," Angela admitted, her cell phone emitting a pleasant warmth against her cheek. Last year, she had been so involved in getting Ruby's Place open again—getting the mold off the old furniture, redecorating, repairing, reinstalling—that these boxes filled with smaller tidbits had largely gone untouched.

"Just bring it over," insisted Toby, the current director of the Sullivan History Museum.

"It's so last-minute," she apologized. "And I didn't have time to go through and organize anything. Just a mishmash of stuff I found in the storage room."

"Mishmashes are my specialty. I've been hoping you'd send something for our upcoming exhibit. 'Uncovered, Untold, and Unbelievable: The Secrets of Sullivan.' I figured, as old as Ruby's Place is, it had to be full of juicy stuff."

* * *

The two-wheeler thunked and squawked and squeaked as Angela dragged it through the front door. It was a bit unsteady, with one wheel tilted at a precarious angle.

She waved back to Officer Vargas and said hello to two women who had emerged from the diner carrying disposable coffee cups. No time to stop and talk today. She had an errand, one she didn't need help with. Her tight grin and her hasty wave ensured them all of that.

Angela had barely made it five feet down the sidewalk when both wheels caught on a sidewalk square nearly three inches higher than the last. A mere three inches—and yet Angela found herself heaving with both hands, as though she were having to hoist the two-wheeler up a front step, or maybe even one of those Ozarks Mountains that populated the state. She tightened her grip, smashed her lips together, and grunted.

The wooden crates teetered. "No—no," Angela pleaded, attempting to right the two-wheeler and steady her load.

But the boxes tumbled, anyway. Items rolled in all directions, sending Angela scrambling to gather it all up.

She snatched the stray papers first—old photographs, newspaper clippings. It wasn't easy, considering so much of it had yellowed over the years and wound up blending in with the last of the scattered November oak leaves.

Her mind remained so focused on the bits and pieces that skittered with the tiniest trickle of wind that she did not notice the antique bottle that had rolled from the box and down toward the alley, coming to rest softly in a patch of unmelted snow.

Nor did she notice the cardinal who swooped down to scoop an envelope up into his beak before taking off again.

5.

December 24, 2019

~Our Journey~

It's good to be on the road, isn't it? There's just something about seeing your hometown's city limits sign in the rearview mirror. Kind of gives you that excited little squirm in your belly.

What's that? Still not sure what kind of place Ruby's is, exactly? Bar is a word that's sometimes used. You know I use it plenty myself. Supper club might be a better term, though it's grown so old-fashioned. I wonder if people even remember those anymore. It's the term Ruby herself liked to use, though, back when she opened up in '55. The sort of classy place that once had people arriving in silk stockings and pockets squares, fresh haircuts and their good perfume. Children were always welcome, too. You've heard that much. Probably why calling it a bar seemed strange to you. Ruby's serves alcoholic eggnog, but the holiday special was always her from-scratch hot cocoa and homemade toasted marshmallows. Not exactly the kind of dark place that has ever catered to heart-heavy guys looking to forget their troubles for a while.

Listen, back when Ruby owned the place, being in that building on the holidays was itself a kind of gift.

Ah, but you grow up, and you think you need to shed all those things that were important when you were a kid. That's part of it, right? You grow up? You move on?

Everybody in Sullivan did just that, it seemed. Little by little. Ruby's was seen as old-fashioned. Heck, maybe it was even already a little old-fashioned when it opened. Coming to the end of the Big Band era. Still, business was down for a while before she passed. And then—the family couldn't make a decent run of it. Closed it down.

Funny thing about moving on, though. You get to a certain point and you wind up looking behind you, realizing for the first time how great something actually was. You start to hunger for it—for something as simple as the taste of homemade marshmallows. You get hungry for the old feelings, too. The feelings you had about yourself or about the world around you that had once accompanied those treats.

No wonder Angela wound up buying the place, right? Who wouldn't want to get closer to that feeling, make it yours permanently?

When we get there, you'll see it just like it always was, back in those early supper club days. Same fixtures, same furniture. Angela's brought it all back to life. Just the way Ruby had it.

Yes, yes, same recipes. Same homemade marshmallows.

Your kids will love them. Trust me.

Look, here's where I get to it. Can't put it off any longer. The other side of Ruby's Place. It's at the root of the mysterious air surrounding it. I know you'll have a hard time believing this. You might even think I'm making it up. But I swear to you, it is one-hundred-percent true:

After Angela turns the "Closed" sign to face the street, the building has a second happy hour. Every night. Ruby herself appears, nodding a hello to Angela. Yes, Ruby. The same Ruby who had owned the place back when Angela was a kid. The same Ruby who had decades ago been a name on the obituary page in *The Sullivan Morning Tribune*. She appears to tend bar. Pours drink after drink—a French 75, a sidecar, a scotch neat—and each time she places a full glass on the bar, a new face emerges to go with it. Whatever their drink was in life, that's what makes them appear now.

See what I mean? I knew you'd have a hard time believing me.

But it's true. At Ruby's Place, during the after-closing happy hour, the term "spirits" refers to far more than just the bottles of top-shelf liquor behind the antique oak bar.

6.

~November 29, 2019~

Back to that old bottle. The one that had rolled from Angela's fruit crate into the little patch of snow at the edge of the alley.

That old alley has had quite the history. Plenty of secrets have lived back there—just the kind of secrets that Toby had been looking to display in his exhibit at the history museum. But that afternoon, the alley was behaving quite innocently, acting as nothing else but a little girl's playground.

Banished from her mother's beauty salon, Maddie Howard had been using that alley to practice jumping rope. Her chanted songs kept her from hearing the old bottle rattle and roll down the hill. But when she paused to untangle her feet, she saw it gleaming in the late afternoon sunlight.

She left her rope in a coil on the alley pavement and raced to scoop it up. She turned it over in her hands, the light brown liquid sloshing slightly toward the top of the bottle.

She squinted at the label: "Maxwell's Special Blend." It had a prize, she thought. Or some kind of branch. Sometimes, Maddie used Red Vines as straws for her soda when her mom took her to the movies. So she really thought little of finding something floating inside. She shrugged and attempted to twist the lid. But all she managed to do was slide her fist around the glass lip. "Huh," she said, realizing the bottle had a cork. "Funny soda," she grumbled, freeing the cork with a *pop*.

She sniffed, wondering if it would smell like Dr. Pepper, her absolute favorite.

But it didn't—it smelled awful. Like nail polish remover, or maybe gasoline.

So she replaced the cork and tossed it. She meant for it to land in the dumpster. But her aim was bad, and it landed in a small snow pile nearby.

Not that it mattered to Maddie.

She had never been past the front door of Ruby's Place— not yet. She had pestered her mother until finally, last spring, she had relented. "Next Christmas," she'd promised, suspecting that Maddie would forget, let go of her obsession with the old place. Maddie hadn't. She had her Christmas Eve dress picked out. It was already hanging on her closet door.

But even with all that interest, Maddie did not know the full story of Ruby's Place. Not the tale about the second happy hour and all the regulars that reappeared. She did not know that spirits materialized when the right cocktail was mixed. So she never could have suspected that opening the bottle that had been hidden inside Ruby's for nearly a century could have unleashed anything but the bitter smell of the whiskey inside.

But not too far away, snow crunched beneath Maxwell Ross's feet as he made his way closer to the town square.

The spirit of Maxwell Ross had been resurrected with the opening of that bottle.

And Maxwell Ross had a score to settle with Sullivan.

7.

~*November 29, 2019*~

High above it all, the cardinal—and letter thief—perched on an ancient phone line, a yellowed envelope still clamped in his beak. The same envelope that had fallen from Angela's turned-over fruit crate. The same one he had snatched up and carried off, as an insurance policy of sorts.

He had watched it all—the bottle, Maddie, Maxwell.

No one else had, though. He needed to draw everyone's attention to the situation that was about to unfold in Sullivan.

Quickly. Before it was too late.

He hopped a few steps, eyeing the square.

Kurt was coming, lugging his bulging bag full of holiday mail.

It was almost too perfect.

He flapped his wings, swooping straight into Kurt's face.

Kurt yelped, throwing his arms up to protect himself. He did not see the cardinal drop the yellowed envelope straight into his mail pouch—cashing in his insurance policy.

The cardinal returned to the phone line. All he needed now was for Kurt to deliver that letter to the address on the front: Ruby's Place.

8.

December 24, 2019

~Our Journey~

You're probably wondering why I thought it was so important for you to spend Christmas Eve at Ruby's Place. Why I came running out to your car, flagging you down before you could take off. Talking you into this alternate route. A detour.

I mean, Christmas is for spending time with loved ones. Your *own* loved ones. Right? You're a stranger to Sullivan. Officer Vargas doesn't know your name. You've never seen this place.

We've been on the road long enough that you're wondering why you agreed to this. You're wondering why you're driving farther away from your family, the warm hearth and the open arms waiting for you…For what? To sit in some old bar? Drink hot cocoa (as though you can't get that drink anywhere else)? To visit some sort of tourist trap with a spooky rumor attached to it—like some of those old Victorian hotels that invite you (or maybe it's dare you) to stay overnight with the ghosts that inhabit the building?

That's not it at all.

Look, on Christmas Eve, the regulars I told you about—the spirits that show up for a second happy hour—don't wait for the bar to close down. They come out during regular business hours to mingle with today's revelers.

Why, you ask?

It's all so simple, really. You have somebody. I know you do. A person you lost. Someone who is still—years, maybe even decades later—an empty seat at the dinner table. The relative or the love or the friend who has come and gone. The person who is no longer in your life, the one you had to let go of. The missing piece of your heart, the pictures in an album, the burning memorial candle. Don't we all have someone we remember with such tender fondness our heart strings begin to vibrate like a guitar at the mere thought of them?

Perhaps the cruelest part of grief is the realization of how much was left unsaid. How much it would mean to us to see that person just once more. If for no other reason than to play them our silly heart-string song. To tell them how strong our love remains. Even now. How much they have been missed. What an important part they played in our lives.

Perhaps, if you were to meet this person one more time, you might like to tell them you are sorry. Maybe, as much as you are filled with fondness, you are also weighed down by some indiscretion you were never fully allowed to explain.

Or, perhaps you long to do nothing but sweep that person into your arms and hold them close. Smell their hair. Feel their lips on your cheek.

On Christmas Eve, Ruby's is just such a place where memories can literally sit beside you. Where meetings with the dearly departed are far more than fantasy. One more time with a long-lost loved one. Wouldn't that be the best Christmas present of all?

That happens. On Christmas Eve. Only one night out of the year.

Why do you think I told you we needed reservations? Because the regulars want to make sure your special someone will be there. Sometimes, Angela has to help them out with that. As bartender, she can coax stories out of those who visit the bar. And she can pass that information on. But don't worry—they already knew who your own loved one is. All they had to do was hear your name.

Don't look at me that way. It's the truth. Just wait. You'll find out when we get there.

Me? It's not important how I know this. How many times I've been in Ruby's myself. What I might or might not have seen last year. I'm telling you all this so you can get ready. Fully experience it for yourself.

All of the regulars? No—you probably won't see every last one of them. Most don't. In fact, I don't think a single person in Ruby's saw the full picture of the place last Christmas Eve. It's just that everything else fades away once people see him. Or her. Whoever it is that's been gone for so long. Might very well happen that way with you, too. Everything else may very well pale in comparison to the missing piece of your own heart. The one you can draw from memory.

Forget the city limits sign in the rearview. Admit it. The excitement of leaving town is *nothing* like the idea that all this time, we've been driving closer and closer to your own loved one.

In the meantime, where was I with our story?

Ah, yes. The mail bag.

9.

~*November 29, 2019*~

The town of Sullivan did not exactly fancy Kurt the keeper of secrets.

Nobody put their secrets in the mail, after all. Secrets had disappeared from mail trucks and carrier bags. They'd *been* disappearing for ages—little by little, ever since the first phone lines cut through Sullivan's skies. These days, Kurt was most often the deliverer of late notices and junk mail. Come November, his back ached beneath the weight of catalogs. In a couple of weeks, it would be cardboard boxes. Gifts. Online orders. Tins of homemade cookies from great aunts and grandmothers.

But not secrets.

That day—Friday, the day after Thanksgiving—was proving to be a rare exception.

It had to be, judging by the yellowed envelope he glanced down to find sticking out of his satchel.

"What in the world," he muttered, pulling it out to examine the old-fashioned, swirling, right-leaning cursive handwriting. He squinted to read the faded postmark: 1955.

"Wow," he breathed. "How did I miss this one?"

Obviously, he thought, he'd been tasked with delivering a letter lost to some back corner of the post office sorting facility.

He'd heard of instances like that from other carriers. But never, not once in all his thirty years as an employee of the USPS, had he ever known it to happen right there in Sullivan, Missouri—let alone on his own route.

Until now, he told himself.

"Hey!" a high-pitched voice cut into his thoughts.

Kurt jumped, startled enough to loosen his grip on the envelope. An early winter gust tugged it from his fingertips and sent it tumbling down the sidewalk.

He gasped and began to run. His uniform was fitting tighter these days than he liked to admit, though, and the weight of his sack was bothering him more this year than it ever had.

A young girl raced ahead of him, her long brown pigtail bouncing in a kind of syncopated rhythm with her feet. She snapped the letter up with ease. Like outrunning the wind was nothing at all.

She brought it back to Kurt, smiling as though she had just broken the world record for letter retrieval. As she offered the envelope, Kurt noticed that her glittery pink nail polish had chipped all the way down to little more than jagged dots in the center of each nail. Her canvas sneakers were covered in hearts she had apparently cut from strips of duct tape. Her jeans had holes in the knees.

Maddie Howard.

"Your mother kick you out of the beauty salon again?" he asked, fighting to catch his breath. "Bet you've been kicked out a thousand times. And since that salon hasn't even been open six months, that's gotta be a record." Again with the heaving of his chest. This was going to be a long delivery season if he was going to keep getting so easily winded. It wasn't nearly as cold as it would be once January rolled around—by then, Kurt would be wearing two ski masks and stuffing his gloves with hand warmers. Already, though, the chill in the air was making his lungs burn. "What'd she evict you for this time? You offer to cut bangs again?"

Maddie frowned. "I'd be fantastic at cutting bangs," she insisted. "If someone would just give me a shot. And for your information, I was only mixing a new shade of red dye that would have looked beautiful on Mrs. Silva."

"Good to know," Kurt said, scooting to the side.

"Speaking of knowing," Maddie said, hopping back into his path again. "I bet you know *all* the good stuff."

"How's that?"

She pointed at the envelope now securely in Kurt's grip. "Who's Ruby?"

Kurt stiffened. "None of your business."

"Is it that Ruby?" She pointed toward the red neon Ruby's Place sign.

Kurt frowned. "I wouldn't know," he lied.

Maddie cocked her head to give him a doubtful, crooked glare. "Mom promised to take me to Ruby's Place this year. On Christmas Eve."

"Did she?"

"People say weird stuff happens in that place."

"If cocoa and marshmallows are strange."

"That's kind of funny stuff to have in a bar, don't you think?" Maddie scrunched her face.

"Ruby's always served some great food, which is why kids have been allowed. I—what do you know about bars, anyway?"

"Look. I've been around. I've lived a very full nine and three quarters years."

"Have you."

"And I've heard people talk. *Straaaaaaange* events," she repeated, in a voice better suited, Kurt thought, for Halloween than for Christmas.

She was right, though. Kurt had heard plenty of stories told by the faces on his regular route. Maybe his mail bag wasn't filled with a ton of secrets, but the people of Sullivan liked to talk. With Kurt, they could really let it fly. They didn't have to worry about either impressing or offending him. He was required to come again the next day, just the same.

Most of the tales about Ruby's Place had been told shortly after the holidays last year. But for the past week or so, they'd been popping up again. Always told in softer, almost faraway tones. Something like, "We lost my dad years ago, but for some reason, he felt so close when I went in. You know, I could almost…It was almost like he was right there beside me."

Or, "…so real, it was like I could *see* him," as the Widow Richardson had said just yesterday, fumbling with the top button on her old housedress. "My Edgar. It was like he was young again, sitting at that bar, patting the stool beside him."

He'd also heard, late last Wednesday: "For a second there, I could smell her perfume. My first love."

On Tuesday: "Even felt a kiss on my forehead. Twenty years after losing him. Can you imagine?"

On Monday: "Felt her hand in mine."

And that very morning: "Could've sworn I saw him in a chair at my table. All I had to do was blink, and I realized, of course, that the chair was empty. But a rusty nail was sitting right there at the table. His own favorite drink! So uncanny. Sometimes, it seems—"

"*So?*" Maddie pressed, making Kurt shake away the echoes of all those stories.

"So what?" He had forgotten what, exactly, Maddie had asked. But he really needed to get a move on if he didn't want to be late on the last half of his route.

"So the letter?" She pointed at the yellowed envelope in his hand.

"Don't ever know anything about what's inside. I just drop the mail off at the right address."

She sighed in utter exasperation. "So where is it addressed *to*? Is it that address? Ruby's Place? Is it going there or not?"

"Don't you have something better to do?"

"Like what?"

"Visit with your family. Read a book. Do homework. Sculpt leftover Thanksgiving Day mashed potatoes into a life-sized replica of Mount Rushmore."

She pursed her lips. "Mrs. Simpson got a new sewing machine delivered the day before yesterday."

"Who is Mrs. Simpson?"

"My neighbor."

"Oh." Kurt began walking. But Maddie followed like a stray hungry for attention.

"Want to know why?" she pressed.

"Not particularly."

"Because her husband is running around with the librarian from the high school. The librarian who got divorced last year."

Kurt paused to glance over at the girl's expectant face. Did she even know what she was talking about? He decided against asking and pressed forward.

"And Mr. Garrison got a new washer, because he's going to be taking in his grandkids. His daughter has *hit the skids*." She made a chopping motion with her hand when she said it.

Kurt laughed. "Now I know you're just repeating that one. What are you, some neighborhood eavesdropper?"

"You don't ever have to eavesdrop, do you?" Maddie asked. "Sure can tell a lot from a person's mail. The stuff that gets delivered to a person's house can tell quite the story. I bet you know everything about everybody."

"Nope."

"Oh, come on."

"Really. I don't snoop. Besides, people put far less personal information in the mail than you think they do."

"And Ms. Krunk—" she started in again, jumping on sidewalk squares as though they'd been branded with some sort of invisible hopscotch markings.

"Good grief, girl," Kurt bellowed. He stopped walking completely to stare down at her. She put her hands on her hips like she was gearing up to argue with whatever he was about to say. "You're going to be the worst busybody this town has ever known," he told her. "And that's saying something."

"If light bulbs could run on rumors, nobody in Sullivan would go dark for a thousand years," the little girl agreed. "My grandpa says that all the time."

"Yeah. Well. He's right." Of course her grandfather was right. In a town as small as Sullivan, where stories were their one and only true commodity, gossip reigned supreme.

Kurt started walking again. He wished she'd go away. He didn't want her to be with him anymore by the time he got to Ruby's. He wanted to deliver this letter alone.

"So. Whatcha got to deliver today?" she pressed, pointing yet again at the yellowed envelope.

"None of your business, I said," Kurt scolded. "Get out of here, kid, and let me do my job, already."

Maddie held up her hands like Kurt had while playing cops and robbers when he was her age.

Kurt felt a guilty pang as he watched her stomp down the sidewalk, straight for the It Ain't Over Yet flea market. The pang intensified when she paused to kick a curbside pile of snow—pushed to the side by a recent snowplow—in complete frustration.

He shouldn't have been so rough with her. He tried to reassure himself that kids had short memories when it came to adults brushing them off. Swore he'd be nicer the next time he saw her on his route. Somehow, though, none of it made him feel any better. Thanksgiving was over. It was Black Friday. Small Business Saturday was tomorrow. The lighting ceremony for the square would take place that very night. It was officially *Christmas*. And there he was, being mostly a jerk to a kid, the very creature Christmas was meant for.

He walked slower, watching the girl cup her hands around her face as she stopped to stare through the flea market's front window.

"Hey!" he shouted, just as she had shouted at him a few minutes earlier.

She pulled her face away, frowning at him.

"You shopping for my Christmas present?"

"What's it to you?"

He laughed and gave her a thumbs-up. "Touché," he said.

Maddie grinned and lunged into the flea market.

Feeling better, Kurt turned back to the letter in his hand. Addressed to Ruby's Place. Clearly postmarked 1955. With the name "Frankie Hall" right there on the return address.

The way he'd heard it from his own grandfather, who'd once owned Sullivan's largest dairy farm, nothing Frankie'd ever touched had ever *not* stirred up trouble in Sullivan. Real trouble, not that silly kid stuff coming from Maddie. And he figured that even now, more than seventy years after Frankie's disappearance from Sullivan, trouble was sure to start up yet again.

10.

~*November 29, 2019*~

"I'm so anxious to see what you found," Toby bellowed, his voice echoing through the Sullivan History Museum. Balding, with a face marked by all the usual lines that appeared after fifty, Toby's sudden excitement made him seem far more middle-schooler than middle-aged.

He launched himself at Angela's two-wheeler and began to unload it, pausing to admire the vintage crates.

"This is fantastic," he said, plopping himself down on the tile floor in the same way kids plopped themselves in front of Christmas trees after Santa had come to visit.

Angela smiled, pleased. Ruby had been absolutely right. "Take that junk," she'd said the night before, as their after-closing happy hour had wound down. "Just a bunch of old stuff left over from a previous owner." Ever since, Angela'd had her fingers crossed that it would satisfy Toby. It would certainly help protect her regulars if Toby believed Frankie Hall was responsible for the one and only real secret her building had ever had.

Really, though, how could Toby not believe it? Angela was herself the trustworthy sort. The kind of woman who refused to dye over the gray creeping into her ash brown hair, the kind who never overinflated the value of her secondhand car, the kind who never insisted she wore a size seven shoe when she really wore a nine and a half.

She is what she is. That was the saying most often attached to Angela.

So when she told Toby, "Hope it's enough," he believed that these boxes really were all she had to offer.

"More than enough," Toby said, examining an old newspaper featuring Frankie's face in black and white. "I mean, this wasn't completely buried. It got written up in the newspaper. But I bet nobody in town knows about this. Not anymore. That makes it a kind of modern-day secret, right? This stuff is great."

"I'll leave this all with you," Angela said, heading back toward the door. But Toby wasn't listening. He grunted a "Thanks, Ang," offering the tiniest wave as he reached back into the crate.

"Frankie Hall," he kept muttering as he sifted through the papers, all of them featuring her name. "Frankie Hall…"

Toby really should have known you can never go sifting through one person's secrets and think it will end there. The secrets belonging to one person will always involve other names. Affairs or underhanded business ventures or shady deals can never be handled alone, after all. Dig up the information on the darker side of one resident of Sullivan, and you're going to wind up unearthing a whole new cast of characters.

Toby certainly did. As soon as he started digging through the stories about Frankie, a new name appeared—Edna.

In fact, the fates of the two women were inextricably

linked. Not that Edna herself would have ever suspected her life taking that turn. At least, not before the night she met Frankie—Christmas Eve, 1930.

Sentimental Journey

linked. Not that Edna herself would have ever suspected her life taking that turn. At least, not before the night she met Frankie—Christmas Eve, 1930.

11.

~*December 24, 1930*~

Edna had too much on the line to be here.

She wasn't a fan of dark alleys. Secrets that grew in alleyways chafed, turning exposed skin pink and irritated.

Once, another life ago, she'd have jumped at the chance to spend Christmas Eve out on the town. A regular poster girl for the 1920s, complete with bobbed hair and the mandatory rouged knees. She'd Charleston-ed and she'd kissed boys recklessly (six of them, in fact, more than any of her girlfriends) before she'd ever met Arthur, the man who had become her husband.

But all of her wildness had taken place in the open. Even her prim and proper mother had chastised her for her daring ways. Edna had never slunk around. Never hidden her actions. Not from anyone.

She did not like the fact that they had to sneak around now.

"Trust me," Arthur murmured in a singsong tone, his breath coming in puffs like a smoking chimney against the icy night air. He took her hand. But his touch offered no comfort. The stars in the winter sky were less like glittering specks and more like a myriad of search lights. Their shoes had come equipped with microphones that broadcast the crunch of their feet in the snow in much the same way the local radio station broadcast "Ain't Misbehavin'."

Why had she agreed to this? Why had Arthur thought of coming here in the first place? They had two children sleeping soundly in their beds, dreaming of Santa. Zelda and Annie. Zelda, the oldest, was not even three. Babies! She had babies. Left at home with her mother and Hank, Arthur's brother. Both of them visiting for the holiday.

At first, she had to admit, the idea had seemed like fun. She'd loved the sparkle in Arthur's eye when he'd murmured his plan into her ear. The smoldering remnants of her youth had come alive again, tingling at the slightest hint of naughtiness.

Earlier, she and Arthur had tried to sneak out, the two of them tiptoeing and twittering and behaving like children themselves.

But Hank had caught them. Grinned at them from the kitchen table while he propped a foot on his knee and struck a match against the sole of his slipper.

"We had a last-minute errand to run," Arthur offered as Hank brought the match to the end of his cigarette, filling the kitchen with a toasty smoky smell. "A Santa run. For the girls."

Hank wheezed a laugh, slumping deep enough in his chair to rumple his nightshirt. He stretched his legs out in front of him, exposing his red woolen long johns. It was a rare smile from the man who had come to Sullivan hoping to snag a job with Arthur at the railroad roundhouse. A carpenter by trade, he'd seemed a different man than Edna had remembered. Older, settled. No longer the bragging Lothario who had kissed more than twice the number of lips Edna had, the man who always had a new money-making scheme and a line of starry-eyed followers, the joke-teller and charmer who was never without company at the café or listeners to his tall tales near the pickle barrel at the downtown general store. Hank was no longer the same man who teased her and winked at her while belting "Yes, Sir, That's My Baby" as he'd polished his signature black leather boots with the bright silver buckles on Edna's back porch. His eyes were different. He was disappointed. Maybe in himself. Maybe in the world. Edna couldn't be sure which.

That Christmas Eve, rather than teasing or playing, Hank simply shook his head at Edna and Arthur. Two years younger than Arthur, he wagged a finger as if to say, *Kids. What can you do?*

"Santa," he murmured, his eyes growing increasingly distant as burned-up ash collected along the edge of his hand-rolled cigarette. "Send him my way when you find him. I got a few Christmas wishes to make myself."

Arthur'd lunged for the back door, acting as though Hank had given them his blessing. An unspoken agreement to take care of the kids and cover for them should Edna's mother snore herself awake on the sofa and rise to make her midnight indigestion remedy of honey and apple cider vinegar.

Edna was about to slip outside when Hank murmured, "You be sure to tell Frankie hi, too."

She'd gasped in fright, tossing her head behind her shoulder before the kitchen door had drifted quietly shut. Through the window, Hank's hair appeared as tangled as a little boy's after sleep, his face marked by every single blunder and disaster that had come his way of late. He looked, in short, too beaten up for his age.

But that was no matter now. Hank had mentioned Frankie. Which meant he knew where they were off to. And if Hank could tell, with a single glance, where they were going, everyone else would, too.

Wouldn't they?

The 1925 Model T Arthur had gotten running again after swapping a month's worth of handyman services for the parts sputtered along, doing all the talking. No longer giggling, Edna and Arthur simply blinked silently at the snowflakes flittering across the windshield.

They rolled forward beneath the giant silver bells and pine garlands that dotted the streets of downtown Sullivan, past the red bows and wreaths on business doors. Past the twenty-foot-tall blue spruce on the town square, decked out in glittering decorations made by the local high school students. They jiggled as they sped past the entrance of Frankie's, "Home of the 5¢ steak!" painted across the plate-glass window.

Frankie's diner was always dark at this time of night—still as a sleeping cat.

At least, it appeared dark and shuttered for the night from the front of the building.

Edna had already known it wouldn't be the same in the

back.

They'd parked down the street, stepping out into the frigid night. Wind whistled, urging Edna to get back in the car, turn around, and go home.

She'd ignored the advice of the wind.

And now here they were, in the alley.

Seeming determined to prove he was every bit as gutsy as his little brother, Arthur circled an arm around Edna's waist. He steered her like she was something bulky and mechanical that didn't intend to cooperate. Something whose parts were frozen and needing to be oiled.

He even pushed her a little.

Not as much as Edna was pushing herself from the inside. She wasn't fighting him. She was simply trying to convince herself to keep moving forward. The galoshes she had buckled over her heels made her feet feel too heavy. Her woolen headscarf did not fit tightly enough to adequately protect her freezing ears.

They stopped at a back door. Under the crescent moon that seemed to have slipped out from behind a bank of clouds just to watch them.

"Exit," the door proclaimed. And yet, she and Arthur were seeking entry.

"Deliveries," another sign on the door instructed, "Ring Bell."

Instead, Arthur knocked.

Edna cringed, glancing up and down the alley. Did he have

to knock so loudly? He could tip somebody off.

This was awful. Edna was too old for this. She had too many children for this. What would people say if word got out that she was here? What if the women at church heard about it?

The door had a window. A tiny one. Arthur whispered.

Edna was trembling, but not from cold.

How did Arthur know what to say?

Hank, she thought. Surely, he'd given Arthur instructions.

Of course. She sighed, telling herself to find comfort in it. If Hank had provided the speakeasy's password, that meant Arthur had clearly told Hank about their plans. Hank hadn't been reading them at the kitchen table—he'd already known for a fact where the two were headed. And besides, Hank wouldn't have sent them someplace dangerous. Maybe this night wasn't going to be as awful as she'd thought. Maybe they wouldn't be found out after all.

Pretty big maybe, though.

Speakeasy. The word sounded lovely, almost like the sweet nothings a boy whispered to the woman who had won his heart.

But now that she was here, this didn't seem lovely at all. It wasn't romantic and it wasn't fun and it didn't feel deliciously naughty. It felt dangerous. Foreboding. The metal door loomed before her like the no-break-out closures that were usually part of a prison.

Oh, Edna found nothing immoral in enjoying a cocktail to celebrate a special day. And it wasn't as though she could personally be arrested. Not for consumption. Prohibition had never outlawed drinking. Just the manufacture, the selling, the distribution.

But she had read the national headlines. She'd heard the stories on the radio. These places were havens for gangsters. Criminals.

What would happen to her children if she and Arthur were caught up in a holiday turf war? They could be hurt or worse. Her mind spun as she imagined one outcome after another in quick succession—each one slightly darker than the last.

Why in the *world* had she agreed to this? She'd heard tell, through the Sullivan grapevine, that Windsor's Cough and Cold syrup made quite the cocktail when paired with soda and (if you could get your hands on one) a wedge of lime. Why hadn't they just bought a bottle and stayed home?

Edna could have kicked herself. And anyone else who had ever uttered the word "speakeasy." It was deceiving. It didn't sound like what it really was.

Maybe, it occurred to Edna, that was part of the disguise.

Locks clicked and the door opened; a woman filled nearly the entire open space. She was thick and sturdy looking, brown hair falling in frizzled waves about her jaw. She slammed her hands on her hips, her heavy, untethered breasts swaying beneath her blouse.

Edna crossed her arms over her chest. She shivered.

"Hank sent *you*?" she asked. Mostly, she asked Edna.

It hit Edna: the woman was suspicious of *her*. She wanted to know if Edna was the kind of weak little ninny who would quiver and hide in a corner, all while making note of everything and everyone inside. The kind of feeble woman who would squeal.

This woman was going to refuse her. Edna knew it. She'd already decided Edna couldn't be trusted with a secret. Suddenly, she was angry. Her anger clouded her fear. Edna hardened her own stare. "Hank told me to tell you hi, Frankie," she said, offering a knowing kind of smirk.

Frankie smirked back. The two women stared each other down. "Well. Guess there's a first time for everything." Frankie pushed the door open a little more.

Arthur and Edna slipped inside.

Music exploded. Loud, lively music. With horns and a powerful woman's voice. A real showstopper. One worthy of any stage. Not just some speakeasy in Sullivan, Missouri.

Frankie plopped them at a small table for two.

Arthur began to fidget in the shadows cast by the candles on the table. He grimaced against the shouts and the stomps. The cheers from dancers. The jostling of their table from rowdy Christmas Eve revelers, everyone singing and hugging and calling out to each other. He seemed to have recognized that he and Edna were outsiders—plain-Jane parents of two—who did not fit in with this crowd.

Edna thought of leaning across the table, telling Arthur it would be fine with her to leave.

But then a trumpet screamed through the room.

And the singer, in a long shiny ivory sateen dress, a gardenia tucked behind one ear, leaned against the piano. She opened her mouth to belt the final verse of "Happy Days Are Here Again."

The woman's vibrato wiggled into Edna's soul. It turned her ribs into a xylophone. Her chest vibrated. Edna was being played—she'd become part of the music of the room.

And she loved it.

The final note struck the air, followed by applause and toasting. The night had become a promise for the new year. Anything bad in life or even slightly uncomfortable could be kicked aside, right now, like too-tight shoes.

Frankie returned with a tray, placing a large silver teapot and two porcelain teacups on their table. She poured from the pot, winked at Edna, and turned away.

Edna instantly lifted the cup. She recognized the smell. Whiskey. Mixed into some sort of cocktail. A sour, maybe. Served in a teapot rather than cocktail glasses. Perhaps Frankie always served cocktails in teapots as another disguise. The fact that her speakeasy was tucked behind a respectable diner, behind a thick wall, open only after closing time, should have been disguise enough. Maybe the teapot offered a reminder to the back door customers to keep the secret of the place. After all, what Frankie was doing was illegal.

And didn't that offer a thrill?

With her first sip, it wasn't just the whiskey that was flowing down Edna's throat—the entire room flowed straight into her, warming her from the inside-out. She was part of it all; the music and the merriment shot straight into her bloodstream. She became the old Edna—audacious as ever—the girl with the short hair and the short skirts that exposed her knees. The girl who just might kiss you if the mood struck.

At that moment in time, it seemed to Edna that she had never outgrown this part of herself. The mature Edna, the woman with a bun and two children, the wife in charge of boiled cabbage and laundry soap flakes and darning socks, was just something she wore on the outside. Like stockings. Something that easily allowed the world at large to believe, with a single glimpse, that she was respectable. A grown-up.

No, *this* was who she was. Wild Edna. Bold Edna. Fearless Edna. Speakeasy Edna. And these were her people.

Edna had come home.

When Frankie next passed by, Edna grabbed her fleshy arm. "Who are they?" she shouted, pointing at the musicians.

"Dorothy's the singer."

Edna squinted, her eyes bouncing between the musicians clustered about the piano. "And the trumpet player?"

"Chester."

"They a couple?"

"Married last week." Frankie slammed her hands on her hips. "How'd you know? Most people look at Dorothy, think she's too young for him. Ten year age difference, you know. That girl's barely eighteen."

Edna shrugged. "Lucky guess," she said, though it was more than that. She could see it on them—the flush of forever that came when marriage was new. That feeling of having won a prize, knowing you were about to conquer the world.

Edna took another gulp, then reached for the teapot.

In the shadows, Arthur continued to fidget. His face clearly showed he was concerned about the amount of liquor Edna might be planning to consume. He shot her a look of warning.

Edna topped up her teacup. And took another quick gulp.

As the music began anew, Edna leaned back in her chair and crossed her legs, letting her skirt fall backward, exposing her long shapely leg all the way to the knee.

If only, she caught herself thinking, *I had a little rouge with me, for my knees. If only I'd worn the silver heels I hid in the back of the closet.*

Yes, this was definitely where Edna belonged.

Watching from across the room, Frankie threw her head back knowingly and laughed.

12.

December 24, 2019

~Our Journey~

Toby was right, you know—few people in town even remember that anymore. Not the stories of Frankie. Or the speakeasy. Kurt was one of the very last.

Mostly, no one remembered it because no one lived it. No one had seen it for themselves.

And also because, somewhere along the way, people stopped talking about it.

Stories, gossip—isn't that how we solidify memories? How we weave them together—yours, mine, other residents of Sullivan—into one cohesive big picture that suddenly becomes the story of *us*? Isn't that how we make certain slices and tidbits of information stick? By rehashing them over and over? Retelling them until they become permanent?

Like I said, Sullivan is a town built on memory. It's the fuel. You'll feel it when we get there. More than electricity. More than gasoline. It makes the engine of the town kick over. Memory is everything there.

The thing is, though—when people stop telling certain stories, that's when the forgetting begins. And then, it's almost like some things (or people, even) never existed at all.

Ah, but that old liquor bottle, the one that fell from Angela's old fruit crate, it's brought back someone who *does* remember Frankie. Maxwell Ross has had her—and her speakeasy—locked in his own memory for the better part of a century.

And now, the secrets that have long been forgotten are all bubbling back up to the surface. Frankie's face is featured on the photos and tidbits and clippings in the fruit crate that Toby sorts through. Her name is on Maxwell's lips—and that yellowed envelope in Kurt's hand.

13.

~*November 29, 2019*~

Angela had just tugged her brown knit hat from her coat pocket—ugly as sin, that was how Ruby always described it, but luckier than a hundred four-leaf clovers—when Kurt popped into her face. "Angela! I'm so glad I found you. I still have a delivery for you. I couldn't leave it at the bar. Not when you weren't there. I mean, it's too important."

"Good grief, Kurt," Angela said, letting go of the handle of her empty two-wheeler. It rattled against the sidewalk. Less than ten minutes had passed since she'd left her fruit crates with Toby, but Kurt's tone and his wide eyes and sweaty red face made her switch gears in a way that made the trip to the history museum seem like something that had happened weeks ago. The burn of worry warmed a spot beneath her ribs as she asked, "What is it?"

Kurt waved a yellowed envelope, babbling, "You hear about things like this. See it on the nightly news, on those spots where they try to highlight good things happening. Especially this time of year. You know, to balance out the bad."

"Kurt!" Angela insisted, holding out her hand.

"This just turned up." He gave her the envelope. Addressed to Ruby. From Frankie Hall. Postmarked 1955.

The skin tightened on the back of Angela's neck. How

could this be? A letter from Frankie? On the same day she dragged a crate of Frankie's stuff to Toby? She couldn't simply shrug that off, label it coincidence.

"How long's old Ruby been gone now?" Kurt asked. "Got to be a good twenty-five years."

That much was true.

Sort of. It was sort of true. It was also true that Angela spoke to the very same Ruby every day, after closing.

So what was the truth about Frankie? Where was she?

Angela ran her finger along the soft edge of the aging envelope.

"Word has it, Frankie was kind of a troublemaker," Kurt rambled on. "Used to hear quite a few wild tales about her from my grandpa."

Angela stared at the woman's name. No return address. Just "Frankie Hall," almost like some sort of warning, right there on the top left corner of the envelope.

"Chances were, she probably wasn't writing to wish Ruby well," Kurt pressed.

When Angela still didn't respond, a decidedly high-pitched voice shouted, "What's in it, already?"

"Where'd you come from?" Kurt grumbled as he and Angela turned to find Maddie with her fists slammed on her hips.

"I followed you," she told Kurt.

"Great. Your mother's probably furious."

"Pah-*lease*. She has no idea. Still has another half hour to work."

"That doesn't matter. You shouldn't be leaving the square without her permission."

"It's three measly blocks!"

"See you two later," Angela called, leaving them to their squabble.

"Look what you did," Kurt scolded Maddie.

"Me?"

"Angela would have let me look at that letter if you hadn't barged in," he said as Angela started to walk away.

"No, I wouldn't," Angela called back. "It's a felony to open someone else's mail. A postal worker should know that."

"But Ruby's not around to open it!"

"So I guess that means we'll never know what's inside." Angela waved one last time.

In truth, Angela would deliver the letter to Ruby later that very night. They'd read it together. During happy hour with the rest of the regulars.

14.

~Happy Hour at Ruby's Place~

Ruby watched through the front window, her heart dancing. This was the first year in ages that the town of Sullivan had decided to decorate the square for Christmas.

Finally—a Thanksgiving weekend lighting ceremony. And it seemed nearly the entire town had come, already in the holiday spirit.

She was getting nervous again. The same way she had once gotten nervous before every one of her stage performances. Even as a prima ballerina, she had fought her undeniable fear of falling—or receiving no applause.

Funny how one life could lead to another, one that in no way resembled the first. How a little bit of savings and a frugal life and good investments could have brought her here. Back home was more like it; Ruby had been a Missouri girl, raised two towns over. Anxious to leave. Just as anxious to return.

Ruby smiled as the crowd counted down, all at once, their voices singing out in unison. Would she be able to pull off another Christmas Eve? All those reunions—so much riding on her old bar.

Her stomach tightened up with another round of nerves.

She edged a bit closer to the window. Stars glimmered, highlighting the beauty of a clear winter sky. At last—a muffled gasp and applause from the revelers outside.

Vintage Christmas lights from Sullivan's past now twinkled above its Christmas present. A silver glow spread across the ancient buildings and illuminated the single red cardinal that sat on Ruby's window ledge.

He tapped softly, as though to get her attention. Ruby could have done the same—knocked on the opposite side of the glass—in an attempt to turn the heads of the passersby. But she knew all they would see was the darkened exterior of the closed bar.

Besides, it was time to resurrect the usual cast of characters. Those who had signed on for an extended run. Time for them all to make their nightly appearance.

She did a petit jeté just for old time's sake as she leapt behind the bar and reached for the scotch. But not for herself. She had never been much of a scotch kind of gal.

No, it was for Walter.

She poured a scotch neat. And as she stood there, next to the open bottle, Walter appeared. Walter, who had run the Sullivan Bank for more than thirty years. He appeared sporting the long sideburns that had been fashionable during the portion of life he would call his favorite. The years when he had both his family and his work, the years when he was established rather than living on a teller's meager salary. When the world had started to suspect he might have actually been forward-thinking for championing several women's businesses, approving their loans at a time when no one was willing to take chances on female-run establishments. Walter reached for his drink, his wrist shooting out from the cuff of his blue polyester suit with light gray pinstripes. "Hey, Rubes," he said with a wink, plopping down on a barstool.

Ruby grinned, poured a glass of champagne, and placed it on the bar, in front of the stool next to Walter.

"Evening, kid," Ruby said when Elizabeth appeared.

Elizabeth greeted her back with a wink.

What was it, Ruby wondered, about seeing your best friend, that always made the world seem instantly more—well—inhabitable? It was the same world as before, with the same tribulations. But suddenly, when that one face appeared, everything seemed softer and easier and sweeter all at once.

She was slow about putting away the champagne bottle, wanting to take Elizabeth in for a moment: there she was, looking no younger than she had at fifty-five, in a blue long-sleeved, form-fitting jersey dress, a large silver brooch fixed to her shoulder. She was a lovely woman—striking as an old-time movie star. Angela was right about that much. Tall and imposing, with a sultry, low voice. Elizabeth, formerly the owner of the most lucrative dress shop in the area—another beneficiary of Walter's forward-thinking.

Elizabeth raked her long red fingernails along the sides of her upswept blond hair, as if expecting her beau to appear at any moment.

Ruby recognized Elizabeth's hair-patting as a silent request—how could she have missed it? She and Elizabeth had long spoken to each other in gestures and knowing looks. How many had they exchanged at that very spot? The uphill climb to success had been nearly identical for both of them. There had been camaraderie in it. A kind of bond that had lasted until Elizabeth's passing.

A bond that had renewed itself after Ruby's death and only strengthened as Ruby and Elizabeth had led the rest of the regulars in chasing away any potential investor who threatened to destroy their meeting place, choosing to wait patiently for the just-right person. Waiting for Angela to literally come falling through the front door.

Angela—Elizabeth's own niece. When she'd shown up in Sullivan, the two women had exchanged another one of their looks—one that said it almost seemed too good to be true.

Ruby poured a beer on tap. Tom appeared at Elizabeth's side.

"Hey girls," he greeted, smiling beneath his dark mustache. He preferred to show up in his police officer's uniform, the one he'd been wearing when he'd first laid eyes on Elizabeth—his late-in-life love, the love that had come to him when he had found himself a single dad with a young daughter.

Sometimes, he and Elizabeth had learned, the love that came accidentally, when you swore you were through with it, when you were officially done looking, was often the sweetest of all.

Tom took a sip of his beer, leaning closer to Elizabeth. They began to talk—murmur was more like it—as couples deep in the throes of the rosiest colored romances always do.

Ruby glanced toward the door expectantly.

"Oh, Angela won't be here until the lighting festivities officially wind down," Elizabeth said, reading Ruby's thoughts. "You'd think they couldn't flip the switch without her."

"They can't," Ruby said softly, remembering the way every head in the crowd had swiveled. And how the search had stopped when they'd seen Angela. She had become synonymous with the square.

"She's got her non-spiked cider to sell," Walter insisted, the former banker still focusing on the bottom line, the business ventures. "Best batch yet. Thought it was pretty smart of her to take a few hot drinks out there. Since this year's been slightly colder than usual."

"Might ruffle the feathers of the coffee shop owner," Elizabeth remarked.

"You kidding? She'll offer him cider, too. Schmooze him with compliments about his house blend until he couldn't possibly get mad."

Ruby laughed, nodding in agreement.

But there was still work to do, and Ruby set about mixing the familiar slew of drinks: the vodka tonics, the gimlets, the cognac. She poured a martini and her regular piano player appeared in a silver sequin jacket, picked up her drink, and carried it over to the upright.

She mixed a gin rickey and Dorothy materialized. Ruby couldn't fathom what the place ever would have been without Dorothy, the old torch singer who had been with her from the very first night she'd turned the "Open" sign to face the street. There Dorothy stood, as always, in her full 1950s-style skirt and her cat-eye glasses, her dark blond hair pulled into a chignon at the back of her head. The music teacher who had moonlighted at Ruby's Place.

"To the original Ruby's Place singer," Ruby announced, taking a step toward the old picture of Dorothy that had always hung behind the bar. The shot of an eighteen-year-old Dorothy in her ivory sateen performing gown and a cloche hat, a gardenia tucked between the brim and her ear. "Sang here before I even *owned* the joint," Ruby added. "Don't get any more first than that." The same line she'd once used to kid her patrons.

Dorothy wished that Ruby would give up her old joke. She wished that she would stop referring to Dorothy as the only regular who had ties to the speakeasy days. There'd been so much heartbreak in it.

That's what Dorothy had always thought, anyway. And it was why Dorothy chose to appear, these nights, looking as she had when she'd worked for Ruby. Looking more like the middle-aged vocal and piano teacher—a graduate of Mrs. Leonard's Music Conservatory, a woman who taught private lessons and eventually led the local high school choir—than she had looked when she'd been a teenage speakeasy singer, working for Frankie Hall.

Only occasionally did she show up looking like her younger self. She had the first night they'd welcomed Angela back. Mostly to get her attention.

It was rare, though.

Without a single complaint, Dorothy raised her glass to acknowledge the regulars toasting her. She then raised her glass to her old boss, thinking, yet again, how fortunate it was that a stiff upper lip could still bend into a smile. She hummed as she made her way toward the upright.

Ruby tossed her cocktail shaker. She rattled ice into highball glasses. She worked her muddler. Oh, she loved this. It was what she was good at. Running this bar—she was better at it, she'd often thought, than she'd ever been a dancer.

Weren't the regulars proof of that? They'd come back to her—and to her bar. They remembered it as powerfully and fondly as she did.

Now, here, the air swelled with the past and the personal lives they'd lived, their losses and triumphs, favorite recipes and facts and…

Ruby knew them all. Knew what they were made of. Just as much as she knew what went into a whiskey sour.

Drink after drink, face after face. Tables filled. Some crowded around the piano to sing along or applaud Dorothy's emotional renditions. They huddled together in candlelight to reminisce and laugh at bygone good times.

A few wandered toward the front window to sip their drinks and admire the soft, pleasant glow of the twinkling lights. Magic felt a heartbeat away.

But that was Ruby's Place. Always. Regardless of whether

it was owned by Ruby or Angela. There had never been a simpler or more accurate description of the old bar than this: Ruby's Place was a cedar box with heirlooms inside. The kind of items that maybe aren't made of precious metals, that maybe aren't worth much in terms of a dollar value. The kind of items that are loaded with sentimental value. The kind of items that, should they ever get displaced, would make you feel lost and hurt. Wounded. Like a piece of yourself had been carved away.

Yes, that was Ruby's Place.

Outside, the crowd slowly began to dissipate, some of them heading to the café for a slice of pie to go with Angela's cider, some of them to window shop, making mental notes and shopping lists ahead of Small Business Saturday.

Angela finally banged through the door in her lucky knit hat, steering her cart filled with leftover Styrofoam cups, dispensers of cider, and boxes of cinnamon sticks.

The regulars cheered, welcoming her inside.

But when Angela didn't immediately respond, the cheers tapered off quickly.

"What's the matter?" Ruby asked. "You look like you've seen a ghost," she joked, attempting to lighten her mood.

Angela took a deep breath as she tugged her hat free and parked her cart near the back wall. "Kurt delivered this today. It's been right here in my pocket ever since. I probably should have given it to you before I left for the lighting. But I just—" Angela finally slipped the envelope from her coat. "I wasn't sure what it would stir up. Could be good, could be…"

"It's from Frankie," Ruby said softly, eyeing the cursive handwriting.

"Frankie?" Dorothy repeated hopefully, weaving through the crowd.

But the room quickly fell eerily silent.

Ruby took a deep breath and popped the yellow envelope open—easy to do after so many years. The glue along the back flap had nearly disintegrated completely.

Angela and the regulars crowded around to read over her shoulder.

"*Ruby,*" Frankie's letter began, "*Good luck with Christmas Eve, girlie. You're going to need it. Keep an eye on your alley door. You never know when you might see a face from the past. —Frankie.*"

"Good thing that never got delivered," Walter said. "Would have really darkened your whole opening night back then."

"There's more to this," Ruby insisted. "There's got to be a reason this came now."

"You can't really think—" Dorothy started.

"I think that Frankie made sure I got this letter today," Ruby interrupted. "I think she's talking to me right now. In the present. Not sixty years ago."

"What do you think she wants?" Angela's voice shook beneath the weight of the question.

"What if," Ruby said, her tone both matter-of-fact and full of dread, "she's coming to take everything back?"

15.

~*November 29, 2019*~

The cardinal ruffled his feathers and pecked on the plate-glass front window. This was not the reaction he'd wanted when he'd dropped that letter in Kurt's bag. They were looking in the wrong place.

Frankie's letter *had* been delivered. All those years ago. By a 1955 mailman who had whistled beneath all those brand-new aluminum stars shining on light poles near the square. But Ruby had been too busy. Too occupied with all the little details. She had opening-night performance nerves. In her rush, all she'd seen was the name on the return. And so she had simply shuffled that envelope off, tucked it into a fruit crate along with some old papers she'd found in storage: all the stuff that had once belonged to Frankie Hall.

It had seemed strange to Ruby back then that those tidbits even existed. There had been several owners since Frankie's days.

But it had also seemed strange, back in 1955, that so many of the passersby kept bringing up her name. They'd pause, shopping bags in hand, and peer through the front window, curious. Ruby would greet them warmly, introduce herself, even give preliminary tours. The older visitors would always sigh, tell her it was a far cry from the joint Frankie ran—"And believe me," they'd say, placing their wrinkled hands, littered in blue veins, on her arm, "it's a good thing. This is a *good thing* you're doing."

Frankie, it was implied—or stated outright—was the opposite of good.

It had rattled Ruby a bit, all the innuendos and half-stories, the indication that something truly horrendous had happened inside her own building, back when Frankie ran it—on a Christmas Eve, no less. The same date that Ruby was scheduled to open.

She tried to press them for more info, but the teller always backed away.

She'd heard just enough for an awful feeling to settle into her chest—the same she'd carry were she to find that her new home was actually the site of a gruesome murder some decades past.

She'd shoved anything associated with Frankie into the shadows, including that letter. She'd been so rattled by it, she had failed to realize the letter was addressed to her. Frankie's was the only name she'd seen.

A few days ago, she'd pointed out the old crates to Angela. "Give those to Toby," she'd insisted, refusing to look inside when Angela suggested she sift through it, just to be sure there was nothing in there she wouldn't want Toby getting his hands on.

Ruby only remembered that the items all related to Frankie somehow—and thought that she'd be glad to finally have those things out of her building. Glad to be able to forget about her completely.

Now, though, here she was. Again.

Again?

Ruby trembled slightly at the possibilities, the scenarios she imagined, the ideas of what it all might mean.

The cardinal let out a few annoyed chirps at Ruby. But she paid him no attention.

What was *wrong* with Ruby? She who could remember the recipe for every drink she ever made? Why couldn't she connect the dots? Remember that this particular letter had also been in that crate? Realize that it had been delivered and tossed aside? Delivered and simply never opened?

Until now, anyway.

The letter was supposed to wake them all, but they were getting everything mixed up. It hadn't been Frankie herself the cardinal had wanted them all to look at. He'd simply wanted them to look back to the days of her speakeasy.

It was Maxwell Ross. Sullivan bad boy from the 1930s. *That* was the danger. He was back.

How could they all be so blind?

The only thing he knew for sure was that they were no more ready for Maxwell Ross's return now than they'd been before the letter.

He had to fix that.

The cardinal flapped his wings, taking off and flying straight for the history museum, housed in one of Sullivan's oldest buildings. Built in the days when gargoyles perched on roofs and Grecian columns surrounded entryways. Hidden by the eaves from any casual passerby, a gap in weather-weakened ventilation slats provided just the right spot for the cardinal to fly through.

He soared down the staircase, landing in the center of the Secrets of Sullivan display, nearly ready for its December premiere.

Angela's crates were still there, the contents of one spread out across the floor.

The cardinal made his way closer to the odds and ends and fragments of yesterday, visible in the moonlight filtering in through the windows—an old candlestick phone, a piece of shiny white metal that could have been a small funnel or maybe some sort of elaborate screw, a small flat disk completely covered in tarnish, a teapot, a few two-cent postage stamps, a dried gardenia, and some sort of glittery confetti.

Antiques. Or fragments of them, anyway. Tina over at the It Ain't Over Yet would be quick to compare the contents to the knickknacks she often purchased by bidding on box lots at auction. Digging through such purchases, she often found scraps of paper taped to the bottoms of Depression glass pitchers or stuffed inside Fenton vases. Sentences describing the owner, how the item had been used. Older women, she'd learned, had an inclination to catalog their homes this way. Their goal had been not just to identify items but preserve the stories behind them.

Those stories, it had often seemed to Tina, were the true value of any antique.

The items inside the fruit crate had tales to tell, too—plenty of them.

How, though?

Why, they needed someone to tell them.

But where to find one person who knew all those anec-dotes?

With no one around to shoo him away, the cardinal picked up the end of the wire that had once connected the old candlestick phone to an earpiece. Using the tip of his beak, he reconnected it.

The wire buzzed and hummed.

With the tap of the beak, he had reawakened Rose Water-ton.

16.

December 24, 2019

~Our Journey~

Oh, I know. You're beginning to think this story of mine is a little far-fetched for your taste. Maybe you're even beginning to regret inviting me along for the drive. You're wondering where the closest Greyhound terminal is. Trying to plan out how you might be able to drop me off and forget all about this little side-trip to Sullivan. Get back on the main highway, the one that will take you to your family.

Enough of this crazy detour. That's exactly what you're thinking.

Isn't it?

Look, I know how it sounds.

But—*Cardinals appear when angels are near.* Haven't you heard that one? And don't you think that in a town like this, where secrets are piled one on top of each other, a little help from a town-wide guardian angel might be in order?

You've noticed it, haven't you? That the secrets of Sullivan are layered? First, we have the secret of Angela's bar—which is that the former, long-deceased owner (and business namesake) is still around. Peel that layer back, you have the secret that Ruby isn't the *only* spirit inside. Peel that layer back, and you find that the regulars in Ruby's Place are reuniting with those still-living loved ones on Christmas Eve. Keep going, peeling back further, and you find that before Ruby even owned the place, the building had a secret after-dark life as a speakeasy. Peel that back, and you've got the secrets surrounding a Depression-era Christmas Eve tragedy—which I'm getting to, bear with me. Peel that back, and suddenly it appears that the old owner—Frankie—is looking to barge in on the town of Sullivan, take back the building. At least, that's what Ruby and her regulars believe. That's what they're preparing for.

But what about Maxwell Ross? The one that the cardinal seems to be trying to warn everyone about? He lived in Sullivan during the days of the old speakeasy. And now he's back. Brought to life by the old bottle of the liquor he'd distilled himself.

All these intersecting, interwoven layers of secrets. Listen, not all of these assumptions or worries will pan out. But *all* of them are pointing toward another impending tragedy at Ruby's Place.

One that's going to occur on Christmas Eve. Which, as you well know, is tonight.

Don't you think that might warrant just a little bit of intervention? Protection? Even—as implausible as it sounds—*angelic protection?*

Cardinals appear when angels are near...

Fine, fine. Forget the cardinal for a moment. There's another important piece of our story to consider. Focus on Rose. Rose Waterton. The original gossip queen of Sullivan.

How'd she manage to win that title, you ask?

By being the switchboard operator. Over at the phone company.

✳ ✳ ✳

Back in the switchboard's heyday, Rose had once used all the criss-crossing wires at her station to connect mothers to their children's doctors and businessmen to the main office ("up there in Kansas City," she'd often heard). Of course, not everyone in town had a home phone. Right about half. Enough that even if you didn't own that particular luxury, you most likely had a friend or a relative with one that you could use for a few minutes. At some point, everyone in Sullivan was on the line with Rose. What she heard ran the gamut. But by far the most interesting calls had consistently come from Frankie Hall over at the diner.

That's right. Frankie—the very same name on the letter Kurt had delivered to Angela.

"*Rose*," Frankie had regularly barked in her signature blunt way, never offering her own name, always expecting to be recognized.

Rose would fight not to sigh in exasperation. Frankie Hall was about as sweet as the horehound candy her grandmother gave her for sore throats. The same bitter lozenges she'd spit into her mother's petunia pots when her granny wasn't looking.

"Get Sam's Grocery on the line for me, will ya?" Frankie would bellow. "Need a delivery of buttermilk. For the pie crusts."

"Good thing a tight pocketbook don't cure a body of a sweet tooth, eh, Frankie?" Rose would ask, playing along. Because no matter how hard times got, Frankie was still making pies. Tons of them. To hear her tell it, anyway. All those midday orders. Buttermilk. Gooseberries. Lard. All for the "pies."

"Benton 1-269," Frankie would bark.

"Yes, ma'am," Rose would agree, even though she knew it was wrong. That number didn't connect to the grocery. It connected to Robert Ludlow's Garage.

Buttermilk, my big toe, Rose would think back then. But because it was her job to please the customer, she'd connect the line. No questions. No corrections.

And then she'd pull the master cord out partway and open the key.

Which meant she could hear Frankie's and Robert's voices flowing through her headset. Even if she hadn't memorized the number for Ludlow's Garage, she would have known who was on the line, just by the sound of his voice.

Anyone in Sullivan could identify Robert Ludlow. All it took was a syllable or two. Ludlow had a voice like no one else's— part misfiring pistons, part injured frog. Remember that. That voice of his is bound to show up again later.

"Buttermilk" was code back then, of course. For whiskey. To be delivered in the alley, behind Frankie's diner.

Because the thing was, since money was so tight, people weren't fixing their cars much anymore. Heck, in Sullivan, they could get along just fine walking everywhere they needed to go. And poor Robert wasn't making the same kind of money.

Neither was Frankie. In hard times, the first thing people decided they did not need was to go out to eat. And no times were any harder than the flat-up Depression.

Frankie, it had seemed, was bound to be the very first person to go belly-up.

But Robert Ludlow was a fixer by nature—whether the fixing centered on carburetors or cash drawers. He had a way to fix the business side of things—for himself and for Frankie, too.

Which meant that Frankie Hall wasn't *just* running her father's old diner. No, after dark, Frankie was running a different sort of place entirely. After she and Ludlow worked out the details of their arrangement, she emptied out her back offices, knocked down a few walls of her own with a sledgehammer. A speakeasy. In such hard times, it was the only thing keeping the old diner afloat.

Rose knew all of that.

Of course, had Frankie been equally aware of what Rose was up to—listening in on her every conversation with Robert Ludlow—she probably would have been more than just a little upset. No one takes kindly to finding out they're being spied on.

Then again, perhaps she already knew. Maybe, when Rose listened in, that phone line filled with a slight clicking noise—the kind of noise that let Frankie onto the fact that someone else was on the line. The switchboard operator wasn't quite as gone as she'd have Frankie believe. And maybe—just maybe—Frankie also knew that the switchboard operator liked to gossip when she wasn't on the clock. And those very whispers Rose uttered were really the only way Frankie could advertise her after-dark establishment.

* * *

The night the cardinal squeezed into the museum, when he brought that old candlestick phone to life, what do you think the phone connected to?

Yes, yes, it connected to Rose—but how?

Don't you think it would need to connect to a switchboard?

Perhaps even—the same switchboard Rose had once sat in front of each day, connecting Sullivanites?

The same switchboard where she suddenly found herself sitting once more.

Yes, once the cardinal had done it—once the old candlestick phone was rewired—there she was: Rose Waterton. Seeming to have just arrived for work, her familiar granite lunch pail in her lap. Back at the same switchboard where she'd once done all her listening.

A few blocks away, back in the history museum, the candlestick phone buzzed slightly. And the other stray items in Angela's fruit crate began to rattle against the wooden slats. A strange metal piece—the little funnel or maybe the elaborate screw—began to do the most rolling back and forth.

Only, that strange metal object wasn't either of those things. Not a screw. Not a funnel. It was an old mouthpiece. From a trumpet. Left behind in Frankie's speakeasy.

That little mouthpiece had a story of its own. One that had yet to reach its conclusion.

To find its ending, that piece needed the cardinal. And the phone.

And Rose.

That cardinal was counting on Rose's curiosity—and her never-ending hunger for the juiciest stories—to make her pick up her headset once more.

She'd done just that when it happened:

A man's voice filled her earpiece.

"Hello, Rose? You there? It's me. Chester."

"Chester?" she whispered.

"Chester," he repeated. "Dorothy's husband. You remember me, don't you? You remember Dorothy, anyway. How could you forget her? Oh, she's so lovely. Sings so sweetly. Just like a bird. Remember that? Remember how the two of us used to play music at Frankie's? Sure, you do. Don't pull the plug on me. Please. I know you think I'm a regular con man. That's right, ain't it? Some no good ne'er-do-well who ran some con game on poor Dorothy. Took advantage of her. Put her heart through the ringer, then left the girl high and dry. Everybody thinks that. I know it. The way I disappeared on her—what else could they think? But to what end? Huh? What good did it get me? To leave my own wife? You ever ask yourself that?"

He rattled on, his voice becoming more emotional with

each word. Sounding as though he'd opened the dam and now here it was, a flood of pleas he'd held back for years.

"Please, Rose…I didn't have a choice. Can'tcha see that? I need to get word to Dorothy. I've been out here trying for ages. And Rose, you're the only one who can do it. Tell her not to give up on me, will ya? Please? Tell her I know I promised. It's not a *broken* promise, Rose. It's just one I haven't made good on yet. There's a difference. I'm coming back. I am. I've done some awful things, I'll admit. The worst being losing my trumpet. I'm on the hunt for it, Rose. Soon as I find it, I'll be on my way home. Our music is still there, right where we left off, see? So is my love. I know it. Tell her I love her. Always have. If nothing else, tell her I love her. And I'm coming home. Thank you, Rose. Thank you…"

"Chester? Chester, wait. Please. Give me a minute," Rose begged.

But he was gone.

All that remained in her headset was the strange sound of something rolling and clattering about—the mouthpiece in the fruit crate back at the history museum.

Rose's head spun as she tried to make sense of what had just happened to her. She glanced around, alarmed that she did not see any of her coworkers—or any other memorable fixtures of Southwestern Telephone.

Only the telephone lines. Those were still visible through the plate-glass window, cutting through the winter-gray sky.

You ever find yourself staring at telephone lines when you're in the passenger seat on long drives, like the one we're on now? I always did. The way they draped between poles—almost like how tinsel drapes around a Christmas tree or across a fireplace mantel. I'd stare at those lines as the family car sped down thoroughfares or circled through old towns. I always tried to imagine how many voices were crisscrossing on that line right then, right at that moment. And what they were talking about.

Anyway. Rose. At the switchboard. The lines were there. Outside. But where was *she?*

Rose began to glance around, seeing only a hodgepodge of items crammed on shelves, all of them marked with prices. Why, amazingly, she and her switchboard were sitting in the back of the old flea market in Sullivan, the one I already mentioned, the one that was turning out to be maybe the most aptly-named store of all time: the It Ain't Over Yet.

17.

~*December 1, 2019*~

The entrance of the flea market flopped open, making three leather straps of antique sleigh bells, a wreath of upcycled tin cans painted green, and a string of outdoor multicolored lights clatter and clang almost violently against the glass door.

Of course the entrance would already be fully decorated. Tina, owner and operator of the It Ain't Over Yet, missed no opportunity to festoon—well, much of anything, really. She was also the only woman in the entirety of Sullivan, Missouri who could wear plastic disco ball earrings and get by with it. Not to mention black velvet platform heels or cat-eye glasses with tiny rhinestones and gold flecks. She was never the beneficiary of snickers or finger-pointing or head-wagging. This particular day—so soon after Thanksgiving that the smell of green bean casserole still lingered in the air—Tina had chosen a pair of red and green plaid bell-bottoms, combined with a black turtleneck and a blond wig in a Twiggy-style cut.

As a woman prone to accessorizing, she loved everything about what was arguably the gaudiest (and most accessorized) holiday of all. Loved the baubles and the shiny tinsel and the ribbons and the twinkle lights.

As the clatter of the sleigh bells began to quiet down, Tina craned her neck from her spot behind the cash register and sighed in undeniable disappointment at the individual who had just burst into her shop.

Nine-year-old Maddie, Tina's youngest and most vocal customer.

Maddie tugged her stocking cap from her head, propped her hands on her hips, and bellowed, "I've got questions!"

"Oh, dear," Tina murmured. Why couldn't she have come the day before, on Small Business Saturday? She'd had the kind of traffic that would have justified kicking her out, telling her she had no time. But today? It was simply a slow and quiet Sunday, not a single soul around.

Or so Tina thought, anyway.

She braced herself for the inevitable exhaustion that always followed one of Maddie's visits as the girl began to tick her questions off on her fingers. "How long does it take an envelope to get yellow! Why would it take a letter a reeeeally long time to get delivered! And who is Fra—"

Thankfully, the door of the flea market clattered and clanged again, announcing another new entrance. Some sort of ancient black case came banging inside, accompanied by both a wintry chill and a familiar figure humming "Silver Bells."

"Hey, there, Lou," Tina called, clearly glad to have someone in the shop other than Maddie. But Maddie's attention didn't wane. She didn't shrug and bounce back out of the shop, leaving the adults to their boring business. Instead, she seemed utterly transfixed by the sight of the mysterious black case. Maddie could be as hard to get rid of as some of Tina's most clingy former boyfriends. Or bathtub rings. Either one.

Long considered the man in Sullivan most likely to do anything for a dime, Lou cleared his throat, working the wooden toothpick sticking out of his mouth. It whipped around, up and down and to the side. Tina chuckled softly, wondering if it was possible Lou was actually conducting some sort of invisible orchestra.

Lou squinted at Maddie as he chucked his winter coat by the door. "Don't 'cher mother need you?" he grumbled.

"For what?"

"I dunno—sweepin' the floor. Fillin' up them shampoo bottles. Over at the—what's that place called?"

"The Curly Girl Beauty Emporium. For your information."

"Cute. So?"

"Mom told me I wasn't allowed back in the salon for two weeks."

"How come?" Lou asked.

"'Cause I helped, that's all."

"Couldn't 'a been such great help."

"Was too. Livened up the blue bottles where they put combs."

"With what?"

"My homemade slime."

Maddie crossed her arms against their laughter. She glared up at Lou, her expression declaring that if he dared to continue with this conversation, she was going to have a zinger or two to shoot right back at him. After all, Lou wasn't exactly a blue ribbon winner himself. He'd been married four times. His hair had grown thin in exact proportion to the thickening of his gut. He'd recently had his fifth cancerous mole removed from his receding hairline, giving his forehead the appearance of having been inscribed with some sort of weird reverse-Braille message.

Maddie knew all about the moles already. And more. She knew far more about Lou, junior busybody that she was.

Lou grunted around his toothpick and clanked his weird black case on the counter in a way that announced he had better things to do than pick fights with third-graders.

But the case he'd come with wasn't a regular square box. It had curves and dips in it. Without hesitation, Maddie inched closer to the counter. She couldn't wait to find out what was inside. Maybe some kind of miniature dragon.

Lou shot her yet another warning look.

She shrugged. With Lou, miniature dragons were certainly possible.

"You selling or trading today, Lou?" Tina asked, glad to put an end to whatever that was developing between him and Maddie. But her question was utterly unnecessary. Lou was sell. Always sell. Cash in hand, that was what Lou came for.

"I don't know anything about this thing," Lou admitted. "My aunt passed away earlier this fall. There was so much stuff."

Maddie snickered through her nose. "Your aunt? Come

clean, Lou. You win that in a poker game? Steal a car with that in the trunk?"

"I could always go down the highway to Fulton," Lou said, wagging his finger toward the door.

"No need," Tina said, making her voice sound smooth and friendly. "We're going to be nice, aren't we? Santa could be listening. We wouldn't want him to pass us by because of something un-funny we happened to say just a few short weeks before Christmas, now, would we, young lady?"

Maddie scowled, obviously agreeing to relent and keep to herself whatever thoughts had zipped through her mind. She threaded her fingers together behind her back in an innocent way.

Lou flicked the clasps. The dry black leather cracked as he lifted the lid, exposing a trumpet.

Tina sucked in a breath.

"What? Bad?" he asked in a worried tone.

"No, I—" Tina pushed her glasses up and leaned forward. "I've never seen anything like it. I get a lot of instruments in here. But never anything like this."

She hesitated to touch it.

"Is it old?"

"I think so." She finally pulled it out, turning the trumpet over in her hands. Made of white metal, the entirety of the instrument was covered in tiny little carved flowers and ivy boughs.

"Your aunt know a professional musician? Someone in your family, maybe?"

"Why would my aunt…" Lou started. Remembering his story, he simply shook his head. "No—not even close. Why?"

"This has to be a professional's instrument," Tina insisted. "Not that I know everything there is to know about trumpets, but you get so you recognize quality. Instruments that have been bought for eighth grade music class aren't the same as those that were part of traveling big bands."

"You really *must* have stolen it," Maddie grumbled.

"Stop," Tina barked. "You never know when you'll run into a nice piece. Just a couple of months back, I went to a farm auction two states away and found that in the barn." She pointed toward an old electronic piece—wooden frame holding tons of crazy open holes with switches and cords trailing everywhere—now displayed in the back of the shop.

"What is that thing?" Maddie wanted to know.

"A switchboard. For the phone. Used to have to call the switchboard operator and ask to have your call connected."

"Weird," Maddie groaned.

"And do you know that switchboard came from right here in Sullivan? Stamp on the back of the item says so: Southwestern Telephone, Sullivan Missouri. Can you believe that? I thought I was going out there to buy up a bunch of old quilts. Instead, I wound up buying a piece of Sullivan history. I've even got Toby on the hunt for more information. He's supposed to email what he finds. What?" she asked, starting to come out from behind the front counter. "Don't believe me about the stamp? Come with me.

I'll show you."

"That's okay," Lou jumped in, blocking her. He didn't care about some old switchboard. He needed to know if Tina was going to help him out with the trumpet.

"Well," Tina said. "Point is, the way we come upon items is awfully strange. You get drawn to things. Inexplicably. Sometimes, it feels providential."

"Provi-*what?*" Maddie tried.

"Each and every item has a story," Tina went on, pointing one of her silver fingernails at Maddie. "*If* you'll listen."

"I'm good at listening," she said. "I've heard all kinds of stories!"

Tina held the end of the trumpet against Maddie's ear, letting her listen like she would to a conch shell.

Maddie gasped. "Voices," she murmured. "Singing."

She seemed so serious—her expression didn't even show the tiniest hint that she might be playing a game. And the way her eyes darted about, it really did seem like she was trying hard to listen to what was inside.

Intrigued by what she saw in Maddie, Tina actually raised the trumpet and placed the sound hole against her own ear.

"I hear it too," she murmured.

But when she lowered the trumpet, she remembered that her radio was playing softly throughout the store.

Still. There'd been a different song inside that instrument—hadn't there?

Before she could listen a second time, Lou pointed at the trumpet, asking, "You really think that's some fancy one, eh?"

"You might want to take it to a music shop to get the most money you can out of it. I'd give you a fair price, but it's based on what I can resell it for. I wouldn't charge as much as a music dealer. Don't have the same clientele. So I'd offer you less."

"Yeah, I just really need money for…" He glanced down at Maddie, who raised her eyebrows. "Christmas shopping," he finished. "It's worth it to take a little less here and not be driving around comparing offers. Thanks for telling me up front, though."

"Sure thing, sug," Tina said. The white metal of the trumpet flashed in the light as she placed it back in the velvet-lined case. She counted three hundred dollar bills and handed them over.

"Seriously?" Lou asked.

"Merry Christmas," Tina offered.

Lou held the hundreds to the light, like he was used to checking large bills for signs of their being counterfeit. "Merry Christmas," he bellowed, and grabbed Maddie into a giant bear hug.

Maddie groaned and wiggled until he put her down.

"And to all a good night!" he thundered, before he scooped up his coat and lunged out of the shop.

"So. I was trying to ask you about Frankie Hall," Maddie blurted. "And letters." But Tina didn't seem anxious in the least to peel her eyes from the old case.

"Good grief, girl. You latch onto something with your

mind and you don't *ever* let go. What's this Frankie Hall stuff all about, anyway?"

"What do you know about her?"

"Nothing. Never met the woman. That's the God's honest truth. Why?"

Maddie shrugged. "Saw her name on some letter that Kurt had." She tried to act like she didn't care one way or another if Tina had any interesting tidbits to share. In truth, she hadn't been able to get it out of her mind. The whole thing had seemed so deliciously mysterious.

"You bothering poor Kurt, Maddie?"

"So that's really a nice trumpet, huh?" Maddie asked, redirecting Tina's attention. She didn't need Tina to get mad at her. She felt like she was already riding a fine line after the way she'd talked to Lou.

"Yep."

"You going to sell it for a lot?"

"Oh, I'll mark it up some," Tina said, scrawling a price on a tag, then tying the tag to the handle of the instrument case. She carried it to the front window, moving other items about to give it the center space, right there in the midst of cotton-ball snow and a miniature aluminum tree and color wheel.

"Just some?"

"When Lou walks by and sees the price tag, I don't want him to feel scammed. Then he brings me something nice again next time."

"Must be a pretty good reason he'd want to get rid of such a nice horn," Maddie said, her voice going singsong.

"Maybe he just doesn't play the trumpet."

"Maybe he's broke. Maybe he spends too much time at the race track. Maybe he owes a bookie—"

"Girl, quit making things up," Tina scolded. She put her hands behind Maddie's shoulders and steered her for the door.

"Wait!" Maddie shouted. "You haven't answered the rest of my questions. How long does it take for an envelope to get all yellowy? How many years?"

"What is with you and this business about old letters? Didn't you see the postmark?"

"The what?"

"The postmark, girl, don't they teach you anything in school? The post office stamps the date. In the right-hand corner."

"Oh. No. I just saw the return. Frankie Hall. And it was addressed to Ruby. Do you think it's the same Ruby as Ruby's Place?"

"Ruby's been gone for ages. Angela runs the place now. You know that. Scat, now, go on."

"But the envelope was *old.* Don't you listen to me? How long does it take an envelope to get yellow?"

"Why you asking me?"

"You're the expert on old stuff," Maddie exclaimed, pointing at the pink Depression glass dishes and the rusted Mobil signs with the flying horse and the souvenir WWII pillow cases.

"*So?*" Maddie urged. "How long?"

Tina dipped behind her checkout counter. She reached into some unseen shelf, removed a business-sized envelope, and pressed it into Maddie's hands. "When this turns yellow, come back and we'll talk about it. Now get going."

18.

~*December 1, 2019*~

Rose did not know Ruby had already been presented with that letter from Frankie. She did not know that Maxwell Ross had shown up. She might have wondered how she fit into the big picture if she had been aware of either of those events. Instead, she felt her sole goal was to reunite Chester and Dorothy. That had to be it. She wasn't sure why, but here, now, the opportunity had opened up for the two of them. Rose had heard Chester's pleading voice. And now, his trumpet had resurfaced again.

This had to be it: Rose, whose job had been to make connections, had been called upon to connect Dorothy and Chester.

It was the only real sense she could make of it.

After Lou's departure, she scrambled for her headset. "Chester!" she hissed. "It's me. Rose. From the switchboard. Can you hear me? Are you still on the line? Chester, I saw your trumpet. *Here*, Chester, at the It Ain't Over Yet flea market in Sullivan. Chester? Are you there? Chester, can you hear me? Chester. Chester…"

Of course she knew his trumpet. Anyone who had lived in Sullivan during the '30s could have instantly recognized that trumpet. One-of-a-kind, made of white metal carved with vines. Chester had been so proud. Showing it off anytime someone asked to see it—or hear him play. But where had it been? How did Lou get it? And how could it look so perfect, after all this time?

Rose smashed the headphone against both ears. It was hard to hear anything over the sounds of all those bells rattling against the entrance as the flea market door swung open and shut, ushering new shoppers inside. Had Chester heard anything she just said? Anything at all?

"Chester?" she tried again. "Please, Chester. You need to get here before your trumpet can be sold."

This was all so strange. That little girl talking about Frankie. Saying something about a letter that had reappeared. And Chester's voice. The trumpet. Where were all the other girls Rose had once worked with? How could she be here, in some old flea market? So many questions, none of them with any discernible answers.

Rose's eyes bounced across the switchboard, until a slot suddenly lit up.

Quickly, she slammed the plug in.

She flinched as her own headset filled with happy squeals and shouts.

Rose leaned forward, still as much of an eavesdropper as she'd ever been. Only this time, there was more at stake.

Everything was riding on her. Without her help, she was certain, Dorothy and Chester would never find each other.

But she still did not understand what, exactly, had brought her back to her old machine. And she was not aware that a few blocks away, glittery confetti had begun to dance across the bottom of the old crate in the history museum. She only knew she was listening in on a celebration—to shouts of "Here's to 1929," and "Happy New Year!"

The very night Chester and Dorothy had met.

19.

~*December 31, 1928*~

Dorothy's feet no longer touched the ground.

But that only seemed appropriate. Feet shouldn't touch the ground on such a splendid, glittering night. And that was exactly what it was for the sixteen-year-old, dressed to perfection in a blue silky dress with long pearl necklaces and matching drop earrings. Dorothy's father, an investment banker, had taken his family to the grand Kemper Hotel to celebrate the incoming year in the ballroom. Crystal tinkled everywhere—chandeliers, cocktail flutes. Gold sparkled on women's fingers and made up centerpieces and jingled in men's pockets.

One more golden night in what promised to be a lifetime of them.

On the side of the stage, Miss 1929 stopped dancing and swinging her sash to purse her lips into an "Oh! Look! Almost time!" expression as she pointed to the giant clock towering behind her.

Dorothy laughed. Five more minutes. A new year—with new possibilities. Around her, revelers called her name and began to chant in unison: "Sing, sing, sing, sing…"

Dorothy's voice had long been the talk of the town—or, at the very least, the talk of her father's inner circle. Described as "the berries" and "the cat's pajamas." And now, here they were, all of them, begging for a tune.

She would oblige. Of course she would. She loved to sing. No butterflies. No hesitation.

The trumpet player hurried forward, reaching down to help her onto the stage. "Take my hand, miss," he told her.

Handsome—Dorothy couldn't help but notice just how handsome he really was. Even though he was older.

He walked her toward the microphone.

Miss 1929 pointed toward the minute hand. Three minutes.

The band began to play.

Dorothy knew this one. Recognized it immediately. "I Can't Give You Anything but Love, Baby." She stepped closer to the microphone. She opened her mouth and let her voice strike the air, clear as a cymbal. The crowd immediately cheered, as though she were a professional singer. The kind people paid money to hear. Not just the daughter of their own business cohort. Not some little girl who had already attended hundreds of golden evenings identical to this one. Who had entertained this sprawling group more than once.

Silly song. Its lyrics were completely out of place for the time in which they were living. Why, just *look* at where they all were! Bathed and surrounded by so many delightful things people could give each other. Not just love. Shiny baubles and soft furs. Woolen topcoats and bath salts that smelled of lilac. Shoes with silver buckles. Brightly colored Bakelite radios. Phonograph players and stacks of records to dance to. Fancy pens that didn't need inkwells.

There would never be a time, Dorothy felt certain, when all she—or someone close to her—would *only* be able to give love. A time when all they could do was pine and dream and wish for lovely things. Lovely things were all around them! They flowed. Opulence was a river that never ran dry.

She sang the chorus like a wink. *We all know better, don't we?*

These were the whoopee years.

In Dorothy's sixteen-year-old mind, she had come to believe that the years of conflict and strife had happened *before*. The older generation had struggled so she would never have to.

She was a lucky girl.

And then came the sound of the trumpet. The perfectly improvised notes agreed with Dorothy: *It's true, you're right*, the trumpet said, *but it could always be better.*

The handsome musician stepped closer to her. Dorothy watched as his hands worked the valves of the shiny white metal instrument. It was a beautiful trumpet. Striking. In the spotlight, it was clear the instrument had been engraved, the entirety of its exterior covered with vines and flowers.

Their individual notes began to twist. They grew, they teased. They were talking now, Dorothy and this trumpet player, leaving behind the literal meaning of the lyrics. They talked as men and women do—the tip of a hat, an introduction. A flirt, a smile. An invitation. Dinners that lingered. And nights and nights and nights…

They challenged, too. They disagreed with each other, their notes diverging, but never so far as to sound dissonant. The trumpet chased her, it caressed her, it caught her when her vocal runs headed out too far, teetering on the edge.

They became part of each other. Their notes promising and collaborating and making something beautiful. Their song built, rising, deviating completely from the original melody line. The band softened behind them, allowing the two of them to control center stage.

This was not the song as it had been written. This was a different song. A song of their own creation, that belonged only to them. To Dorothy and Chester, who had, in the length of two verses and a chorus, experienced an entire courtship.

As the second hand ticked toward the final moments of 1928, they held onto the last note as long as they could, teetering, teetering—

Miss 1929 squealed, pointing at the clock. The drummer thundered. The other horns onstage screeched.

The crowd screamed, turning away from the stage as confetti fluttered down from the chandelier above the ballroom.

But this was no common confetti. As the clock struck midnight, it rained both golden flecks and dollar bills. Flying down toward a giggling crowd who grabbed and stuffed the dollars into their pockets, purses, and dress tops.

Not that any of them needed the money. The tumbling confetti might as well have been made of mere strips of worthless green scraps of paper. A child's play money. It was all a game.

Life itself was a game.

Onstage, Chester and Dorothy paid no attention to the chaos before them.

Instead, Chester took Dorothy's hand. The emotions they had experienced with their music was far more valuable than any silly old money.

Forget money. Cash was boring. It was common.

Dorothy and Chester had something far more important. Rare. They had discovered the much-ballyhooed pot of gold at the end of the rainbow. That's what it felt like, this thing between them. Suddenly, the song they'd just played seemed wrong for a new reason. Love wasn't cheap. It wasn't something you had when you were down on your luck. It was what you found when luck was with you all the way.

Already. That's what they'd come to believe. In just a few minutes' time.

Here, in the first seconds of a new year, they were at the beginning of their own new tomorrow—together. They had so much more to learn.

Like each other's names.

20.

~December 4, 2019~

Rose's knitting needles clacked away as she added a new row to her muffler. It gave her something to do until she got another call. Hard to believe the sounds of that faraway New Year's Eve had faded away in Rose's ear three days ago already. It seemed dream-like as she thought about it, and as she waited for the switchboard to light up or hum or buzz. As she waited—and waited—for voices to come through her headset. Someone. Anyone.

Three days of silence meant Rose's mind was filled with nothing but thoughts of times gone by—even with the distraction of her knitting. Recollections of how the good times had faded, just like that opulent New Year's Eve of so long ago. How harsher times, leaner times had followed for them all. The Great Depression. A punch in the stomach to that night's revelers—and, of course, to poor Dorothy and Chester.

Enough with the waiting. Rose crumpled her knitting in her lap, deciding to try the switchboard again. Where *was* Chester? Why was she suddenly so bad at the job she'd held for decades? She had never once failed before. Stretched the limits, perhaps, with all her listening. But never, not once, had she let down one of the

Sullivan Southwestern Telephone customers trying to get in touch with someone they had no number for—or even a last name. With a few questions, she'd always been able to pinpoint the person they needed to talk to. And bring a comforting voice to fill their ear.

But she struggled now. She slammed her headset on and clenched her jaw, connecting lines, asking, "Hello? Hello, you there? Anybody?" while the muffled sounds of a pickup truck engine filled the It Ain't Over Yet. Had Rose turned around in her chair, she would have seen Rob of the *Rob & Geena 4Ever* sidewalk graffiti fame turning into the parking space reserved for him across the street, just outside the bookstore he had owned for going on the better part of a decade.

He used not-so-specific phrases like that sometimes, to himself: *better part of a decade.* Made it sound like he'd been making a go of it for a substantial amount of time.

But Rob didn't immediately remove the key from the ignition. Instead, he idled, the smell of a late lunch for two swirling through the cab. He was certain the sounds of Nat King Cole's voice bled through the rolled-up windows in the same way the sounds of late-'80s hair bands had once bled through the windows of his ancient old Chevy Caprice, his very first (and still favorite) car.

He'd never been a lover of holiday music. He'd always found it corny and trite, and by the second week of December, those incessant bells running behind every single song began to sound to him more like screeches from an angry cat. This year, though, instead of avoiding songs on the radio, he'd actually purchased Christmas albums. Ten of them so far. Bing Crosby and Booker T and the M.G.'s and Bob Dylan and the Brian Setzer Orchestra. Last week, on a whim, he'd even bought a polka band Christmas album from Tina over at the It Ain't Over Yet flea market.

He couldn't get enough.

He was in the holiday spirit. All because of Geena, his first love—the same girl who had, in the late '80s, filled that old Caprice with the smell of her Exclamation perfume.

For way too long, Geena had been one of those dark, squishy spots in a heart that you try to sidestep, like it was made of quicksand. One of those bitter sections of the past that could suck you in and refuse to let you out again, leaving you to drown in a swirl of what-ifs.

After spending time together last Christmas, though, Geena had become someone he could count on. She was, quite simply and perfectly, *his.* A regular voice on his phone. Someone who was going to roll back into town and into his arms in just a few days, as soon as she'd finished grading her last American Lit final.

His first love had become his current love. This kind of thing never happened. People didn't get second chances. It was the stuff of schmaltzy holiday movies. Or the silliest of the paperback romances that he sold in his bookstore. Books he'd always assumed readers gravitated to because they were filled with sweet, lovely events that never actually took place in real life.

And yet...

Those happily-ending paperbacks were turning out to be far more realistic than Rob could have imagined.

The absurd *wonderfulness* of it all had even been taking his mind away from his finances—which was something of a miracle in itself. Sales were down at The Page Turner. A perplexing amount, actually. The kind of down that had him wondering, late last summer, how much longer he'd be able to keep Kelly, his one and only employee. The kind of down that made him even question, at the worst of times, keeping the old place. Which tore him up. But no matter what he tried—sidewalk sales, direct mail flyers—it just wasn't bringing people to the shop.

He couldn't understand it. The rest of the businesses on the square seemed to be on an upswing. Why not his?

The holiday shopping binge had to do it. It just had to. If it didn't…

He stopped the Nat King Cole song. And he shoved another tape into the ancient deck in the dash of his truck. Another one he'd bought over at Tina's place.

Doris Day's voice filled the cab with her soft, soulful rendition of "Sentimental Journey."

He chuckled at himself. Doris Day? The old Metallica-blaring seventeen-year-old would have grimaced at the sight of what he'd turned into. But he couldn't help it. He liked the idea of a journey being nothing more than going back in your mind. Reliving old memories. That's what that old song was about.

As he listened, a vibrant red cardinal swooped down to

land on the hood of his truck. He watched through the frosty windshield as the bird cocked his head and hopped forward a few times. The bird tilted his head in the opposite direction, as though trying to figure Rob out.

"Cardinals appear when angels are near," Rob recited, an old saying he'd often heard Angela repeat. He chuckled. Funny the things that stuck with you, that wound up popping into your mind.

Maybe angels also liked Doris Day. Rob turned up the volume, but the cardinal hopped to the edge of his hood and flapped his wing, as if wordlessly asking Rob to follow him.

Rob chuckled for thinking something so utterly ludicrous. He killed the radio, and gathered the lunch he'd just picked up for himself and Kelly.

The cardinal fluttered to the sidewalk and hopped forward again, this time toward The Page Turner.

"You looking for seasonal work?" Rob joked.

The bird spread his red wings and took to an unusually low flight. He zipped over the sidewalk, straight for the bookstore entrance.

Rob yelped, cringing, expecting the bird to whack his head against the glass panel in the door. Birds did that sometimes, especially in the spring, when nest building was at its zenith.

But the cardinal twisted through the air at the last second, turning and swooping and disappearing into the gray-blue winter sky.

Lunch in his hand, Rob started to reach for the door handle. But he stopped short. A strange brown rumpled pile filled the space in front of the entrance. Had the cardinal been trying to warn Rob? Point it out to him?

Don't be ridiculous, he scolded himself.

What was that brown heap, though? Some sort of book delivery? Why hadn't Kelly taken the delivery inside? She hadn't left, had she? Sure enough, through the front window, Rob could see Kelly shelving books.

What was going on?

As Rob cautiously approached, the brown lump let out a long, low-toned groan.

Rob blinked. That lump was a man. Curled up in his doorway. A disheveled one. With a long, ratty-looking beard.

Rob knelt, placing his takeout container on the ground. "Sir?" he asked. "Sir? Are you all right?" Was he asleep? Who fell asleep in the doorways of random businesses in the middle of the day? Had he passed out? Was he hurt?

The man lifted his head, cleared his throat, and coughed. His bright blue eyes popped open.

"Sir?" Rob repeated. The man's clothes were old. Not just worn. He hadn't seen clothes in that style since he was a little boy visiting his great-grandfather, a farmer who'd viewed all of his possessions in terms of their usefulness. A pair of pants that fit, his grandfather had often bellowed, that had a working zipper? Why, that was not something you threw out. Not ever. And leather boots?

A man held onto those till the very end. Scuffs and all.

Still. Wool pants. Who wore wool pants anymore?

"Sir?"

The man seemed to be coming back to reality in tiny incremental steps. Rob shivered when they locked eyes. He had never seen such despair on a man's face. Not even during his days in the service. This man's expression broadcast he'd seen far too much. More than he'd ever wanted to.

"I—I'm trying to get home," the man blubbered. "I promised. By Christmas Eve, I said."

"Somebody's waiting on you?" Rob asked.

The man nodded, using his hands to push himself upright, sit tall. "Yes. She's been waiting a long time, I'm afraid."

"Let me buy you a bus ticket," Rob announced, assuming that the man was far from home. Anyone that weathered had to be. "You want to call someone first?" He pulled his phone from his pocket.

His words didn't seem to have the positive effect Rob had intended. Instead of grateful, the man seemed more scared or confused. He pushed Rob away as he hoisted himself to him feet.

"Had enough of phones," the stranger grumbled. "Been calling and calling. Finally, though, somebody got through to me. I've been looking—"

"Looking for what?" Rob asked. He grabbed the paper bag from the sidewalk. "Here. Let me give my employee her lunch, and I'll drive you to the bus station. You can eat my lunch on the way."

The man adjusted his hat, pulling the brim down over his eyes. And gasped. "What is that?" he demanded, pointing across the square, toward the It Ain't Over Yet.

"It's—a flea market," Rob said. It was pretty obvious, frankly. Why did the man need to ask? He was back to suspecting the man had been hurt. Some sort of head injury, maybe? Did he need to go to the hospital instead of the bus station?

"No—*that*," the man said.

Rob wasn't sure what he was pointing at. He only saw Tina in the front window, arranging some potential Christmas presents in her front display. She'd apparently selected a few antique toys, a group of something that sparkled—probably some sort of gaudy costume jewelry. And she'd propped a large black case open, showcasing a silver object inside. Rob wasn't sure what it was. The black case reminded him of the one that had carried his son's saxophone to and from after-school practice during his only semester of middle school band.

"Why don't you come inside for a minute?" Rob asked, reaching for the entrance. "Get warm. Get you a cup of coffee." And find out if this man needed medical attention while he was at it. "Don't have anything fancy in here, not like a coffee shop," Rob went on, "but who needs anything other than strong and black, right? You know, my girlfriend—"

But when he turned to usher the man inside, the sidewalk was empty.

Except for one little girl skipping into view.

"Hey, Maddie," Rob greeted. The two were well acquainted. Sometimes, she sat cross-legged on the floor in the back, reading Harry Potters. Rob didn't mind. He pretended not to know about the bookmark in the copy she hid behind the dusty old history books. But he never offered to give her the copy, either. Sneaking around was part of the fun. Most of the fun, maybe. He knew that. He wouldn't dream of spoiling it for her.

"Did you see a man out here?"

"The mailman?" she asked hopefully, her cheeks stained a deep pink from the winter chill.

"No. No. Just a man. In old brown clothes."

Maddie shuddered. Rob took it as a shake of the head. A way to answer no.

Rob hadn't imagined him. He knew that much. And he couldn't have just dissolved into the sidewalk. He had to be somewhere close by.

"I don't want him to wander around out here aimlessly," Rob muttered. "I really should find him."

"Find *who?*" Maddie frowned at him.

"You really didn't see him?" Rob asked.

Maddie stared back, horrified. She had seen him, in fact. She'd seen him evaporate in that slice of time that Rob had turned his back, reaching for the door to the bookstore. And she'd just as quickly discounted what she had seen as some kind of trick of the eye. Like a mirage, only one somehow caused by the winter cold instead of heat.

But now—Rob had seen the man too?

Rob did not suspect that his eyes worked any differently than they had before. Yes, getting Geena back had made him feel happy endings were possible. Second chances existed. Paperback stories no longer seemed schmaltzy and unrealistic. He'd often told himself getting Geena back had turned him into a bit of a misty-eyed softy. All those carols. Doris Day recordings in his truck, for heaven's sake.

But he never would have suspected that an open, happy heart could change what he saw standing right in front of him. No more than Maddie would have ever thought hearing a carol echoing inside an old trumpet in the It Ain't Over Yet could have made her aware that there were voices and music floating through the air. Melodies that she had never paid attention to before.

But it had. Both of those things had changed the way the two of them saw and heard the world around them.

And that was why they were both aware that Chester was back in town. Even if the details of his story were still unknown. They had seen him—which was something that had not happened to Chester.

Not for a very long time.

21.

~December 4, 2019~

Across the street, Rose had also seen Chester. Only, was it really? She couldn't be sure. It had been a man. Old and unkempt and desperate looking. Out in the street. Had it really been him, or had she simply been hoping? She hurried to the front window to try for a better look.

Could it be? If it was Chester, did he know where she'd called him from? Did he know where the It Ain't Over Yet was? Did she need to signal to him, wave him across the street?

Behind her, Tina continued to work undisturbed. She still had not seen Rose. Not once since her reappearance. Neither had Maddie.

Rose squinted. The man had been right outside. She was sure of it. Where was he now? As she tried to spot him again, a woman ran down the sidewalk in front of the It Ain't Over Yet.

Not just any woman, though—Linda Bryant, who had recently been put in charge of the secrets of Sullivan. Or the history museum's exhibit regarding the secrets of Sullivan, anyway.

Tina burst through the flea market door to wave her down. "Just wanted to wish you luck," she announced.

Rose grimaced, standing on her toes, leaning to the side,

squatting. But the two women were completely blocking her view.

Linda paused to stare at her reflection in the window. "Maddie's mother insisted I'd look good as a blonde," she muttered, smoothing her bangs into place, not noticing Rose on the opposite side of the glass.

Was Rose actually invisible?

No—there she was. Her image hovering right on top of Linda's.

Linda continued to try to arrange her bangs, acting like she was staring into a mirror.

Rose waved. She danced a few steps of the Charleston. She stuck out her tongue.

Nothing.

"Picture perfect as a blonde," Tina insisted, adding, "and the sweater's great," while pointing at the poinsettia-covered cardigan peeking out from the opening of Linda's parka.

"Fifteen minutes till the first tour," Linda muttered sourly, bemoaning the fact that she did not have more time to change everything about the way she looked.

"Don't worry, Ms. Bryant," Tina told her, "If you can make reading old Latin texts fun, this tour will be a breeze."

Linda brightened. "I figured all my old students had long forgotten that."

"Reading the *Odyssey* with assigned parts and costumes and live music? Who could forget? Best class I ever took. I'm sure Toby over at the museum remembers it fondly, too, and that's why he tapped you to be in charge of the Sullivan Secrets tour. You'll be a hit."

Linda checked her watch. "Thirteen minutes," she announced, and took off running again.

"You'll be a *hit!*" Tina repeated as Linda raced away. Linda raised an arm, indicating she had heard.

Rose craned her neck now that her view was unobstructed, looking one way down the street and then the other.

But the disheveled man—whoever he had been—was gone.

She slumped back into her seat. None of this made sense. She had reappeared so suddenly herself—but did that sort of thing happen differently for everyone? Might it have actually taken Chester a few days to travel to Sullivan?

She chuckled at herself. "Travel on what, Rose? The train? What conductor punched his ticket?"

Maybe it was only wishful thinking, the idea that it had been Chester.

Her eyes bounced across her old switchboard again. She had connected with the past before—rather than a person. Connected to a New Year's Eve. Maybe she could do it now. Maybe that would mean more to Chester than anything she could say over the phone line.

Her own strange camouflage had taught her the power of being seen. Maybe, she thought, if Chester could somehow see with his own eyes that Dorothy could never give up on him, it would bring him inside the flea market. Where he could finally put his hands on his trumpet.

Rose crossed her fingers. And she set to work. The red cardinal swooped to land on the old phone line outside.

A few blocks over, at the Sullivan History Museum, as Linda's feet thundered on the stairs, the old fruit crate rattled yet again from a shadowy back corner. Toby' d gotten everything important out—or so he'd thought. A few stray bits and pieces, he'd said, were all that remained. He'd stacked the remnants up neatly in the old fruit crate, placing the box where it would be undisturbed. He'd return all of Angela's things at once, after the exhibit wrapped.

But those supposedly useless bits and pieces—and the stories they held—were exactly the pieces the cardinal had made sure Rose could connect to.

And now that she was working the switchboard, the two-cent postage stamps slid from one side of the crate to the other.

22.

~*December 24, 1931*~

"**N**ever seen him so late," called Mrs. Latchy, Dorothy's aging neighbor. *Rubberneck*, that was the word the rest of the neighbors most often used to describe her.

Dorothy cringed. Around her block, her husband Chester was known as a disaster of a man, one of the pretty ones whose empty promises swirled around him like sweet-smelling lilacs. A woman couldn't help but be drawn to his soft voice as he looked into her eyes as though she were the only one in the world who mattered. He offered enormous bouquets of ideas and dreams as colorful as spring blooms. But what good were pretty flowers? Once they'd been placed in the cut glass vase on the table, they never did anything but wilt.

So it was with Chester. Or so neighbors like Mrs. Latchy believed, based on nothing more than a bunch of unverified observations.

Had she—or anyone else on the block—ever had a single decent conversation with Chester? Had they tried to get to know him?

No. They hadn't. They had all made easy, stereotypical assumptions. And now, Mrs. Latchy was using her own prejudices to tease Dorothy.

On Christmas Eve, no less.

Dorothy glanced up and down the street. She still believed. Any minute now, she would see him.

Mrs. Latchy made a kind of *tsk* noise with her tongue. A mix of disapproval and pity.

Dorothy made a fist. Mrs. Latchy had never paid enough attention to know that she and Chester were perfect for each other. Capable of making beautiful music together. Literally. His trumpet, her voice. Which, as far as Dorothy was concerned, was like spinning gold out of thin air. Children were miracles. Wasn't that the word that people cooed around newborns? But why not give the same value to their music?

To the audience, their music was *alive.* It pulsed. It touched everyone who had ever heard them in Frankie's speakeasy. No one left feeling the same as they had walking in. Hearts were happier. Burdens were lighter. The world wasn't quite so dark. How many couples right there in Sullivan could claim the same ability? Was that not a miracle as well?

Dorothy and Chester weren't going to be a speakeasy ensemble forever. It was why he'd left town all those weeks ago—to find them a regular job in a nice establishment. A place where they could make an honest living. Where people would stand in line *out front* to get in.

But how could Dorothy tell Mrs. Latchy that? Wouldn't it sound pie in the sky? Besides, Dorothy and Chester had never been

able to be out in the open about their nightly work—which had to
be true of anyone involved with a speakeasy, she assumed. They'd
had to keep it to themselves.

So Dorothy had no choice but to simply take whatever disapproval Mrs. Latchy chose to dole out.

"I got a check coming," Mrs. Latchy announced, like she
had won a prize. "Did some alterations for the choir." She sighed,
hugging herself against the wintry cold. "No, I never did see the
postman quite so late before. After four already. Sun'll set soon.
Bank'll be closed. Late on Christmas Eve! Can you believe it?"

Dorothy relaxed a bit. It was the postman's absence she was
bemoaning, not Chester's. She chided herself silently for jumping
to conclusions. Especially since Mrs. Latchy did not know where
Chester had gone.

A cardinal drifted down out of the sky, landing on a nearby
branch. Dorothy had seen him before, his red feathers standing out
from the pine trees that lined the neighborhood.

"Looking pretty as a picture this evening," Mrs. Latchy remarked, bringing Dorothy's attention back toward her again.

Still overly cautious, Dorothy wasn't sure if she should accept the compliment. Would it only lead to more criticism? She
eyed Mrs. Latchy's appearance, the plain brown wool coat and large
red Bakelite pin in the shape of a poinsettia. Probably planning on
going to Midnight Mass with her own husband, who was nothing
special himself. Bald and overweight and as old as Dorothy's grandfather. A man who smelled of stale pipe smoke and factory grease.

A man who had accomplished nothing extraordinary.

He had probably never promised Mrs. Latchy anything extraordinary, either. A life of dinner plates and socks and newspapers and pipe smoke. But he had kept those ordinary promises, and that, in Mrs. Latchy's mind, made him a superior husband.

Dorothy wasn't so sure.

She glanced down at her own charcoal-colored gored skirt and the red sweater her mother had knitted years ago. She'd had her hair styled by the woman who lived next door to her in the boarding house. Arranged in chin-length waves with a marcel iron.

"Just—waiting for the postman. Like you," Dorothy lied. In truth, she thought she'd see Chester rounding the edge of the street at any moment. She'd gotten herself all dolled up for him. He'd promised her. He'd be back in time for Christmas Eve. That was what he'd said.

"Never seen him so late," Mrs. Latchy repeated in agreement.

Dorothy nodded distantly, shivering as she glanced through the snow-covered branches lining her street.

Where *was* he?

She edged closer to the sycamore where the cardinal had landed, expecting the bird to decide she was too close and skitter away.

But he did not move.

"You got presents coming, maybe?" Latchy called out. "Looking for something from your folks?"

Dorothy cringed against the mention of her parents, who had never approved of Chester, either. They had warned her. They'd also thought Chester spoke in bouquets. Dorothy hadn't received a present or a birthday card from them since he'd slipped the thin gold band on her finger. They had threatened as much when she'd announced their engagement—and her plans to leave school for him. All in the attempt to force her into a different decision.

"You're too young," they'd both insisted. "Think of what you'd be giving up!"

But Chester was giving up, too. Giving up the road, anyway. She failed to see the difference. Besides, wouldn't they both be gaining something far more important than anything they could leave behind?

"Chester told me he would write before the holiday," Dorothy announced. She said it only because she still believed Chester would come through and return in person. Just like he'd said the day he left. She liked the idea of acting as though there would be nothing more than a crummy letter and then, suddenly—Chester himself, not just coming through, but appearing to do far *more* than what had been expected of him, for once.

There, Chester, she thought. *I set the stage for you. Now all you have to do is show up.*

Mrs. Latchy's face fell. "Chester," she repeated sourly. There it was, all over again: judgment. Mrs. Latchy thought Dorothy was a fool.

As if trying to brighten Dorothy's mood, the red cardinal

hopped from branch to branch. It worked; her spirits began to lift enough that she hummed to his movement, creating a new song. Dorothy found herself thinking of lyrics to match his syncopated rhythm:

Look over here.

I'm red as the ribbons on your favorite gifts.

The color of holiday cheer.

Look at me, the bright spot on stark winter snow.

It's Christmas, the time of miracles.

Believe—believe—believe—even if the rest of the world doesn't know…

"Yes," Mrs. Latchy said, glancing down the street a final time, "it sure is getting late."

But Dorothy did not hear her. She kept her eyes on the cardinal. And even as the cold bit through her stockings, she felt her red lips spreading into a hopeful smile.

No—a *knowing* smile. She was going to see her Chester again.

On Christmas Eve. Just like he promised.

"Even if," she sang softly, under her breath, "the rest of the world doesn't know…"

23.

~The Bank of Sullivan~

The vault had always stored more than just cash.

Or so Walter had regularly informed his son. "Those are goals and ambitions we've got in there," he'd told Scott. "Wishes. Hopes for the future. Somebody's house. The business they want to open. The car they're saving up to buy. Yes," he'd often said, "we don't deal in money here. We deal in dreams."

The day that Angela showed up to talk to Scott, though, it seemed to him that the Bank of Sullivan was primarily filled with yesterdays.

It was all Scott could think of while Angela squirmed on the other side of his desk.

Mostly, he was thinking of high school debate.

Angela had chewed gum all through their high school debate tournaments. It was probably something of a nervous tic, but to Scott, it was like she was preparing to chew up and spit out the competition.

She would lower herself into one of those metal folding chairs along the back of the stage, and she would chomp away, her jaw moving up and down viciously.

When she was called up to the podium, she would always stick the pink wad under the wooden lip—but only temporarily. She'd make her argument, annihilating the competition. Then she'd remove the gum, hiding it in her palm all the way back to her seat, and pop it into her mouth again.

Everybody else hauled giant three-ring binders of information to debate tournaments. Scott did. But Angela? She brought her gum.

And her memory. She brought that, too—and it was far more effective than anybody else's binder. She read incessantly, and everything she read she stored up there in her head, to be pulled out, connected to other tidbits, and used against the poor souls on opposing teams, the ones who drew the short straw and got stuck debating Angela.

One December—junior year, Scott remembered—their bus broke down on the way to the state tournament. To make matters worse, it was snowing and help was having a difficult time getting to them.

The team offered a mixed response—especially as time ticked on, and their driver was appearing less and less successful getting the bus started again. Especially as it grew clear to them all that they were probably going to be a no-show. Some of their fellow debaters and bus occupants crossed their arms and slumped, angry. Others seemed relieved. But the holidays were on the horizon, too, and yet another handful drew the outlines of Christmas trees on the frosty bus windows. Someone brought out a pocket transistor radio, and the sounds of John Lennon's "Happy Xmas (War Is Over)" filled the spaces between the uncomfortable vinyl seats.

Angela nudged Scott, asking him to follow with the curl of a finger.

They slipped out through the door the driver had left open. He followed along as she threw herself in the field, flapping her arms and legs to make snow angels.

They laughed, their breath sending white clouds into the air, not caring that the wet snow was seeping through the backs of their dress clothes.

This was his favorite side of Angela—the silly side. He was flattered to be the one she chose out of everyone on that bus to share it with that day.

Suddenly, she sat up and began to speak in the same authoritative voice usually reserved for her rebuttals. "Wilson Bentley was the first person to ever photograph snowflakes. He took five thousand of them in his lifetime. We didn't have a clue what snowflakes looked like up close until he came along."

Yet another fact she had stored in her memory bank.

Scott snorted a laugh. "You aren't going to say something corny about how we're all unique, are you?"

"No—I was thinking about how we assume we can see everything in front of us. But we don't. We miss so much. Ever wonder what you walk right by and never see? All because someone like Wilson Bentley hasn't come along yet to show us the details."

✳ ✳ ✳

The long-ago scene came back to Scott again as Angela continued to squirm in the chair in front of his desk at the bank. The squirming was beyond odd. The fact that she'd made an appointment seemed still stranger. The fifth of December, eleven in the morning.

He wasn't really sure why she felt she needed any of it. They'd grown up together. The scene in the snow was rare enough to stick out in both of their recollections of high school, but it was not exactly an isolated incident. Their paths had crossed repeatedly, as paths tended to do in small towns.

Besides, they'd cultivated a kind of renewed adult, professional friendship over the past couple of years. She'd spent quite a few hours in the chair in front of his desk, securing the appropriate small business loans to buy Ruby's and later, to finance the renovations. She had often paid her mortgage in person. Even occasionally stopping by to simply say hello. Maybe they still weren't each other's emergency contacts, but they were close enough that Scott had actually thought to invite her to his family's Fourth of July barbecue the summer before.

Now, she was squirreling around in that chair like she had been worried and fretting for days on end what Scott's response to her question would be.

"Let me get this straight," Scott said. "You want to know about the—what do you want to know about the deed?" He twisted his face into a confused expression. "Hasn't all of this been settled for ages? What problem could have possibly crept up at this stage of the game?"

He leaned forward, plopping his forearms on some scattered manila folders.

He wished she would come right out with it—tell him what this was all about. What trouble she thought might be around the bend.

Instead, Angela attempted to avoid his full-on glare by looking at the front corner of the desk, near the inbox. The same corner where he'd arranged a cluster of framed photographs. One, Angela noted, was of his father, Walter, who looked in that photo very much like he always did each night when he still showed up for her after-closing happy hour.

She could not tell Scott that, of course. Though she ached to. He'd seen his father the year before. She was certain of it. She wanted to blurt it out, tell him seeing his father had been made possible because of her.

This new life—running Ruby's—made Angela feel, in a way, like she once had when she was young. Like she had something about her that turned heads, something that was noticed everywhere she went in Sullivan.

This time around, the attention-snagging wasn't because she was pretty. Or young. She'd acquired a recognition as a successful businesswoman—that was true. The people of Sullivan knew she was doing something marvelous. But the finer details—the real responsibility that lay across her shoulders, regarding the after-hours regulars—she felt was both real and undiscussed. Not even completely seen in full.

Almost like those snowflakes she had told Scott about on that long-ago debate trip.

The regulars had chosen her when they had never chosen anyone else. They'd discouraged any semi-interested potential investor with one disaster after another until Angela had shown up. Her own memories were the strongest—and pure. They'd believed, and Angela had come through for them.

This kind of thing was once in a lifetime. It never came back around again.

But what if it was suddenly in danger? What if Frankie really did pose a threat to everything she'd worked to achieve? Angela would never find a way to start over. This was it—for her and for those unseen faces she had grown to love.

"Angela?" Scott pressed.

"Sorry—I got distracted by your collection of family shots," Angela admitted, pointing.

"The kids are getting big—"

"I was looking at your dad. That's exactly the way he looked when we were kids ourselves," Angela said, pretending she had not talked to Walter the night before. Pretending he was not the one who bellowed, every single evening, "To the Christmas *spirits* who are all alive and well!"

Scott shrugged. "I guess—well. I guess that I've been thinking of my father a lot lately. Christmas coming and all. You know how it is."

Angela hated this. All this dancing around the truth.

"Now," Scott said. "The deed? What were you saying?"

She hadn't said anything. Nothing about what she was really afraid of. That Ruby had potentially received a warning shot from Frankie Hall. How did Angela fight back? How did she protect her bar from whatever Frankie was now?

It felt a little like trying to have a fistfight with the wind.

Angela's stomach twisted with fear. She hated that, too. Because it felt like weakness. That was mostly what fear was, wasn't it? Proof that someone else had the upper hand?

"It's silly, I suppose," she finally admitted. "But I was wondering—well. If the bar is completely mine. I guess I mean—what I'm asking—can anyone question my ownership?"

"I don't understand."

"Frankie was the original owner, right?"

"Frankie…" Scott thumbed through some files on his desk. "I have a Frances. Frances Hall."

"That's her."

"She wasn't the original owner. Looks like her father was. Still. That building has changed hands—I'm not sure how many times, actually. There were several owners before Ruby. Why are you asking about Frances?"

"I heard that she didn't leave under the best circumstances."

"I don't have that information—"

"Yeah," Angela said, her face flaming beneath her fringe of gray bangs. "I know. You—you wouldn't. It's silly, really. I mean,

I've had the place now for two years. I know that you would have made sure the title was clear. But it's just…"

She stopped talking and stared at him, long enough to remind him it was still her, Angela. The same logical, smart Angela who had regularly beaten him in debate (and the Language Arts Fair, come to think of it) at Sullivan High and had never, in any way, seemed like someone prone to shadowboxing, fighting imaginary opponents.

Scott might have been concerned—he might have been wondering where that tough Angela had gone, the one who had chewed up her opponents—if she had not mentioned his father. It had distracted him. Completely.

"You going to be having a big Christmas Eve shindig?" he asked, his eyes landing, for the briefest of moments, on his father's picture.

This was torture. Utterly. He could not see the details. Angela couldn't show them to him without also betraying the regulars.

Why had she even thought any information could be gleaned from this meeting? She fidgeted beneath the heat of her own embarrassment.

For some reason, Walter's old saying found her—the one she'd often heard him repeating to Scott, about the bank dealing in wishes—and she knew that if she could wish for anything, it would be some sort of police officer she could turn to. Not Officer Vargas, who would have wrinkled his forehead in confusion, unsure of what Angela was afraid of.

A police officer who understood the full story of Ruby's Place. Who knew the regulars were there. One who had maybe even patrolled the streets back when Frankie had owned the place.

Angela had to shake it away, tell herself she was wasting her time with such a wish. No such officer existed.

She was utterly wrong about that.

But right then, she couldn't see how wrong she was. All she could do was extend her hand and thank Scott for his time.

24.

~*December 15, 1931*~

"Still can't believe you took this job," Hank told Edna, exhaling a plume of smoke in her face.

Edna batted the toasted-smelling wisps away and stared him down. "I pestered Frankie for it," she corrected.

Hank shook his head, lifting a glass filled with whiskey. "My brother's wife. Breakin' the law every night. At a juice joint."

"Aw, come on," Edna moaned. "It's not as dramatic as all that."

Hank tossed her a crooked, knowing smile.

"It's not," Edna insisted. "You and I aren't doing a thing we didn't do when we were young. Sneaking out for a drink of who-knew-what when we all knew what we *really* had a taste for was a bit of youthful naughtiness."

"And now?"

"And now, it's about the extra cash we need. You know that."

"Come on—way I heard it, you had quite the time here last Christmas Eve."

Edna shrugged. "What if I did? Can't maintain that feeling forever. You live the thrills enough, they begin to feel common-place. Like your car."

"My car?"

"Sure. I remember the first time you let me drive it, back when I'd met Arthur. First car I'd ever driven. Out there on a dirt path behind Old Man Ritter's farm. Barely made it to fifteen miles an hour, and never did quite get the hang of shifting that day, which involved just magically knowing how far down to press the clutch. It had been thrilling, though, to be in the driver's seat, the gears grinding and the vehicle bucking…even though you did shout at me the whole time to pay attention."

"You never did listen. Tore my gears to smithereens."

"Oh, I did not," she said, making a face. "Still. I've driven daily now for years, and I rarely ever get the same feeling. Even going twice as fast. Just turning the wheel does not make me laugh."

"Too bad," Hank said. "You got a great laugh."

Edna ignored this. "I am a waitress in a speakeasy. I serve bootleg liquor to Sullivan's good and bad. I have memorized all Frankie's cocktail recipes. I sing along at night as Dorothy entertains the crowd."

"Good thing," Hank said. "You got a pretty voice."

"I haven't sung a single song on key in my entire life."

"Who said anything about keys?"

Edna had to force herself not to smile. But she could feel her cheeks turn red.

"What?" Hank asked, seeming proud to have flustered her.

"I wish Arthur thought all this was as amusing as you seem to." She acted as though it was all in good fun—a joke, a jest. But in truth, her husband had never approved of her taking an actual job. Especially at Frankie's. Arthur's repeated frowns of disapproval had found her with not a small amount of hurt. In Arthur's mind, a married woman who took on a job was telling her husband that he had failed. That he was not earning enough, doing enough. That his one and only purpose in life—to provide for a family—had not gone as planned.

Yes, in Arthur's mind, Edna had told him that she was passing judgment on him, simply because she had taken one of the few jobs open to her, or to anyone in Sullivan.

And so, in return, Arthur had lobbed his own judgment on her. Each time she left for work and returned.

"Arthur's a stick in the mud," Hank assessed. "Always has been. Never did understand what you saw in him."

"He's your *brother*."

"Right." Hank exhaled another stream of smoke, and held his glass toward her, wordlessly asking for a refill.

Before she could turn away, Hank grabbed her wrist. He gave her more than just a knowing look.

It was uncomfortable. Until he murmured, "Come clean, Edna. It never completely stops being a thrill. And you never stopped being the kind of woman who thirsts for it." He offered a crooked, boyish grin. The kind of grin he often wore in Frankie's, wild storytelling Lothario he still managed to be, given the right setting.

Edna laughed. Mostly, she laughed because she could easily

decode the look he had just given her. He was saying he understood her—in a way few others did. Because they were the same. Two people who never did stop thirsting for adventure.

Edna had forgotten that until last Christmas.

Still, she would have made some sort of remark back if a knock hadn't hammered against the alley door, drawing Edna's attention.

She took a moment to glance across the bar. Frankie, currently involved in some long-winded conversation with a couple at a nearby table, motioned for Edna to see who it was.

Edna nodded, then shook her finger at Hank, reminding him to behave while she was away.

She didn't realize she still had her cocktail muddler in her hand until she pressed her ear against the tiny window in the back door. When she heard the murmured password, she slid the lock free.

And found herself staring at the deep blue uniform of a Sullivan police officer.

Her muddler slipped from her fingers to clatter onto the floor.

The officer's handcuffs rattled as he squatted. He raised the mashing tool to his nose.

"Get folks in here sometimes with upset stomachs," Edna explained.

"Do you, now."

Edna nodded, looking straight into his eyes. The way any

innocent person might.

"That smell, though," the officer said, taking another sniff. "Smells like—"

"Ginger ale and peppermint."

The officer gave her a stern look. "I'd much rather have a Tom Collins." And offered her a wink.

Edna backed away, letting the officer inside.

"Nice cover, though, Edna," Officer Charlie Barister said, handing the muddler over. "Your calm conviction very nearly made me forget the smell of bathtub gin."

"One Tom Collins, coming up, Charlie," Edna announced, making sure to lock the alley door again—it was Frankie's number-one rule: that alley door had to be locked. Every single time someone new came in, it was locked again. No excuses. No forgetting. "I know it's your usual, though. You don't have to order it every single time. Not when I'm here."

Officer Barister took a seat next to Hank. "Charlie," Hank greeted in the same manner he would any old friend, one you weren't surprised in the least to see inside Frankie's.

Hank and Edna both knew how Frankie's operated. On the goodwill of the Sullivan police department, that was how.

The cops came. Not all of them, but not just Charlie, either. The Sullivan police department had its fair share of by-the-book officers who would have closed the place down in a second. But the rest showed up with an unspoken agreement never to blab about what was going on. They knocked and repeated the password—in uniform—had a drink or two—then left with a wink and a tip of their hat. Maybe a pat on the behind for one of the waitresses. But never for Frankie. Not if they knew what was good for them. Not if they wanted to keep that hand of theirs.

Edna mixed Charlie's drink, sliding it into place in front of him. He was young. Twenty. A nice round number—and the youngest on the force. The age Edna was when she was smoking and kissing and dancing along the edge of wildness.

She wondered about Charlie. Was he a good guy or bad? So what if he enjoyed a Tom Collins now and then? What did that mean really? Was Charlie truly watching out for Frankie—a woman on her own in a cutthroat business? Was he maybe on Frankie's payroll, like so many others in Sullivan? Was he getting a slice of the profits, a little payment every single month, in exchange for his silence, his protection? Was he keeping any Sullivan journalist or new cop who might have an itch to make a few headlines from bursting into the speakeasy after dark? Was he making sure that everyone involved with Frankie's—the waitresses like Edna or Ludlow the liquor distributor—remained safe from arrest?

Then again, a bust like the one Frankie's could provide would certainly make a lawman's career. Charlie could end up on the front page—and not just in Sullivan. The Feds could offer him some high-up job. As much as she liked him, part of Edna wondered if Charlie was just biding his time.

He was so painfully *young*. The kind of young that maybe even indicated he hadn't yet decided if he was good or bad. The kind of young that maybe couldn't anticipate what kind of offers might come his way. The kind of young that couldn't know he might eventually find himself pushed in a corner, needing an escape hatch. The kind of young that did not know that sometimes, escape only happened by hurting someone else.

Charlie was either a guard dog Edna could scratch behind the ears or one she needed to steer clear from. One of these days, Edna figured she'd find out one way or the other.

She just hoped the finding out wouldn't put herself—or anyone else who frequented Frankie's—in harm's way.

Another knock rattled the back door.

Edna kept her eye on Charlie as she once more made her way down the small hallway toward that back exit.

She grasped the small metal hook, sliding the tiny opening to the side. Two eyes peered at her as the whispered code word floated through the space.

Edna squinted back, into the darkness of the alleyway. She had perfected the art of recognizing a person by only his or her eyes. Window to the soul and all that.

But it was more. Eyes weren't just round; they came in a variety of different shapes. They had different patterns of wrinkles surrounding them. Eyebrows could be sculpted or overgrown. Women had natural lashes or had applied cake mascara.

These eyes, though...Edna had no idea who they belonged to.

Still. He (and it was clearly a "he") knew the password.

Edna still felt she needed to get Frankie. Tap her on the shoulder and whisper into her ear. But Frankie would probably have a hard time hearing her tonight, in the midst of this racket. And besides, she'd been pushing Edna to take care of things on her own more and more. Frankie would get annoyed if she tugged at her arm too many times, asking too frequently for her help or approval, almost like a child.

Yes, Frankie would undoubtedly be annoyed with Edna if she pestered her now.

Besides, she reminded herself yet again, the man knew the password.

So Edna took a deep breath and swung the back door open.

He took a shallow step backward, seeming surprised to find her standing there. He'd clearly been expecting Frankie. His eyes popped, his head jutted backward, then his face spread outward into a pleased smile.

A crocodile kind of smile, as far as Edna was concerned. Did he think he was about to get a kinder reception from Edna? Did he view her as an easy target?

Edna fought a shiver.

"Ma'am," he greeted, tipping his ratty brown hat.

She nodded once, crossing her arms over her chest.

A truck parked in the alley leaned to one side, the load in the bed putting the kind of pressure on the frame that threatened to snap the back axle.

What could possibly weigh so much?

Liquid. Edna knew the answer before she was even quite ready for it.

She squinted at the wooden barrels. This stranger had a truck full of whiskey. Bathtub gin. Moonshine.

But he was not Frankie's regular distributor. That was Robert Ludlow's job. Robert, whom Frankie had always said could fix anything.

Robert. So what did this guy want?

"Can I help you?" she asked. She wasn't sure what to do with her tone. Perturbed? Curious?

"Let me introduce myself. I'm Maxwell," he said, holding out his hand for her to shake. "Maxwell Ross."

Edna did not budge. She didn't know any Maxwell Ross.

Maxwell's smile faded. He withdrew his empty hand, cleared his throat, and attempted to regain his composure.

"I got quite a deal for Frankie," he said. "But maybe you're the woman who can close on it."

That did it: Edna realized the need to speak calmly in a high-pitched, childlike tone of innocence. "Sir, we already get deliveries from Sam's Grocery. He cuts the fairest deal in town."

"I think you and I both know I'm not talking about chicken fried steak and pie, right peaches?"

Maxwell grinned again. Edna didn't like it.

"I know who she's been workin' with," he insisted. "I know which distributor. And I got a better deal for her than Ludlow. Boy, do I have a deal."

Edna tensed. Loyalty, she had learned quickly, was itself a currency in Frankie's after-dark business. And this man was out to drive a wedge in Frankie's loyalty to her distributor. Which would be dangerous if not fatal for her business.

But if she said no to him, that could be dangerous, too. She knew nothing about this person—she did not literally know everyone in Sullivan, and this man had never, to her knowledge, ever visited Frankie's before. She only knew that in a business already not on the up-and-up, he obviously had to be a crook.

She wanted to back up enough to signal to Hank that she needed help. But that showed weakness, didn't it? The kind of weakness that meant this stranger would know he could take advantage of her? And besides, if she signaled to Hank, wouldn't Charlie also see?

And what would Charlie, a uniformed cop, do with this information?

She could not take the chance. Which meant this situation—right here, in the alley, with a man who wanted to sell her his own bootlegged liquor, who obviously did not follow the unwritten code of behavior in an illegal business, who could get angry at this exchange (and then use his anger as a weapon)—was hers alone to deal with.

It was hers to navigate or completely mess up.

She raised one of her own eyebrows (penciled in a slightly darker brown in order to contrast with her auburn hair) and asked, "Not about pie? Then it must be about our pot roast. If not, I have no idea what you're referring to."

"It's gonna be that way, is it?" Maxwell smirked, the smile disappearing from his face. He turned, his feet punching the sidewalk as he hurried to his truck, stopping once to glare her way.

Edna stayed in the doorway, refusing to move until she was out of the truck's rearview mirror.

Once the truck's engine grew faint, she told herself it was over. No sense in bothering Frankie with the details of it all.

In reality, she had absolutely no idea what she had just done.

25.

~*December 5, 2019*~

Yes, who *was* Charlie Barister? Hero admired by boys all throughout Sullivan, though none quite so much as his own little boy, his Tom? A corrupt police officer, one who was on the take? A police officer biding his time, waiting to make a name for himself?

Did anyone in Sullivan know for sure?

Was it possible for a person to ever truly know anyone?

That last question had been haunting Dorothy ever since the appearance of Frankie's old letter.

It was a question that tortured her all over again, with a kind of renewed viciousness, the night Angela returned from her visit with Scott. Dorothy sipped her gin rickey, listening as the regulars pestered Angela for details regarding what she'd learned at the bank—which was nothing. Angela had gotten nowhere.

Discussions quickly turned toward rehashing story after story of Frankie Hall:

"Smashed a baseball bat against his Model T…"

"Now, I don't know that the woman *actually* had mob connections, but let me tell you…"

"Threatened my grandfather with a pistol…"

"And then when my uncle flat-up disappeared…"

Where had these stories come from? Had they always float-ed among the regulars, and Dorothy had simply closed herself off to them? Or were the tales currently all being embellished—right then, right in front of Dorothy? After all, sometimes, not knowing something for certain could make a person's brain go haywire. It meant all you could do was imagine the possible answers—which were often far wilder and more sinister than reality.

Were the regulars all doing that to Frankie—turning her into a villain? How could Dorothy have never heard these tales?

Each story hit Dorothy with a new wave of sadness.

"Frankie was a great comfort to me," she tried. "You know, when I was young—"

But no one was listening. Not to her. Not to her own story about Frankie Hall. Her favorite story. About the two of them in the alley out behind that very building. It was still so clear to her— she didn't see the old scene from her eyes, but from Frankie's.

That was how well she'd felt she'd known her.

Dorothy retreated from the crowd and plopped down onto the piano bench, where the shadows could find her and her own memories of Frankie would be easier to tap into.

26.

~*October 3, 1931*~

Frankie hated taking the garbage out. She grabbed the indoor container—filled with sour smelling kitchen scraps—and headed into the dark alley, quickly dumping it into the even fouler-smelling larger container with the same disgusted force she might use on a troublesome speakeasy customer who'd had one too many and was looking to start a fight.

She had just started to head back inside when she began to realize the large alley trash container was sniffing.

Frankie scowled. She didn't have patience for anything that cried. Not even metal objects Frankie was flat-up abusing. *Get tough, stupid can*, she nearly barked.

But no, the can wasn't crying. Of course it wasn't. As her eyes grew better accustomed to the dark, Frankie could make out a familiar female form attempting to cower, tucking her face behind her hand. The ivory sateen skirt trailing out from underneath a heavy black wool coat with the patch on one elbow was instantly recognizable. Dorothy. Frankie's vocalist. Half of the nightly musical duo. Sniffing and shuddering and full-on sobbing.

"He left, didn't he?" Frankie wiped her hands on the back of her skirt. "Chester, I mean." He had already mentioned as much. Even if he hadn't, it wouldn't have been a surprise. In Frankie's world, men did that when their backs got pressed into a corner. They began to dream of distant lands.

Women, in Frankie's observations, tended to hunker down and work on whatever tiny postage stamp of a home they'd claimed for their own. Even Frankie had.

Not that Dorothy was much of a woman. Poor thing had asked Frankie for ice the other night to soothe the wisdom tooth she was beginning to cut.

Dorothy was a kid. Which made Frankie a little angry at Chester. What had he been thinking, leaving her alone? Not only had she lost her companion, she had lost her family because of him, and this was the first time she'd ever found herself on her own.

Frankie fumed. It seemed so foolish for Chester to take off to find something better. As if money was as commonplace as leaves and a job could be had for a smile in some other state.

"How long till I can expect him back?" Frankie finally asked. "I do hope he'll take my stage again. Even temporarily."

Dorothy shook her head.

"I'm not being cute. I mean it. I wish he'd come back. Maybe not as much as you do, but the man plays a mean trumpet. It'd be impossible to replace him."

"Three months," Dorothy answered around another sob. She wiped her eyes. "He said he'd give it three months. And then he'd come for me."

Frankie sighed. As if three months was some sort of magical length of time. All it would take for Chester to establish a new life. He truly was a dreamer. Especially in times as bad as these.

Dorothy staggered toward the back door. Overcome by emotion, she stopped abruptly and collapsed onto the speakeasy step.

Frankie groaned. There was no way around the poor woman—even if she'd wanted to leave her there, she couldn't. She was stuck. Sympathizer in Chief. Bad back and all.

Frankie grabbed hold of the handle on the back door and slid to the cold step, groaning and grumbling and huffing the entire way. The concrete beneath her was freezing. It radiated straight through the fabric of her skirt to send a painful chill across her backside.

She struggled to figure out where to put her legs. She was tall. Taller than most men. Nearly a foot taller than Dorothy. Everything about her was bigger than normal. She had to travel to Columbia, Missouri twice a year to find shoes big enough. With her heels flat on the ground, her knees poked up like two knobby mountains. When she put her legs down, her toes pointed skyward, and her feet appeared to have become an audience of two, watching and listening uncomfortably to this exchange.

Dorothy snickered.

"I'm glad you find this entertaining," Frankie barked. "You do understand that me being down here is supposed to be comforting. Is it comforting?" She leaned closer, getting right up in Dorothy's face. "Are you comforted yet?"

Dorothy let out a wild belly laugh.

Frankie leaned back. Her laughter was a good sign, anyway.

"I've got one important question," Frankie said. "Did he take that trumpet of his?"

Dorothy's face grew serious again as she nodded.

"Then it will be fine," Frankie offered.

Dorothy shook her head sadly.

"Look, we all do what we have to do. For me, that was knocking down a wall in the back of my diner and going into the after-hours business. Never would've crossed my mind until the crash and a pile of really dumb laws. Seems, in rough times, the only thing that can make any money at all is something that makes people put aside their troubles. Doesn't matter if their feeling better is only temporary. That's the service I provide. I never would've made it on the diner alone. Never. But this little place back here, where folks can pretend, for a while, that the outside world doesn't exist? That's where my real money is. Yes, ma'am. A slice of escape. That's my specialty."

Frankie eyed Dorothy, trying to figure out whether to tell her the next part or not. Her mouth started moving before she'd even realized she'd made the decision. "I offered him more money," she admitted.

Dorothy's eyes swelled. "You did?"

"He told me it wasn't enough."

Before Dorothy had time to fully process this new revelation, Frankie explained, "He didn't mean money. He meant that this life wasn't enough for the two of you. He wanted something better. An honest life. It was eating him up. You two have other dreams to chase outside of this place. I know that. Dreams of a home of your own. A real home. Of—kids, eventually. Even though you still seem so young to me."

Frankie jutted to the side in a way that made Dorothy turn toward her, look her square in the face. "Did you know I almost belted Chester the first time he walked in with you?"

"You did?" Dorothy asked, her eyes big and wet, her nose and mouth red. "Why?"

"Because I thought—what a creep, coming in here with that girl. But you know, when I heard the two of you sing, it was just—"

"What?"

"Meant to be. You two. I mean you, on your own—never did hear anybody sing so sweetly. But put the two of you together?" Frankie whistled. "Never in my whole life did I ever see two people better fit for each other. And that's the straight-up truth."

She nudged Dorothy. "Be-ooo-te-ful music together," she said, in an overexaggerated way, tugging a smile out of her.

"I know you two want a life that doesn't include sneaking around. He wants to give you all that. He's a good man, your Chester. And you're lucky to have found him. Your perfect match."

Dorothy perked a bit, like a thirsty flower getting a much-needed drink of water.

"*And* he has the ability to sell people a little slice of happiness—him and that trumpet of his. Like I said, I deal in slices of happiness every single day. I know how important they are. So you two will be just fine. You keep on singing right here, earning your own wages, like always, nothing different about that. And come— what date did he promise you?"

"Christmas Eve."

"Come Christmas Eve, he'll be on his way home to get you. Take you right off to that better life."

Dorothy threw her arms around Frankie's neck. "Thanks," Dorothy muttered.

"I didn't fix a thing, gal."

"A little slice of escape," she muttered.

The two women sat together for a while. Frankie was waiting for Dorothy to make the first move, be the first to signal it was time to get up.

Dorothy knew that. And in that moment, she loved her for it.

27.

December 24, 2019

~Our Journey~

Huh. I hope we didn't take a wrong turn back there. The landmarks have changed a bit. There used to be an old gas station on the right—must've been knocked down. Made that turnoff look completely different.

I guess gossip does the same thing, doesn't it? Hear somebody else's version of events too many times, and suddenly, it's almost like they've knocked down the landmarks and changed the landscape of the trips we take down memory lane.

Sometimes, hearing stories from other people's viewpoint can make things clearer, I suppose. Most times, it seems, it really just leads us astray.

But how do you know for sure?

Poor Dorothy was beginning to wonder the same thing. Because Frankie—or, at least, the Frankie lodged in her own memory—was not the kind of woman who would ever write a threatening letter.

As the stories swirled around Dorothy, she started to remember the whispers that had once filled her own music classroom. Little girls with their hands cupped around their mouths, whispering into their best friends' ears. Sometimes, the tidbit was so juicy, the listener would turn and repeat it to the person sitting on her other side.

A silly old game of telephone. By the time the whispered sentence reached the end of the classroom, it was *never* the same sentence they'd started out with. In fact, by the time it got to the end, the sentence was usually completely unrecognizable.

Is that what this is? Dorothy wondered. Had the regulars gotten their stories about Frankie twisted up? Had they forgotten where these tales originated? Did they now believe that distorted and inflated stories were actually made of the same kind of verifiable facts that Toby preferred to deal in over at the history museum?

Had gossip grown stronger with the telling, become less rumor and more town legend? What *was* the truth of Sullivan? What had been cleaned up? Reinvented? Embellished? What had been darkened? Turned into something more sinister? Had Frankie?

Dorothy wasn't sure anymore. Even armed with a slew of her own memories. After all, what she remembered wasn't entirely objective, was it? We all pretty up our own stories. Tidy up the details to make them work out in our favor. What had Dorothy prettied up? Had she turned Frankie into a good person simply trying to make a buck in a bad time?

It would be understandable if she did, wouldn't it? I mean, poor Dorothy. Her husband disappears during the Depression, never to be heard from again, not by a single soul. He never returns, and neither does the truth of what happened to him.

I heard that wasn't unusual at the time. Happened to a lot of men. Probably met some pretty gruesome ends, most of them.

So why not make her own past a little less awful? Why not make Frankie into a hero?

Had Dorothy really done that?

Maybe *I* have. After all, the details I'm sharing with you are things I've heard, too. Secondhand, third-hand…

Maybe I'm tidying things up as I tell this wild story, here in the backseat of your car.

All the more reason for us to continue on our journey to Sullivan.

Where you'll be able to see it unfold for yourself.

28.

~*December 6, 2019*~

A black, shadowy figure cupped his eyes with his hands and peered through the front window of the It Ain't Over Yet.

Tina yelped, startled enough to drop the vintage Superman lunch box in her hand. It clattered against the tile floor, the racket bouncing through aisle after aisle of yesterday.

The man peering through the window didn't look up, seemingly oblivious to the noise inside.

Tina made no attempt to retrieve the box. Instead, she took a cautious step toward the glass. Tina tended to see the same basic circle of faces, over and over. But she had never seen this face be-fore.

…Or had she? *Was* that someone she had already met? Someone who had since become a poster boy for hard times?

He was certainly rough looking. Overgrown. Could the dirty long hair and the beard be acting as disguises? Would she be able to call the man by name without them?

His ice blue eyes remained fixed. He was staring, but not at Tina. At an object in the front window display.

She took yet another step forward.

Finally, the man looked up.

Tina definitely did not know him.

He paused, then reached for the door. Tina regretted getting his attention. For a split second, she actually wondered if she could lie to him and tell him that she was just about to close. Right then, in the middle of the day. That some disaster had happened. The roof was leaking in the back. The plumbing was all backed up. Or…there had been a small fire near the coffee pot left out for customers. Or…

Too late. He was inside.

"Ma'am," he greeted, removing his hat and smoothing his hair back from his grimy face. "Would you mind if I looked at your trumpet there in the front window?"

Tina flinched. Should she let him? Or should she reach for the phone in the back pocket of her bell-bottom jeans?

He sensed her hesitation and took a step back, pointing at the window. "I'm a musician. Or I was. And that trumpet is so beautiful. Silver plate. Might be a Buescher. I'm guessing mid-1920s."

Tina was intrigued. He seemed to know what he was talking about. She inched her way between her '50s-era life-sized laughing Santa, an old tricycle, and the enamel heater—all those winter objects she'd hauled out of her storage facility, hoping they would draw Christmas shoppers.

She closed the lid on the instrument case, carried it gingerly to the front counter. "Think you'll have more space here," she said, reopening the case again.

The man hurriedly followed, gripping his hat brim tightly in both hands. He leaned forward, the way people sometimes leaned over cribs, not wanting to disturb a sleeping baby.

He sighed an "Ooooh," as he smiled briefly. Tilted his head. Got a teary glint in his eye.

A strange sense of calm engulfed Tina. Something about the stranger put her completely at ease.

"Feel free to take it out of the case," Tina offered.

"Really?" he asked.

"Sure, sure. Take your hat for you."

She hadn't been prepared for the feel of the fabric in her hand. Rougher than modern fabrics. And yet also slightly fragile. A bit moth-eaten. It looked like it had come out of someone's attic. Maybe he'd gotten it for free at the homeless shelter off the highway. She knew the place kept boxes of hats and gloves and even new packages of socks through the winter months.

She hated herself for the moment of judgment that had passed through her as he had stepped inside. It was Christmas. Where was her compassion?

He lifted the instrument gently.

"Still think it's a—what name did you say again?"

He shook his head. "It's unique," he said. "Custom. One of a kind. Specially made."

"Try it out," Tina offered.

The man looked shocked. Seemed to hesitate a moment. But he placed the instrument to his lips and he played a few notes.

Four of them.

Tina recognized them instantly. The opening notes of "Silent Night." Only, the way this man played them, they sounded mournful. Pleading. As though he was begging, *Wait out this one cold night. Just sit it out with me. At the end of it, something better will be.*

Four notes. Tina sighed and touched her chest, her fingers resting on the soft angora of her vintage sweater set.

"Would you be open to a barter?" the man asked.

"What kind of barter?"

"I can't afford that trumpet. But if you need some help at the store here, now that Christmas is coming, I'd work off the cost."

Tina didn't need any help. She'd owned and worked that store herself for the better part of thirty years. All through the hard decades, when Sullivan looked like one of the dime-a-dozen mid-sized towns all through the US, cities that had fallen on bad times and didn't know how to dig themselves out, she had made the store work. Even when her business had occasionally been discounted—some old place that sold a bunch of used junk, it had sometimes been said, not like a real business with shiny new everything inside—even then, she had survived. And now that traffic had started to trickle back? Why, she didn't begrudge the extra work. She reveled in it.

She needed no help.

And yet…

She had never seen anyone so instantly attached to an object in her shop.

Tina knew nothing of this man. Except for the fact that he needed that trumpet. No way would anyone else in Sullivan have the same reaction. She'd never seen anyone respond like that, not in all her years behind the counter. Mrs. Anderson hadn't even behaved like that, and she'd been paying off the same brooch in layaway for nearly two years.

Like Mrs. Anderson, he did not ask for the trumpet to be lowered in price. It would tarnish his dignity.

"I can't tell you how much I've been hoping someone like you would walk through my door," Tina lied. She stretched out her hand. "Help is exactly what I need. Welcome to my staff. I'm Tina."

"Chester."

They shook.

Tina removed the price tag and tucked the instrument behind the counter.

She needed to come up with a job that would make it seem she actually needed him. That her offer wasn't pure charity.

And fast.

29.

~*December 10, 2019*~

Geena Barister walked slowly down the familiar sidewalk, her mind flooded with an odd swirl of emotions. She was back home. But the warm, comforting feeling of home was gone. Because her dad was gone.

Just outside of Ruby's Place, she stopped to stare at the letters that had been carved into wet sidewalk cement all those years ago: *Rob & Geena 4Ever 1987.*

Another lifetime. But as she traced the edges with the toe of her sneaker, the sentiment no longer felt like a *what-if.* Funny how time worked. Back when she was young, the future had seemed unobtainable. Untouchable. Light years away. Now, here, in her forties, it was the past that seemed so. The past was a place she could not get back—at least, not by any other vehicle than her own mind.

She hoisted her tortoiseshell glasses up higher on her nose as she glanced across the street. She could see Rob moving around inside the front window of The Page Turner bookstore. Feelings of nostalgia—of missing the past—really shouldn't have been interrupting her every thought, not this year. Rob wasn't some old piece of graffiti, not a chunk of old times gone by carved deep into her heart. He was a present tense.

But Rob, this year, had nothing to do with these feelings. She knew the real reason she was turning so wistfully sentimental: her father.

Technically, last Christmas had been Geena's first without him. But this holiday season, as she'd returned to town, Geena had found herself flooded with memories of her dad: Bounding down the stairs in his police uniform, running late because he'd taken the time to braid her hair. Standing on the porch, grilling poor Rob, her high school sweetheart. She chuckled, remembering the skin-tight acid washed Palmetto jeans she'd loved and he'd hated. The blond hair she'd highlighted with Sun-In and a blow-dryer until it was crunchy—the same hair he'd joked would look *fantastic* under a hat. The old hair band power ballads she'd played over and over, until she often caught him whistling their melodies.

Maybe, she tried to tell herself, you weren't ever supposed to have everything you wanted all at once. Life was dealt out in spurts. In slices.

But this idea rang hollow. There *had* been a time when she'd had Rob and her dad both. Back in 1987—when Rob was carving their names into the freshly-poured sidewalk square, and her dad was shaking his head at her, telling her such public displays were inevitably foolish—back then, why couldn't she have realized how lucky a person was to be the recipient of so much affection? It wasn't like you could just go out and buy more, the same way you could exchange one worn-out pair of jeans for another.

It had taken her a while to figure that out. Almost like Geena's much-loved books: the true, full meaning of any one period of life could never really be understood until the last page was read.

Her phone went off. She fished it from the pocket of her old-fashioned man's wool Pendleton jacket, finding another text had come in from the Head of the University of Iowa English Department. "Sorry I didn't catch you before you left for the holiday," it read. "We need to talk about your contract."

Geena grimaced. She'd hoped avoiding the department head before leaving for winter break would mean putting this discussion off until she returned for the spring semester.

Really, though, it only made sense that he'd be after her for an answer.

Her teaching contract would be up next May. They had offered her an extension. Three more years. Geena had always imagined she would jump at the chance—but once it had arrived, she wasn't so sure.

The truth was, Geena had inherited a nice sum of money when her father had passed away last winter. That, and her childhood home, which she now owned outright. After crunching the numbers, it was clear: Geena didn't have to teach next year at all. If she really watched what she spent, she could live off her inheritance, stay right there in her old childhood home, and...

Did she even dare think it?

...she could write.

It seemed like the world's greatest luxury: time to do nothing but get up in the morning and work on her Great American

Novel. Didn't every English professor believe she had one inside her somewhere?

But what would she write *about?* If she had an outline— even a rough idea—she'd be all in. But what if she took next year off, and never found her direction? Wouldn't it be a year wasted?

Somehow, Geena had thought everything would be a little less confusing once she got home. And yet, all it seemed to do was change the scenery around her torn-in-two-directions heart.

Geena slipped her phone back into her pocket without texting the department head back. If only, she thought, turning to face Ruby's Place, she still had her dad to talk to.

And suddenly, that simple little passing thought brought back all the visions and memories of last Christmas Eve. It flooded her heart. Last year, in the midst of the festivities, she thought she had seen him inside the bar—thought she'd actually talked to her father.

Maybe, she mused, *if I go in there right now. Maybe if I sit there long enough, conflicted enough, needing him enough, he will reappear. We'll be able to hash everything out, like we used to at the dinner table, and I'll have my answer…*

She quickly rolled her eyes at herself. How many glasses of red wine had she also had last Christmas Eve? More than a few.

Come to think of it, she'd imagined far more than her father last December. She'd actually pictured him meeting up with a woman—Elizabeth, that was what he'd called her. A lovely, older woman. The one who had run the dress shop in town.

Mrs. Cranston, the Baristers' next-door-neighbor, had told Geena her father'd had a secret love after her mother was gone. Had Elizabeth only seemed like the right fit to Geena? Had she been so saddened by her father's death that she'd felt the need to give him a happy ending? Like somehow, he'd ridden off into the sunset instead of passed away?

Your dad is gone, Geena, she scolded herself. *Seeing your dad last year was a symptom of grief. Wishful thinking. So was all that stuff about Elizabeth. He's not here to talk to about your problems anymore. You have to let it go.*

She raced across the street and knocked loudly against the plate-glass window of The Page Turner.

Rob turned from the cash register, flashing an annoyed frown until he saw it was her. His frown instantly turned into a look of pure joy.

Geena smiled back. Yes, she thought, at least that much was clear: Rob loved her. You just couldn't fake split-second reactions like that.

He raced outside and grabbed her up into his arms. "I thought this was finals week."

"It is," Geena agreed. "Technically. But the classes I taught this semester were structured around papers rather than tests. The only class with a timed final was scheduled for Monday. Started grading as soon as they all walked out the door. Term papers were all graded a week ago. Submitted my final grades last night and hit the road before dawn this morning. Hoped I'd get here in time to maybe put together dinner for you, me, and Justin tonight."

Rob cocked his head to the side in that way of his, the one that said it had pleased him that she'd thought to include his teenage son.

"You had this planned all along."

"Maybe," Geena said proudly. "Surprised you, didn't I?"

"I'm just glad you're here," Rob said. "Probably won't see too much of Justin, though. He's getting awfully serious about that girlfriend of his," he added, leading her into the store.

"Kelly!" he shouted at his lone employee, seated behind the cash register. "Look who's here!"

"I can see that," Kelly chuckled. She stuck a finger into her white hair to retrieve one of three pencils stuck into her bun. "You get over to your dad's place yet?" And then caught herself, realizing what she was asking.

It seemed no one in the town of Sullivan had come to grips with the idea that the tough and hardy Tom Barister could actually be gone.

Geena brushed it off, recognizing Kelly's embarrassment. "I did, actually," she answered. "Dumped my stuff off, got the house opened up. Heat cranked so it'll be warm when I get back. Although, I did see someone's been keeping my front walk cleared of snow—even though I asked him not to," she said, wagging a finger at Rob. "Spread some Ice Melt, too. And opened the cabinets under the kitchen sink to make sure the pipes wouldn't burst."

"Whoever that guy is, he deserves a prize," Rob announced.

"I mean, that guy is a keeper."

"You think?"

"I think."

"Must be nice to have a whole month off," Kelly commented. "I remember the free-as-a-breeze feeling of the last day of school…"

Geena nodded, gravitating toward a counter display of paperbacks. "What's this?" she asked. "You guys don't deal in new releases—or do you these days?"

"Oh, that's on consignment," Kelly said as Rob drifted toward the front window. "Lovely lady put that together. With the rest of the genealogical society. Pictorial history of the area. Self-published. They did such a nice job…"

Kelly got up from her seat to pick up a copy. "Some of these pictures are so great. Let me show you my favorites," she started.

But Rob was shaking his head and muttering, "Could have sworn…"

"Sworn what?" Geena asked.

"Sworn I saw him again," Rob said. "In Tina's window. The other day, there was this guy."

"What guy?" Geena pressed.

"Found him in this kind of sad looking heap near The Page Turner's door. Obviously down on his luck. He said he needed to get in touch with someone. I tried to buy him a bus ticket. But he disappeared on me. Almost like he vanished in a puff. Haven't seen him since. Until a second ago—maybe…"

"Rob's been looking for that guy all over town," Kelly broke in, still flipping through the pages in her book. "Been so long now—seems like it was right after Thanksgiving he saw him. I keep telling him the guy's surely found who he was looking for by now." She flopped the book open and pointed. "There," she showed Geena. "This one. Don't you love it?"

"Who are they?" Geena asked, staring at the image of musicians.

"Don't know, really," Kelly admitted as Rob left the window, his forehead still wrinkled. Geena slipped her arm around his waist, but even that didn't seem to bring him fully back to the present, to erase the nagging worries carved into his face. "Not much of a caption," Kelly went on. "I'm not sure who even submitted it to the collection. Those musicians have such personality, though, don't they?"

"That's him!" Rob exclaimed, pointing.

"Him who?" Geena asked.

"The guy. The one I saw."

"Can't be," Kelly argued. "This picture goes back to the 1930s."

Rob sighed. "So similar," he muttered, squinting at the trumpet player.

"This guy really got to you," Geena observed.

"I just worry about him," Rob said with a shrug. "The whole thing was kind of weird."

"I don't need a bus ticket," Geena said, shutting Kelly's

book and feeling the need to change the subject, "but you can buy me and Kelly a couple of burgers."

"Might I be getting something in return for that, Professor Barister?" Rob joked, leaning in closer, as though to steal a kiss.

He stopped, frowning. "What is it? You look like you want to say something."

She did—so much. She wanted to tell him about how she'd imagined seeing her father last year, over in Ruby's Place. She wanted to unload the weight of how much she still missed him. She wanted to tell him about her contract, and the department head who was hounding her for an answer. She wanted to talk about her dream of writing. But she didn't really know where to start.

Mostly, she worried that if she said anything of it out loud, it would wind up sounding ridiculous and foolish—especially the part about how real her dad had felt sitting at the same table with her last Christmas Eve. She didn't want to lose it—even if it had been nothing more than a wine-infused daydream.

"Nothing," she said, reaching again for her coat. "You guys are busy. Why don't I pick up the grub? After lunch, I might even stick around to help out at the store. If you're lucky."

She offered a sweet smile—one that Rob couldn't argue with. She stepped back out into the winter chill, giving the front window of Ruby's a gaze full of impossible Christmas wishes.

30.

~*December 10, 2019*~

Later that night, behind the "Closed" sign, the regulars all began to gather inside Ruby's Place.

Elizabeth—the same woman Geena had yet again managed to convince herself was merely a figment of her own imagination—climbed onto a barstool. She had yet to take her first sip of champagne when Tom appeared.

He squeezed Elizabeth's shoulder. Instead of sitting right next to his lady love, though, he headed straight for the front window.

"Geena made it back in town," Angela informed him with a smile.

"Was she in the bar? Or across the street? At the bookstore? How'd she look?"

"Looked great. Like her usual self. She and Rob left the bookstore together a few hours ago."

He seemed disappointed. But reminded himself, "It's probably just as well that I didn't see her."

Elizabeth stood, wrapped her long slender arms around Tom's shoulders, and steered him toward a stool at the bar and the mug of Pabst waiting for him.

Elizabeth and Ruby exchanged a look. Ruby nodded, understanding. "I agree, kid," she said.

"Agree with what?" Tom asked.

"Maybe you should let Geena see you again this Christmas," Ruby offered nonchalantly, wiping down the counter with a rag. She turned toward Angela. "Didn't you say earlier that Geena looked good—healthy—but also a little—"

"Troubled?" Elizabeth finished.

"Like she's got something on her mind, is all," Angela said, now trying to downplay it. "She stood out there on the sidewalk for kind of a long time. Her face was all distant, like she was really mulling something over."

"When I saw her last year, I made things right between the two of us," Tom reminded her.

"It would be good for both of you," Angela prodded. "This is going to be a really hard Christmas for her again. Maybe even worse this year. She was probably still in shock last year. You passed so close to Christmas."

"That goes against what we all agreed on," Tom said, his voice getting louder and more upset. "We said one time. Do you know how packed this place would be if we let everyone meet up with all their missed loved ones every single year, over and over again?"

"I just thought maybe last year didn't count," Angela said. "As close as it was and all."

"No—the truth about this place has to remain…enigmatic. Peculiar and incomprehensible. People can whisper about it.

They can wonder. But it can never be proven for sure. Right? Ruby, you said it yourself. A mystery is what will draw a crowd. And nobody knows crowds like Ruby. *Right?*"

Before anyone could respond, Tom reminded them, "Geena has to wonder if she ever really did see me—just like everyone else who has a brief reunion on Christmas Eve. She won't wonder if she sees me two years in a row. Our cover will be blown.

"Besides," Tom murmured, "she has to live her life on her own terms."

"She is," Elizabeth said. "She's Dr. Barister. Literature professor extraordinaire."

"It's different when the old safety net is gone," Tom said. "I know that. She still has the house, but there's no one in it to help out if she hits hard times. If the English Department cuts back and she can't find another teaching gig for a year or two, I won't be with her the same way. Not like I was in the past.

"If she thinks I'm still here," he went on, gaining steam again, "in this bar, it might change her mind about how she lives the rest of her life. I don't want her to feel tethered to Sullivan. If she wants to stay, she should stay. If she wants to sell the house and teach in Zimbabwe, she should. It's her life. But it should all be on her own terms."

"Rob's here," Elizabeth offered. "You don't think he'll tether her to the place anyway?"

"She and Rob aren't married," Tom argued. "They called it quits once. Maybe that was just youth—wanting to test the waters elsewhere. Then again, maybe it was a gut instinct telling them both they weren't right for each other. Maybe she starts to feel that way again after a few more months."

"You don't think they'll make it?" Angela asked.

"What's making it?" Tom wanted to know. "You get a chance to love somebody. That's a beautiful thing. Maybe it lasts fifty years and maybe that lasts five. Why's it any less if it's five instead of fifty?"

He glanced over at Elizabeth, saying everything he was feeling with a single look: That their own somewhat brief late-in-life love affair had been powerful enough for Tom to come back to Elizabeth once his life was over. Theirs was the love that had never diminished—for either of them.

"I thought—the way you acted last year, you sort of approved of Rob," Angela said.

"I like Rob fine. But Geena's mine."

"You'll always be her father," Elizabeth said. "And you'll always feel that way about your kid. No matter what, you want to be the one protecting her. From anything. Everything."

Tom's eyes grew hazy. "Might even be worse for a cop." He started to raise his mug to his lips, but stopped. "My dad was a cop."

"I didn't know that," Angela said.

"A better cop than I was."

"Oh, pfff," Elizabeth said, waving her hand. "Not true."

"It is, though."

"Why? Because he died on the job? Made the ultimate sacrifice? Is that what you think?" Elizabeth pressed.

"Because he had harder times to navigate." Tom's eyes grew distant as he confessed, "I always wished I could have known him as an adult. Strange the things you focus on as a kid. With me, it was the way adults shook hands when they met. It's so funny, you know, I always hated attention of any kind—birthdays, having to go accept some kind of award at school…It followed me my entire life. But my greatest fantasy was always that my dad could have been around long enough to shake my hand. Because it would have meant he saw me as an adult. Not just his kid. And it would have meant he approved, too. It would have felt like the world's greatest award—one I would have actually welcomed. I hope—when I saw her last year—I gave Geena that feeling. That I *saw* her. That I think she's incredible." His voice broke on the last word.

Elizabeth slipped her hand around his in comfort.

"What was his name?" Angela asked, leaning her elbows against the surface of the bar. "Your dad, I mean."

"Charlie," Tom said. "His name was Charlie."

31.

December 24, 2019

~Our Journey~

Somebody needs to trim that pine tree up ahead. The branches bend when they get heavy with snow, hanging in the exact-wrong place. Creates a blind spot. Can't see around the corner.

Stories have blind spots, too. There's one in this story, keeping you from seeing Charlie.

You've been wondering about Charlie for a while now. I know that. I've been watching you in the rearview mirror. I can see part of your face from my spot in the backseat—your kids and your dog both fell asleep about twenty minutes ago, and here I am, pinned in, not wanting to move and disturb them.

It's okay. I don't mind. It's kind of a nice feeling. Cozy.

But Charlie. Remember when I told you about the night Edna met up with Maxwell Ross in the alley behind the speakeasy?

Sure, you do. That night he'd wanted Edna to buy up his liquor, and she wouldn't.

Well, let me tell you, Edna was not quite as on-her-own in that alley as she'd thought that night. Charlie was right there, standing at the back of the speakeasy, drink in hand, watching through the crack in the door she'd left slightly ajar.

He was dead tired—completely zapped. He'd survived a couple of shop-lifting incidents, three fender benders (one involving a couple of bicycles), a robbery, and two domestic altercations in his seven-hour shift. As much as he'd just wanted to sit at the bar, nursing his drink, the sounds of loud voices had drawn his attention.

He was still in full-on cop mode. Not that he was ever truly out of cop mode. So when Edna hadn't immediately returned from answering the alley door, he'd made his own trek down the hallway to find out what was going on.

There he stood, like I said. Staring through that crack in the door.

"I got quite a deal for Frankie," he heard a man informing Edna. "But maybe you're the woman who can close on it."

Charlie could only see Edna from the back—and the way she was standing, she was blocking him from seeing the man she was talking to.

But when her hands disappeared from her sides and her back stiffened, Charlie knew she'd crossed her arms over her chest to make a defensive shield of sorts. "Sir, we already get deliveries from Sam's Grocery. He cuts the fairest deal in town." She was clearly nervous. Her words may have sounded the perfect blend of polite and discouraging, but her voice was as tight as the highwire that had stretched across the insides of the previous summer's traveling circus tent.

"It's gonna be that way, is it?" the man asked. When Edna swayed slightly, Charlie got a better look at the man's face. Charlie grunted, finally recognizing him. Maxwell Ross.

Maybe you've also been wondering about Maxwell, this man who has held a grudge against Sullivan for so long. I can tell you the exact same thing about Maxwell that Charlie would have said, back then: Maxwell Ross was the sort of man trouble easily found. Without him even having to look for it.

It went that way sometimes. Some men could put their fingers into a Cracker Jack box and find nothing but twenty dollar bills. Some could open an elevator and come face-to-face with The Rockettes.

And other men—men like Maxwell—they could put their fingers into their own pockets and find nothing but holes. They could open elevators only to be greeted by a congregation of alligators.

Some men met their loves and married and had families.

Maxwell met his love—a brunette, green-eyed beauty—and watched her run off with someone else.

For others, the stars aligned.

For Maxwell, the stars simply crossed their eyes and stuck out their tongues.

In the winter of 1931, Maxwell Ross was forty-three years old. His father had died young. His mother was legally blind. His hunting dog had a goiter the size of a cantaloupe. And he was about to lose the family farm on the outskirts of town—the same farm that had been in the family for five generations.

I'm not making this up. I'm not trying to be funny.

That was life for Maxwell.

Hard economic times had struck for everyone in Sullivan—it had struck for the entire country. But that didn't mean that everyone was suddenly on the same playing field as Maxwell. It meant that Maxwell was getting hit harder than anyone else.

Out of necessity, he'd learned what it took to be become a one-man distillery, investing every cent he had received from selling off his livestock and most of his farm equipment.

But where would he unload it all? Try to sell a jug here and there for a few pennies to broke farmers?

Or sell gallon after gallon to someone who needed a large supply each night?

In that alley, that December evening of 1931, Edna was bound to do nothing but shake her head at him, insisting he leave. She had no authority to speak for Frankie. She liked Robert Ludlow, the mechanic turned moonshiner. And she simply did not like the way Maxwell Ross had shown up with no warning, stepping out of the dark to demand she deal with him. His manner was sneaky. He frightened her—even without knowing he had a bad reputation. Edna took his mere appearance as a bad omen. An upside-down horseshoe. A broken mirror. A black cat. The number thirteen.

Still standing in the doorway, eavesdropping on the alley scene, Charlie would have surely told you he began to consider

Maxwell Ross not just unlucky, but dangerous. Staring at him, he could have sworn he was looking at a loaded gun waiting to go off. Simply being near Maxwell meant something dangerous and painful was most likely bound to happen.

Charlie also knew that with a guy like Maxwell, there really was no safe resolution to any argument. At least with an actual loaded gun, removing the bullets meant an end to danger; things could return to normal.

Removing Maxwell Ross from the premises did no such thing.

One way or another, Charlie knew, Maxwell Ross would be back.

32.

~*December 11, 2019*~

The square seemed busier than usual—everyone with a *hello* and a *how have you been*, everyone sharing their own Christmas plans, giving each other peeks into their shopping bags.

Everybody but Linda, anyway.

She simply glowered and hurried on, wondering why anyone with holiday cheer had to go rubbing it in.

She stomped all the way to the Sullivan History Museum, where she brushed the snow from her coat and her hair and wished she could do the same with all her bad feelings.

How could this happen? How could it be that no one had any interest in the exhibit? The town of Sullivan? Gossip capital of the whole United States? Nobody had interest in an exhibit about the secrets of their own *town?*

It was inexplicable. Unexpected. Disappointing. The groups Linda'd had for her tour had all been in the single digits, each one a little smaller than the last. Surely, by now, she was down to zip. Zilch. Nil.

And she'd been so excited leading up to it. A chance to teach again. She hadn't realized how much she'd missed it until Toby had approached her with this opportunity. To change a person's mind, Linda had always thought, was delicious. She had relished the years spent convincing seventeen-year-olds that Latin was exciting—adventurous—the most interesting class they would take in high school.

Just like that old choir teacher of Linda's—what was her name? It was a funny one. Dodd. Mrs. Dodd. Why had they giggled at that? It was the first name, that was it—Dorothy. No. Dotty. *Dotty Dodd.* Silly the things you could get fixated on when you were young and bored and in class.

"Fine," Linda remembered the teacher saying, her words dripping with exasperation. "Call me Dorothy. Heck, call me Queen of the Eighth Notes if you want. Call me anything as long as you show up to choir."

Linda had. And Dorothy had changed her mind about music. So much so that later on, music was part of Linda's own Latin classes. She'd regularly brought in percussion instruments to emphasize the rhythm of the texts. A way to get the kids' attention. She'd often wished she'd had a chance to tell Dorothy about that.

But that was all a past tense. And here it was, Wednesday. The perfect day to be lost in one's own to-do lists, both for work and for home. It was eleven in the morning. Too early for lunch hour. Too late for—well, Linda wasn't sure for what exactly. But the upcoming holidays and life and schedules were keeping everyone from stopping by the history museum. At least, she tried to tell herself that was the reason. Today was no exception. Actually, come to think of it, today—right smack in the middle of the week—they might have more on their plates. Might be more likely than ever to have other things to do. Weekday obligations, weekend preparations.

Maybe, she thought as she hung her coat in the break room, she could go down and talk to Toby. Jokingly ask him if it would be okay for the two of them to *mitterent ad auras*. See if he could figure out that was a loose Latin translation for *shoot the breeze*.

How much of Latin II did he even remember?

She was about to find out.

Humming, she stepped from the break room and stopped in her tracks.

The main entryway was full. Completely. A giant clog of bodies stretched from wall to wall.

"You're here for—?" Linda croaked.

"The Secrets tour," a voice piped up. "Aren't you running it? It's time, right?"

Linda's head spun. How could this be?

Just go with it, she told herself, worried that questioning this sudden surge in attendance might bring a deluge of bad luck—or make this crowd disappear, all in a blink.

"Yes! Yes, I am. And it is," Linda announced, offering a flourish with her arm. "This way, please," she called. A somewhat pleasant cloud of confusion hung over her, making her feel dazed, as if she'd won an unexpected prize.

* * *

Later on, as she wrapped up the last tidbit about the old bar, the one that had once housed the speakeasy, the questions came roaring back to Linda: Where had these people come from? Why now? Had word somehow spread about the exhibit?

That might have made some sense. Everyone showing up all at once, though?

Not so much.

Linda stepped from the exhibit room into the hallway when she was stopped by an unfamiliar young man.

"It's not quite as easy as all that," he informed her.

"Not as easy as what?"

"That exhibit of yours. It's oversimplified."

Linda frowned. First the unexpected crowd, and now, for some reason, this person had stayed behind—not rushing out the museum's front door with the rest. What had she said that he'd found incorrect enough to confront her about it?

He turned to point at the display highlighting the police force. "Not during Prohibition. All that speakeasy stuff. Good story. But times like that, nothing's ever black or white. Is it?"

"No," Linda agreed. "It isn't."

"Good versus bad—where's the line, right? When you give everything to protect one person, sometimes, you don't stop to realize somebody else is getting hurt in the process. Especially when the someone you want to protect is young—or a kid, really. Makes every last one of your fatherly instincts kick in."

Linda wasn't sure where this was going. But she let him continue to talk.

"My little boy wants to be an officer—like most kids his age, I suppose," the man went on. Which surprised Linda. He seemed far too young to have a boy old enough to have dreams of his own. He shrugged. "They see the blue uniform and how people respond to it."

The man before her was currently dressed in a leather coat and a newsboy cap, but he had a certain confidence. He obviously knew what he was speaking of. A police officer too, surely.

"Maybe he just wants to be like you," Linda offered.

"That transparent, am I?" He shrugged. "We all want our kids to look up to us. Does everybody else question whether or not we really deserve being looked up to? I do. I do quite often, actually," he admitted quietly.

Linda walked over to the display, which contained old precinct photos, black and whites, a few mugshots from the Roaring Twenties, old handcuffs, a master key from the jail.

"How would you fix it?" she started to ask. "What would you change—" But when she turned, he was already slipping through the door.

She sighed. Maybe, she thought, there was something she'd missed in that old fruit crate of Angela's. She checked her watch. She had time to look before her next tour.

33.

~*December 12, 2019*~

Maddie thundered into the flea market. She stomped up toward the cash register and slammed her hands down on the front counter.

"I need to open an account. *Pronto.*"

Tina eyed Maddie over the rim of her black and white checkered glasses. "What kind of an account?"

"A charge account. Do you have any idea how close it is to Christmas?"

Tina threw her head back and laughed. "Dream on," she said, turning again toward the display she was currently working on.

Maddie leaned over the counter. "What is that thing?"

"Clearly," Tina said, "it's a Christmas tree which I am cleverly cutting from a piece of green felt."

"Oh. Looks more like a green shark."

Tina sighed, pushing the sleeves of her sweater up. Her vintage riding pants fit a bit tight, and her black go-go boots were about half a size too small, but to be beautiful, a woman had to suffer. Or so her own mother had frequently said.

"Why did you want to cut out a Christmas tree?" Maddie pressed.

"So I could attach earrings onto it. To hang near the front counter here, see? People like jewelry for Christmas."

"Ahhhh," Maddie said.

"Yes. Ahhhh." Tina turned her head back down to her work.

"So?"

"So what?"

Maddie held up her hands. "The charge account? You gave one to Mrs. Anderson. Right? For her brooch? It's a special brooch. Just like the one she gave her very best friend when they were young. The one that got lost in a move. She's paying on it so she can give it to her again for Christmas this year."

"How do you know that?"

"I know everything about this town."

"No. The answer is no. And besides, Mrs. Anderson does not have an account. Not like you think it is. It's layaway."

"No? What do you mean, 'no'?"

"I mean that you are asking me to open an account that will never be paid, my dear."

Tina was tired of talking to Maddie. She bent forward to appear lost in concentration as she continued to cut out her tree.

"I need presents!" Maddie exclaimed. "Lots of them. My mom, my best friend, my…"

"No, Maddie. No. You will never pay me back. I am not in the business of providing presents for freeloaders."

"This is impossible," Maddie groaned, slapping her thighs.

"How am I supposed to get enough money to buy anything good? How about you give me an account for just my mom's present?"

"Maddie—" Tina started.

"Why do you need to buy it?" a man's voice interrupted.

Maddie and Tina turned at the same time. Chester stood at the far side of the store, where he had been rearranging furniture to make space for an antique buffet. One of dozens of little tasks he'd been completing for Tina.

Maddie's face registered something between surprise and fear. Here she was, suddenly staring at the man she had seen outside of Rob's bookstore. The man who had seemed to disappear, like a magic trick.

She wasn't sure if he was about to disappear all over again—before she could get out a single word. Besides, what did this man know about presents? He didn't exactly look like Santa Claus. More like someone so down on his luck, he was going to need every single one of the goodies in Santa's sleigh in order to get himself back on track.

"Why do you have to buy presents?" Chester pressed. "In my day, when times got tough, we simply made gifts."

"What can I make?" Maddie asked in disbelief.

"What are you good at?" Chester took a step closer.

Maddie pouted. "Nothing."

"You have to be able to make something."

"I made a jump rope once out of Mom's clothesline. Oh! And this other time, I drew pictures on her sponges."

"How did *that* work?" Tina asked.

"They were still dry. She hadn't used them yet. But then when she wet them, all the paint stuff ran all over the place."

Chester and Tina laughed. "I guess you weren't too popular in the house that day," Tina said.

Maddie's pout turned into more of a scowl.

"You could probably cut out a tree of your own," Tina offered. "I've got some felt left."

Maddie seemed unimpressed.

"What if you learned something?" Chester offered.

"In time for Christmas?" Maddie bellowed. "Do you know what date it is? Besides, all my teachers say I'm a slow learner."

Chester shrugged. "Up to you."

Maddie was obviously intrigued. "Learn *what?*"

Chester turned, pointing at the early twentieth century upright piano pushed against the interior wall.

"You gotta be kidding," Maddie moaned.

34.

~December 12, 2019~

Rose's mind filled with prickly exclamation points.

She slammed a plug into the switchboard. "Hello? Ruby's Place? Dorothy? Are you there? Can you hear me? Anyone? Chester's here. I've tried to connect before. He's been working at the It Ain't Over Yet. Now, he's teaching a little girl to play the piano. Maddie. That's her name. She's here, and she can see Chester and—"

She stopped. Why, she found herself wondering all over again, couldn't Maddie and Tina see *her*?

But it was no real matter—not in the grand scheme of things. Not with a love story hanging in the balance.

"Dorothy?" she croaked. "Are you there? Do you have any idea that the very man you hoped throughout most of your life to see once again is right here? Just a few doors down from you? On the same block?"

She heard nothing.

"I've tried," she went on. "I've heard all the regulars. I know about them. I know you're with them, too. The only one from the speakeasy days who comes. Why is that? Why do you come and no one else?"

No answer.

"I've heard the stories. The wild tales the regulars tell about Frankie. I've shouted into this earpiece. Trying to tell you what I know. What I've always known. And no one responds. Why can't you hear me? Please hear me!"

Silence.

"Am I even connected?" Rose sighed, staring at the familiar board in front of her. "This used to be so easy."

She shook her head, wondering. Had her words—announcing that the trumpet had shown up in the flea market—really been responsible for drawing Chester out? What else could have done it? There he was, at the front of the store, introducing Maddie to the black and white pattern of the piano keys. And yet, he was seemingly oblivious to her own presence. Every bit as oblivious as Maddie and Tina.

"He's never once even looked at me," Rose muttered.

"What carol should I play?" Maddie asked. "Something good. But easy. Jessie in the fifth grade, *she* said that she heard this one song once about…"

"Hello?" Rose called out, trying to get their attention.

But Chester only thought a minute, then snapped his fingers. "'Jingle Bells'! The perfect song to play for your mother."

"Hello! Chester. *Chester!*" Rose tried again.

"Wait a minute," Maddie said. "Where am I going to perform this concert?"

"It's a whole concert now, is it?" Tina asked.

"Well, where am I going to play this for Mom? We don't

have a piano in our house."

"Hey! Back here! Look here!" Rose shouted, waving her arms over her head like she was trying to land a plane.

"Why not perform for your mother right here in the shop?" Tina asked. "We could make her an invitation out of some of my construction paper. I could even decorate the piano!" She smiled, already designing a whole Christmas scene for the top of the upright.

"First things first," Chester insisted.

But Rose had run out of patience—mostly with her own inabilities. Lips tightened up angrily, she slammed her cord into the switchboard. And connected with the old fruit crate Angela had loaned to the history museum—the one with all the tidbits from Frankie's speakeasy days still inside.

She opened the key—slower this time. Every tiny twist of the key brought her a completely different set of sounds. Slowly, she realized that she was connecting with a different piece of history each time she moved the key. That explained the different voices. Different levels of joy, sadness, fear. Each click allowed her to listen in on a different day, a different year.

She bit the tip of her red fingernail.

Her hand stopped when the sounds of a celebration hit her ears. *Of course!* Rose thought. She pulled her headset off and turned the volume up, so that the voices would have a better chance of being heard by the group at the front of the shop.

Christmas Eve. 1931. The date everything changed in Sullivan.

The date that might be powerful enough to change everything now.

190

35.

~*December 24, 1931*~

Dorothy paused beside the boarding house's line of mailboxes. The postman had come and gone. She'd heard him get an earful from Mrs. Latchy about the late hour of her delivery and had watched him receive a peppermint candy from the widow who lived on the first floor. She crossed her fingers and held her breath, saying a quick prayer. When she lifted the lid to her own box and peeked inside one last time—nothing. No letter from Chester. Not a word.

There had also been no phone call on the one line everyone at 1165 Elm Street shared. No chance she had missed his call, either—the phone had simply never rung. Chester, it seemed, would not be surprising her by showing up just in time to join her for their Christmas Eve set at Frankie's.

Dorothy took a step away from her mailbox, only to bump into another body.

"Got my check!" Mrs. Latchy announced, waving it in the air.

Dorothy nodded limply, assuming Mrs. Latchy was gleefully eating this up. Loving the fact that Chester had failed her again. Loved not that Dorothy was suffering, but that Latchy herself was right. She savored it, working her mouth like one of the widow's peppermint candies was dissolving on her tongue.

"Changed your clothes, I see," Mrs. Latchy said.

Dorothy had. In fact, she was now wearing the same fancy dress she always donned on performance nights. Funny how a fancy dress could get stained and need mending, the same as any other dress. And when you wore it like a uniform, slipping your arms into the same sleeves over and over, it didn't give you the assurance you were a woman of substance, of success. It made you feel like you had no choice. Same dress. Every single Friday and Saturday night.

As of late, she had begun to detest the dress.

"So nice that you've got plans of your own on Christmas Eve, even without your husband," Mrs. Latchy said as she headed back inside, in a tone that implied she didn't think it was really that nice at all.

Dorothy did her best to ignore her, catching a bus filled with happy voices heading to the downtown square. Christmas Eve was everywhere—in the crisp night air and the stars and the smell of pine. In the twinkle of the eyes she encountered. Folks gearing up for Mass or racing to a family member's house with a tray of covered treats.

Loneliness attacked, attempting to crush Dorothy as she found herself enmeshed in a Christmas in which gifts were not— could not—be as important as they had in years past. Simple gestures had risen to the top: using the last of the sugar for a few cookies, maybe. Knitting a new scarf. Making a handkerchief cut from the fabric of a worn-thin cotton shirt, with initials hand-embroidered in the corner.

And if the cupboard was quite literally bare? No matter. So many in Sullivan were sharing the simple gift of togetherness. Knitting a handful of moments into a single memory. Who needed some old object in a stocking when you had each other?

But Dorothy did not even have that. She had no family. No husband. No parents. It made her feel like an object that could be discarded, during a time when people had so little that practically nothing was being thrown away.

Dorothy was rotten. Soured. Used-up. And she was nineteen years old.

Dorothy fought the awful weight of Christmas as she stepped from the bus and walked toward Frankie's.

The moment she drifted into the dark alley, a trickle of voices seeped into her ears.

She recognized one—Frankie's. The other belonged to a man.

In that moment, Dorothy's heart lurched. Could it be?

Had Chester come to Frankie's directly? Not even stopped by the boarding house first? Was he here, wishing Frankie a Merry Christmas?

Dorothy raced forward, the galoshes she'd slipped on over her heels kicking up the recent powdery snow. Magical things happened on Christmas. Everyone said that. Why had she doubted it? Why had she ever doubted Chester? She had been a fool. It was all true, all the stories she had grown up with, the tales of wonder and magic.

In the glow of a streetlight, Frankie turned. She waved and called out, "Don't worry, Dotty. You're not late. In fact, I think you're a little early."

What was Frankie talking about? Of course she was late. It didn't matter what the hour said. If Chester had gotten there first, if he had spent a single minute standing in the alley without her, then Dorothy was late. She had not arrived on time. Hurt and anger and fear instantly receded. *Chester!* Here he was. And he was beautiful. Chester and all his music and his promises. They were glorious.

Frankie turned toward him to say, "I can't for the life of me figure who might have called you."

I would, I would, I would, Dorothy thought. *If I'd only known the number.* "Chest—" she started to cry out.

But then it happened: the man croaked, "Ma'am—"

That was all it took. That strangely gruff, frog-like voice— was it really a frog, or was it more like a car trying to kick over? Regardless, Dorothy recognized it instantly.

The same way everyone in town always could.

"Robert," Dorothy said.

The same Robert Ludlow who owned the garage. Whose conversations with Frankie were always overheard by Rose at the switchboard.

Robert Ludlow, Frankie's liquor supplier.

Of course, right then, it didn't seem like that much of a big deal that Ludlow's frog-like, gruff voice was filling the alley. Not to Dorothy.

Well. It didn't seem like a danger, anyway. It didn't seem like something was off. Didn't seem like some catastrophe was on the horizon.

All Dorothy knew right then was that he was not Chester. The disappointment nearly knocked her off her feet. She had called Chester's name. Or part of it, anyway. Like a fool. Her emotions slapped her, every bit as intensely as the winter wind attacking her cheeks and undoing the marcelled waves in her hair.

Robert Ludlow shook his head. "Strangest thing," he said, turning toward Dorothy. "Somebody called the garage. Could hear the phone ringing from my place upstairs. Went down to answer, and—come to think of it now, it was hard to hear whoever called. Lots of background noise. So much, I think it was a man, but I'm not sure. Telling me Frankie was going to need an emergency delivery. So many people had decided to come for Christmas Eve. That's what they *said.*"

"Well, I don't know who placed that call," Frankie said. "But it doesn't matter now. You just come right on inside with me and we'll get you a little Christmas Eve cheer of your own. Ought to offer a man something for coming out here in a hurry on a holiday." She linked her arm in Robert's and they all three made their way for the back door.

"Get that lock, will you, Robert?" Frankie called.

"Sure thing," he croaked. But he was so entrenched in Christmas Eve and happiness and loud voices and jokes and friends and a good drink on its way that he did not realize the lock swiveled but didn't turn any tumblers inside. He did not know that the lock had been broken—just as Frankie was unaware of it.

No one knew that the alley door was actually wide open.

They never could have suspected that this simple detail, in a matter of only a few more minutes, would wind up helping to cause their own downfall.

36.

~December 24, 1931~

Dorothy swallowed a sob, tossed her head back, and belted: "Ho, ho, ho," as part of her own rendition of "Up on the House Top."

Music, as always, offered her a momentary pause. A place where she could forget everything—Mrs. Latchy's judgment and even the platform where she was standing. Slowly, as she began to give in to the music swirling all about her, she even stopped worrying about Chester.

Why? Because music was its own universe. Untouchable and unchanging. It didn't matter what had happened earlier that day, that week, that year; the tune was unwavering. Notes and melodies were unaffected by the tragedies of life.

That, to a great extent, was the beauty of music. Notes never moved. They never aged. They remained as young and vibrant and lovely as the day they'd been written on a staff. They never broke promises. They never changed their minds. Tonight, the notes were allowing Dorothy's voice to put smiles on faces. Every last person in Frankie's. As they all toasted and shouted and engaged in Christmas Eve well-wishing.

Even Edna was a happy participant. Singing along with Dorothy as she mixed cocktails, raising her own glass in toast after toast. Laughing along as Hank, who had become her constant companion, told his wild tales to a swelling audience.

Here it was, as Frankie had always said—a bubble, a shelter, a place to escape.

All because Dorothy was singing such a silly, peppy Christmas song. So upbeat. The simple tune had lifted their spirits. Infected their bodies. Moved their feet in rhythm. Allowed them all to believe, for a while, that the potential for a better year was drifting through the air—thousands of possibilities, waiting to be breathed in.

"Ho, ho, ho," she belted, proudly this time. "Ho, ho, ho…"

37.

~*December 12, 2019*~

Chester got up from the piano bench and turned to look at the back of the store, toward Rose and her switchboard.

Rose gasped. Had he heard the voices she had tapped into? Were any of the words discernible? Or had it all sounded to him like some old radio that didn't quite have the station tuned in?

He shook his head and brought his attention back toward his new student.

A disappointed Rose sank deeper into her chair. She had just started to remove the cord when Chester asked Maddie, "Now, where were we? Ah, yes. 'Ho, ho, ho…'"

"No!" Maddie squealed. "Jingle bells!"

He *had* heard! Voices and words and…Rose really was getting through. She had to keep at it. Grabbing the same cord, she frantically sought to reconnect with that fateful night—Christmas Eve, 1931.

38.

~December 24, 1931~

"Hank," Edna said. She said it three times to get her brother-in-law's attention, in fact.

He turned, abandoning his latest tale of heart-pounding adventure, probably eighty-five-percent fiction. Maybe ninety. "What in the world's got you so pushy—?" he started. But when he saw the look on her face, the tease he was about to lob at her dissolved.

"You going straight home?" Edna asked.

Hank glanced back toward the table of men who awaited the rest of this tale of—what could this one have possibly been? Some exploit with a beautiful woman? A hunting or fishing expedition in the Antarctic? Some brief and unexpected encounter with royalty?

He raised a finger, saying he needed a moment. He stood, taking Edna by the arm and steering her out of earshot.

"Is everything all right?" he asked. His eyes showed genuine concern.

"I'm not sure," Edna whispered, her own eyes darting about the room.

"Why not?" Hank pressed. "The kids were fine when we left, and Arthur—"

Edna sucked in a deep breath at the sound of his name.

"What about Arthur?" Hank asked, falling into his role as protective brother.

"Someone called Robert," Edna said. "Frankie and Dorothy met up with him in the alley. Frankie just told me about it. She acted like it was all in good fun, but now I'm worried. Somebody *called* him."

"Why do you think that's so strange? It is Christmas Eve, after all. It's busy. I'm sure Frankie thought you'd need an extra delivery—"

"Aren't you listening? Frankie didn't call."

A flash of concern lit Hank's eyes as the details finally began to sink in. But he shrugged. "Come on. Christmas Eve? You really think somebody's trying to set Frankie up on Christmas Eve."

He eyed her in a way meant to calm any fears she had.

"Go home," she said, obviously still upset. "Go be with Arthur."

"Why would I go and leave you?"

"Look, I'm sure you're right. It's probably nothing. But I—" Her eyes pleaded with him.

"Edna, if you have the slightest suspicion, you should come with me."

She tossed her hand as though to wave away the tension in the air. "That's not the only reason I'm asking. It's Christmas Eve, and poor Arthur is home all by himself. Stick in the mud that he is. He won't come here, but I do feel bad about the two of us leaving him on a holiday. Please. You guys have a Christmas Eve of your own. My mother's at the house to watch the kids. Tell her—I don't know—that I decided to go to church with our friends. The ones you and I went to see *together*." She emphasized the last word to remind him of the lie they'd told to get out of the house.

"Where do you think the two of us can go on Christmas Eve? Isn't this place the only one still open?"

He was right; she hadn't thought of that. "Then don't go out. Curl up with some coffee."

"You've been saving that coffee for Christmas morning."

"I know it, and it's mine to give away. I'm telling you, go home. Keep Arthur company. It's Christmas, and you still need to give me a gift, and that's what I want. A brotherly Christmas Eve together."

"I see right through this brother stuff," Hank said, wagging a finger. "I'm telling you, when tomorrow morning comes, and there's not a single shred of Christmas Eve trouble in the paper, be prepared. You're never going to live this one down. What a nervous Nellie you can be."

He chuckled as he propped his hat on his head.

"Thank you," Edna told him, holding his coat for him.

But when he started toward the alley door, Edna blocked him. "Follow me. This way. Out the front. I'll lock the door behind you."

"The honest door, eh?" Hank asked, then repeated, "You really are a nervous Nellie."

"No detours," she insisted. "Go straight home. To Arthur."

"All right, all right," Hank grumbled.

"Hurry. Please," Edna insisted.

"Yeah, yeah," Hank moaned. "Perfectly good story left only half-told back in there. All for what?" He swiveled, holding his hands out from his sides.

Hank wasn't complaining. He was asking, once more, *If it's so dangerous to be here tonight, shouldn't I be taking you with me? Why am I leaving you behind? It's not right.*

She refused to answer beyond waving her fingers at him in a *go on, shoo* kind of motion. "I'm fine," she insisted.

"For a nervous Nellie." The third time he'd used the term. This time, though, it didn't sound like a tease.

"I'll be fine. Like you said, it's Christmas Eve. Right?"

Hank hesitated.

Edna shrugged, saying, "Hurry," before shutting the door behind her and returning to her post at the bar.

39.

~December 24, 1931~

Edna had just started to reach for her cocktail shaker when she heard footsteps coming from the tiny hallway leading to the alley. Thundering. Clomping.

How could that be? The alley door was always locked. People were supposed to knock. She hadn't let anyone new in. And Frankie was right there, leaning against the edge of the bar. She hadn't let anyone new in, either.

The piano faltered, even though Dorothy hadn't reached the end of her song. The sour notes hit the air painfully, like strikes intended to bruise.

Dorothy's knees buckled at the first glimpse of blue uniforms. What was happening? Police officers were often in the crowd, but not in a group like this. And not holding billy clubs and pistols. Not sporting angry faces.

Edna had a similar reaction. Who were these men, anyway? Edna had never seen any of them before. Where was Charlie—Officer Barister? Why was he not here?

There really had been a setup.

As it sank in, Edna made a wish. She wished for the blind gutsiness of youth. For the ability to act without second thought. She wished for a backbone of steel. She also made a wish that Hank was already home. She wished that her children would be fine with their father, and her own mother would not resent her choice of a job or think less of her.

The strange part of it all was that while Edna was making these wishes, she was also moving. Edna ducked, swooped around the far edge of the bar and lunged forward, wrapping her arms around Frankie's waist. She tugged her closer to the floor, hiding her behind a large group of revelers.

Frankie grimaced. "My back," she grumbled, struggling to free herself from Edna's hold.

Merrymakers closest to the clump of officers laughed, still believing this was some sort of prank. Pointing. Calling out, "Hold your horses! Close this place down after we finish our drinks!" Or, "It's Christmas! Bust Frankie next week, why don't 'cha?"

Until the first angry shout from one of the officers. The first garbled command.

Jokes faded to silence as everyone finally understood: this was real.

A chill rippled through the room in the second before the speakeasy erupted in a kind of drunken confusion. Nonsensical shouts and toppled chairs.

"Frankie!" came the police officers' shouts. "Ludlow!"

The uniformed men pointed their pistols, the tips of the barrels glimmering like silver stars.

Frankie stopped fighting to free herself. She gave in to Edna, allowing her to steer her, still unseen by the police, through the chaos.

"Raid!" someone shouted, slurring the word heavily as Dorothy continued to wring her hands from the small platform near the piano.

Liquor and guns rarely mix well. One of the patrons pulled his own pistol—maybe to try to protect Frankie. Maybe because he wanted to finish his drink in peace. He pulled the trigger. The sound of a gunshot punched the air.

And that was when the speakeasy descended into a kind of frantic lawlessness. Even with the police on site.

Suddenly, someone's hands were on Dorothy's arms, pulling her down. *Get down.*

"Who's shooting?" Dorothy asked. "Who would come to Frankie's with a gun?"

Before she got an answer, the police fired back.

The chaos doubled, tripled. Feet on the floor. Racing. Shouting. Bodies crawling under tables. Screams and shouts about protecting the ladies.

Dorothy was being pushed. She did not know where she was going, only that on this incredible night, with the magic of Christmas Eve all around her, she was about to be spared from the ongoing disaster. She believed.

Just a few feet away from Dorothy, Edna curled her body like a shield around Frankie's back. They ran in tandem, with Edna navigating.

Bullets screeched through the air, buzzing and zipping.

Hitting the walls, the tables, and customers who screamed out in pain.

Edna's feet kept moving, weaving through overturned tables and broken glass and clumps of screaming people. A chair slammed into her back. A man's elbow hit her in the cheek. Frankie lost her footing, bringing the two women down to their knees. Edna pressed her fingers against the floor, into something wet and sticky. Hoping against hope that it was spilled liquor and not someone's blood.

She fought back against her own screams and tears, bringing herself to her feet again and shielding Frankie all the way to the office, which held a side door to the diner. The honest half of her business.

They scrambled for the front door, fighting to unlock it.

The two women lunged onto the sidewalk.

But Edna gasped when a man appeared in front of them. "No, no, no—" she cried out, certain he was an arresting officer. Instead of saving Frankie, she'd delivered her straight into the arms of punishment.

"Shhhh," the man scolded. The nearby streetlight illuminated the face beneath the hat.

"Hank," Edna breathed.

"Come on," Hank urged. "I turned around soon as I heard the shots. Car's this way. Hurry."

On the opposite side of the building, Dorothy found herself being pushed through the back door and into the alley.

Safe! She exhaled beneath the glittering stars, letting out a soft laugh of utter relief. She thought to herself what a great story it would make when Chester found his way back to her.

Grateful, she swiveled to thank whoever it was that had just rescued her. Of course it was rescue. Even with bullets flying, Dorothy believed the best would happen. Christmas could not let her be injured twice in one night. It could not keep Chester from her, breaking her heart, then allow her be wounded in the speakeasy.

Then again, Christmas might have already sent Dorothy's rescuer back into the building, to help others still huddling inside.

Yes, that probably happened, she thought. Her kindhearted gentleman, sent by Christmas, would probably already be gone when she looked behind her.

But when Dorothy finished turning, she found herself staring into the face of a man in a police uniform.

Before she could say anything, he whipped her about to face forward, clicked her hands together behind her back.

Click? Dorothy tried to pull her hands out from behind her, only to feel the sharp pinch of metal. She'd been handcuffed.

But how could that be?

He steered her again, this time toward a police wagon already crammed with frightened faces.

As she fought her skirt and her wobbly legs, Dorothy clamored into the back of the wagon. In the distance, a lonely ambulance siren began to wail.

40.

~*December 12, 2019*~

own the street, inside Ruby's Place, it was simply business as usual—the expected mid-afternoon lull. Rob and Geena had finally taken time for a bite to eat, though whether it was a late lunch or an early dinner at that point was anyone's best guess. And Kurt had shown up with the daily deliveries.

"…used to get so many cards…" Kurt was babbling.

Angela nodded, sifting through her mail. "…lost art," she was agreeing. The simple joy of a Christmas card, the idea that someone had thought of you, taken the time to address an envelope, bring the card to the post office.

As they talked, a strange buzzing sound attacked them—powerful enough that Kurt and Angela both winced, forgot what they had been speaking of just a moment before.

"It's coming from your phone," Rob shouted, pointing at the landline attached to the wall.

Angela shook her head, unsure how he could possibly know that. It sounded to her like the very air was permeated in a sound coming from everywhere and nowhere all at the same time.

Rob stood, leaving behind his half-eaten cheeseburger, and pointed again toward the phone that hung behind the bar.

Angela took it off the hook. But before she could bring the

receiver to her ear, a horrible rattle exploded—like Fourth of July bottle rockets…or gunshots. Geena yelped and Kurt squatted, as though to dodge whatever might come flying out of the receiver.

Voices screeched. Shouts of something like, "Raid!" exploded through the earpiece.

Angela leaned away, terrified. But she hesitated to hang up before she knew for sure what she was listening to. She held the earpiece slightly closer. Was she overhearing some sort of tragedy that needed to be reported? Was someone's home being broken into? Did she need to flag down Officer Vargas, get him to listen to this?

The phone began to shake in her palm with each bang, each high-pitched whizzing noise. The receiver turned hot to the touch. She dropped it and watched in horror as smoke began to pour from the holes in the earpiece.

Angela lunged into the kitchen to grab the fire extinguisher. When she returned, Rob was already slapping the smoking phone with a bar towel.

"Back, back!" Angela shouted.

When Rob cleared away, she sprayed the receiver, white foam spewing out everywhere.

Panting, her gray hair tumbled down over one of her eyes.

"Whaddaya think that was all about?" Kurt asked, leaning over the bar. "Never seen anything like that."

"I need a drink," Angela moaned.

But it was too early for stopping to catch her breath. Angela knew that as soon as she saw her. Standing on the sidewalk and staring through the front window. A large woman—tall, with chin-length hair, in rumpled clothing. With blood on her gray skirt.

Angela shuddered. She knew that face. She had seen it on the pictures that had blown out of the old fruit crate. Pictures she had chased down on the sidewalk. Pictures that Ruby had given to her to take to the Sullivan History Museum.

"Frankie," Angela muttered.

She scurried outside.

But the sidewalk was empty. In the blink of time that it had taken for her to throw the door open, Frankie had disappeared.

Angela feared that Frankie had somehow been behind whatever had just happened with her telephone. That Frankie was trying to send her a message—a fairly violent sounding one at that.

Above, a cardinal perched on the phone line, surveying the episode below as though he'd somehow seen this all before.

41.

~*December 12, 2019*~

"Angela?" Rose barked into her headphones. "Angela? Can you hear me? It's me—Rose. I guess you wouldn't know that name. But Dorothy would. Angela, you've got to talk to her. Can you hear me?" She paused a moment, hearing only commotion on the other end of the line. "Angela? Tell Dorothy that Chest—"

She gasped as her headset was snatched from her head.

He was there. Standing beside her. Chester. Glaring down at her. Before Rose had a chance to celebrate the fact that he could see her, he barked, "Don't you do it."

"But why? You asked me to," Rose defended herself. "On the phone. The first time I heard your voice, you asked me to connect to Dorothy. To tell her—"

"I thought it was what I wanted. But now—" He sighed, coming to squat beside her. "Rose, I haven't been ignoring you. But it's so hard to be this close. And I didn't know—not what happened to her, not about the arrest—not until right now."

The sadness and shock in his eyes proved that much.

"There's far more to this story than I could have imagined. There can't be even the slightest chance of any false promises. That's what people thought I made her all along. I want—no more con-tact. I see. You showed me. Dorothy isn't the kind of person who would ever give up. She believes. Let me come to her *with* that trumpet. Finally. That trumpet is our magic. It can't be any other way."

42.

December 24, 2019
~Our Journey~

Sometimes, on long drives like this, you almost grow blind to what's speeding by outside your window. Guess that's a little like life, isn't it? You get to moving so fast through your day-to-day, you're so intent on getting to the next goal, you go blind to the little things around you. All the ordinary furniture of everyday life.

Often, it takes something completely out of place to make you stop and really take notice.

And seeing Frankie for a slice of a moment did that for Angela. More, even, than that letter had. Seeing the old speakeasy owner made Angela stand still long enough to take it all in. Everything that had been happening. Everything around her. The sidewalk squares and the sign on The Page Turner across the street, the graffiti carved into the nearby sidewalk. A lone cardinal, currently sitting on the phone line. The brilliant red spot in the sky stared back at Angela—in no hurry himself—as if to ask, "Did you see her too?"

Angela squinted at him. Cardinals were showing up everywhere, it seemed—on the ledge, the front walk, up there on the phone line. But always one at a time.

Maybe, Angela caught herself thinking, it was always the same bird.

She shook her head at herself—but wasn't quite able to shake off the uncertainty that suddenly filled her as she stared up at the red dot against that winter gray sky.

That day, nobody who lived in Sullivan—not one of the people speeding by, phones in their pockets, anxious to get to the next store, the next errand, all those extra little things that needed to get done before Christmas Day, gifts and trinkets and decorations and soaps and towels and blankets for the guest room where the in-laws were going to stay—would have ever bothered to pay any attention to some old phone line. Who cared? Who had landlines anymore? Hardly anybody other than Angela, who had revived the old phone line like she'd revived everything else: the original neon sign out front, the original hardwood floors and heavy, wooden tables and chairs, not to mention the ornate bar. The business, Angela had insisted, wouldn't be the same without the phone ringing regularly—some nights, off the hook, as they all used to say.

Most of the Sullivan residents only considered that ringing phone background noise. It didn't really register the same way. Not in modern ears. That old phone line was nearly as outdated as Kurt's letters.

It wasn't, though. Now Angela was more certain of it than she ever had been. Something quite out of the ordinary had happened on her phone—coming across the line where the cardinal sat watching.

That phone line was alive.

Angela didn't know it, but I can tell you—it was all because of Rose.

Strung across the full length of the city, the line was suddenly jammed with the voices of everyone who had been involved in that fateful night in 1931. All of them wanting to tell their own story. How their own life had changed.

Why wouldn't they? Rose had plugged into the big event itself. The headlines and the chatter and the overheard conversations that had followed that violent night had turned Frankie into a bad guy. Frankie, once Dorothy's comforter, her friend—the woman who'd helped everyone, including police officers like Charlie Barister, forget the outside world for a little slice of time.

Did she deserve it? Was it unfair? It didn't matter. The label was hers.

We all do that. Don't we? Without even realizing it sometimes. We tag people. It's easy. Especially when everyone picks out the same tag. *Yes, yes, Frankie the troublemaker.*

Don't you think Edna, who disappeared that very night, leaving town with her kids, got a similar brand? Don't you think she was labeled an unfit mother, a cheating wife? Don't you think the people of Sullivan shook their heads, muttering, "Those poor little girls," as though agreeing that Edna was simply not the mother her daughters needed? Especially since she and Hank cut out of town with the kids, leaving poor Arthur behind?

Yes, Frankie the troublemaker. Edna, the floozy. Hank, the boastful storyteller. Arthur, the stick in the mud turned unappreciated husband. Dorothy the child with the fragile broken heart.

It's so easy. Give everyone a title. Some way to sum them up, all at once, in a single sentence.

Even if it's based in some kind of truth, easy brands are never the full picture.

And that day, the voices on the line were all scrambling to say just that. Fighting to be heard. To tell a bigger story. All of them insisting on adding their own tidbit, details. What they had seen. Who they had been. Which tags were right. Which were undeserved.

Angela trembled with fear, not sure what had happened. Too many muffled voices filled the air. Angela couldn't pry them apart from one another, figure out what they were trying to say. Were they seeking help? Offering a warning?

It wasn't as though she could express these fears to Geena or Rob. Kurt? Absolutely not.

Without any of the after-hours regulars nearby, all Angela could do was stare up at that cardinal and wonder what he knew that she didn't, at least not yet. Why wouldn't someone *tell* her? Letters and voices and strange messages weren't enough. She'd thought her worries last year were bad, but they were nothing compared to this. Last year, she'd had doubts about her business, fears that her dreams wouldn't pan out. This year? Something almost sinister crackled against the air.

But what, exactly?

At the flea market a few doors down, Rose grew flustered as she reconnected her lines. But not just to the old box at the history museum. Not anymore.

There were too many voices reaching out to have come from one location.

"Hang on," she pleaded. "Hold your horses. Wait your turn!"

But no one was willing to wait. They couldn't, now that a chance had opened up for them to speak. "Gossip," so many of them were grumbling. "That rotten gossip." Over time, too many of the stories that had hardened into legend were slanted. Or twisted. Or plain wrong.

Now they were scrambling to let their own version be heard. This was their chance to set the story straight.

43.

~January 3, 1932~

Ruth Latchy knew what so many in Sullivan thought about her. That she was *particular*. And that was putting it kindly. *Persnickety* was the word she knew Martha over at Sullivan Drug preferred. She also knew that Martha's husband's description couldn't be repeated in mixed company.

James Wilmington had owned the Sullivan Drug Store for the past ten years. He and his wife Martha had mixed treatments for Ruth Latchy's coughs and recommended creams for her aching feet. They had prepared toasted ham sandwiches that she ate at the counter on Thursday afternoons after her weekly trip to the library. She knew they had grown to expect her to inform them (politely and succinctly, of course) when there was too much pickle juice in the potato salad, too many bubbles in her seltzer water, a missing button on Mr. Wilmington's shirt.

They were wrong about her, though. Ruth Latchy wasn't picky. If you asked her for the truth of the matter, she would say she was simply a woman of precision. A woman who knew how to manage her husband's meager paycheck, stretch a dime, with no waste left over. How to consume what only needed to be consumed. No extra treats allowed. *Cheap*—that word trailed her, too. But it wasn't right, either.

People got so much wrong about her. As people do.

Mrs. Latchy understood it had more to do with the people who received her advice than it did with her. Not that it stopped her in any way. But the bottom line was, Mrs. Latchy did not believe in dreaming. Simple as that. She believed, instead, in raising or lowering hems rather than buying new skirts when fashion changed. She believed in starched collars to prop up old work shirts. In scrubbing kitchen floors daily. Silly dreams were a waste of time; dreaming didn't get the laundry done or dinner cooked. Wasteful thoughts needed to be redirected.

People did not like to be told that dreaming was a waste of time. So the town of Sullivan snickered and grimaced at her. They did their best to dismiss her.

One of these days, they'd realize she was right. She was sure of it. They'd wish they'd come to their senses earlier. She expected someone to tell her that any day.

Besides, Mrs. Latchy knew that feeling bad about her own criticism was also a waste of time. Hurt feelings did not get the bathroom clean or beat the dirt out of the rugs.

That morning, when she stopped by for a cup of coffee (make that *half* a cup of coffee, with one-fourth of a teaspoon of cream), Martha asked, "Anything good in the paper this morning?" as she placed the cup and saucer down on Mrs. Latchy's left-hand side, right where she preferred it to be.

Ruth Latchy could not answer. Not when the local *Sullivan Morning Tribune* (left by the man who'd been sitting there earlier—no need to buy a new paper when a perfectly good one was right there for the reading) had been folded to display the shocking headline: "SPEAKEASY BUST IN SULLIVAN."

"This the first you're hearing of it?" Martha asked. "Paper's been doing a whole bunch of stories on it. Hard to believe, though, isn't it?"

"I—had no idea," Ruth remarked, clutching the collar of her shirt.

Martha placed her elbows on the counter, staring at the newsprint. "You see there that Frankie's disappeared? On the *run*. Must'a snuck out during all the gunfire." She made pistols with her hands, pretending to fire a few rounds, then blew on her index finger gun barrel. She was young enough—the May of the May-December romance with her husband of two years—that such a gesture still did not seem foolish.

Ruth squirmed.

"James and I came to check on everything Christmas Day. You know how word spreads around here. What with the drug store being so close to the diner…"

Ruth raised wide, frightened eyes at Martha.

"Well," Martha said. "Anyway. Our place was fine. Obviously. But the *diner*." She shook her head. People around here, they all pitched in to make sure everything got cleaned up quick. But you should have seen it on Christmas. Bullet holes all through the front window. Glass scattered everywhere. Front door was completely busted. And the alley. Like some sort of explosion went off back there."

Ruth placed her finger on the newsprint. She leaned forward, as though to more closely examine the letters.

"What is it?" Martha pressed.

"This woman. She lives in my building," Ruth said.

"Who's that?"

"Dorothy—she—and Chester. Dorothy was arrested at the speakeasy? She *sang* there?" Ruth gasped, horrified.

"Never can tell about people, huh?" Martha asked. It was the statement that had been floating through her drug store ever since the bust. For the most part, it was the kind of thing people said to fill up the air while they were all busy fixing new labels onto old names. *Frankie the bad guy, Edna the disrespectable woman, Dorothy the...*

"Well—I can," Mrs. Latchy declared. "I can always tell about people. I always suspected there was more to her story. She was gone in the evenings, most times. She was so young, I had assumed she had another man, maybe—but not this. Never this."

Martha laughed. "As if cheatin's better than singin'," she joked.

Ruth kept shaking her head, completely taken aback by the news of what had occurred in quiet little Sullivan on Christmas Eve. In the tiny slice of time that it had taken her to read the newspaper story, the world had gotten immediately darker—corrupt and malevolent. The kind of place where gunfights broke out and the police arrested people she knew.

Martha's face fell. She hadn't meant to upset Mrs. Latchy. Teasing wasn't as much fun as it had been a few seconds ago.

"Got some fresh apple pie," Martha offered, lifting the lid on the glass display. "Come on, hon. No charge. What do you say?"

Ruth caught her reflection in the shiny side of the napkin dispenser. She looked grotesque. Persnickety and uptight, just like everyone liked to say. She pushed it out of sight and finally shook her head against Martha's offer. She had not come for apple pie, and she did not approve of unnecessary treats, even if they were on the house.

44.

~*December 14, 2019*~

Once Angela calmed down, she began to place calls, pacing the sidewalk outside with her cell pressed tightly against her ear: An electrician. A locksmith. The phone company.

The electrician found nothing. No sign of faulty wiring. Remote tests done by the phone company confirmed this diagnosis.

On hearing of Angela's fears, Officer Vargas promised a doubling of police presence on the Sullivan square. Of course, that amounted to a second occasional officer coming by—mostly Vargas's weekend fill-in.

"We ought to be out here deterring petty theft during the shopping season anyway," Officer Vargas had proclaimed.

Was he placating Angela? Most likely. But it wasn't as though she could fight him on the issue. What would she say? That Frankie Hall was itching to make a comeback?

The only time she questioned whether it might actually be safe to say something about it—about seeing Frankie, standing out there on the sidewalk—was when Scott showed up on his way home from the bank a couple of days after the incident.

"I heard you had some trouble," Scott said, standing near the bar, staring anxiously at the phone.

"Word travels," Angela answered, quickly wondering if he could be fishing for additional details.

"This place, though—" Scott started. He shifted his weight, his face twisted up almost like a kid with a stomachache.

"This place what?" Angela pressed.

"When you stopped by the bank, I thought it was all so strange, but—" He looked right at Angela. *There was a reason you tried to ask me about the deed*, his eyes said. *Just like the snowflakes you talked about on the debate trip. You've seen something that the rest of us haven't. We're all walking right by it. Aren't we? What are we missing?*

Angela tried to respond in kind, to agree with her own look.

But she should have remembered that Scott was not a man who spent time trying to translate looks. Not even when he was in the midst of dealing them out himself. He was a man of reason. Of bottom lines and making sure the last pennies were always accounted for. A man of interest rates and logic. The kind who quickly shook away whatever strange thoughts might try to percolate to the surface.

"I'm glad it turned out to be nothing," he said with a smile.

Angela nodded. "Right," she agreed. "Nothing."

But before he stepped out her door, he tossed one more look behind his shoulder. There they were again, the same questions, returning. He offered a slight, almost apologetic smile, as if to tell Angela he regretted not offering her something more. For not being able to calm her worries.

Angela was worried, all right. And no matter what steps she took, they all felt flimsy. She contacted the locksmith a second time, less than an hour after shiny new deadbolts had been installed on her front door and the alleyway entrance, to ask about additional security features.

The regulars shook their heads at her as she flicked the deadbolts back and forth each night, just before for her after-closing happy hour. They insisted the solution had very little to do with physical doors and locks. Angela knew they were right—but how else could she protect herself? Her bar?

"No doubt about it," Ruby said, pacing the floor. "Frankie's back. She's looking for a way to barge in…shove me out." She peered thoughtfully through the front window. "Don't know why she'd show her face to Angela, but to no one else since. Why not show herself to me if I'm the one she wants to kick out of this place?"

The question only hung in the air unanswered. Mostly because they were all having the same thought: It wasn't just Rose Frankie wanted out of the way. It was all of them. Including Angela.

Southwestern Telephone had of course promised to install a new phone. But they were backlogged, the service rep explained, having loaned so many of their linemen out to Arkansas to help restore the lines that had been torn from transformers during an early December ice storm. *Might not be there till next week*, that was how they'd put it.

Angela had understood. She still had her cell, of course. But she hated being without her old landline—it was the number she'd included in all her ads and the mailers she'd sent out after Thanksgiving. All year, she'd been working her customers. Using her bartender charm to collect stories and a visitors' book to collect addresses. What would happen when those customers—especially the out-of-towners who had accidentally found the place—tried to make reservations using the number included on Angela's mailer, but couldn't complete their call? The Sullivanites might still stop by, but the others would no doubt call some other establishment. Maybe even assume the place had gone out of business yet again.

A holiday bottom line wasn't the only thing in jeopardy, either—it was all those meetings with loved ones. That was what was really on the line. Would all those "ghosts of Christmas Eve" appear on the twenty-fourth only to weave through the crowd, searching, but never finding the face they had hoped to see? No—not hoped. *Expected* to see, after reading the story notations Angela had meticulously recorded all year long. Would they miss out, all because Angela's phone had been out of order?

Was this part of Frankie's plan? Was she trying to shut down the one-night-only reunions? Did she want Angela's business to go under? Was that how she would steal it back from Ruby and the rest of the regulars?

What was she planning to do with the place once she got it back?

So it was with an enthusiasm usually reserved for elementary-schoolers on Christmas morning that Angela greeted the Southwestern Telephone truck as it pulled to a stop in front of the bar.

"Oh, am I glad to see you," Angela breathed. "I can't believe you're here so quickly. Only been two days. I was told next week at the earliest…" Simply having him in her building made her feel she was putting some sort of a roadblock in front of Frankie's plans.

The man nodded and set right to work. Unbeknownst to Angela, the tools he carried in a professional-looking, polished box were nothing but ruses. The job he had to finish had nothing to do with pliers and cable testers.

The technician whistled as he disconnected her old phone.

"I didn't quite trust myself plugging in this new one," Angela explained, attempting to hand him the phone she had purchased herself, just the day before. "Thought I needed someone to test all the wires here in the wall. That poor salesman in the electronics store didn't know where to find his own landline phones anymore." She chuckled.

"No need, ma'am," the technician said, refusing to chuckle back or even look up from his work. "I've got a phone. Courtesy of the phone company."

"Oh," Angela said, her face wrinkling in confusion. "I guess—I suppose I can take mine back."

The technician nodded and returned to whistling as he set about installing the phone he had brought.

Perhaps, if Angela had not been confused by his statement

regarding the new phone (she could have sworn her contract had provided for no such equipment), she might have noticed that the tune he whistled was not a recognizable song, but repeating notes that mimicked the call of a cardinal. And, had she looked closer, she would have seen that the patch on the back of his work coveralls featured a similar red bird perched on a phone line.

45.

~Rose~

Rose kept working the switchboard, waiting for someone—anyone—to ask her what *she'd* heard about that Christmas Eve in 1931.

Not just beg her to repeat their own stories.

They once had. Didn't they remember? Back when Rose was part of a whole slew of young women working the switchboards, she was the only one people gravitated toward if they wanted to know the latest. She always had a crowd, anytime she showed up in public.

Why wouldn't she? Secrets were constantly spilling out of her. All you had to do was smile. Mention the weather, maybe. Nod a hello. And suddenly, the flood gates were open. Even without the mention of a specific name, the folks of Sullivan could guess (with surprising accuracy) who the current whispered story was about—and Rose would not be fired for talking out of turn.

A bit underhanded, maybe. Sneaky. But also utterly delicious.

She did have another cover story. One that involved the courthouse.

Rose Waterton did not listen to the radio on the rare day she had off from the phone company. She did not enjoy *The Shad-*

ow or tune in to any of those silly soap operas that filled Sullivan's airways every afternoon. She did, however, enjoy being present at local trials. Wiggling her backside into one of the hard wooden seats in the back row of the courthouse, her knitting needles clacking all through cross-examinations. While she had been guilty of plenty of switchboard snooping, she might have enjoyed arming herself with the latest tidbits of courtroom drama even more—spinning what she had observed into stories in ways that local journalists and even writers of pulp fiction could not. Or so Rose had always prided herself.

Each time she appeared coming down the courthouse stairs, the out-of-work daily laborers perked up their ears and began thumbing through the papers at the nearby newsstand where she always stopped before heading for home. What headline was Rose looking at? Did it mean something? What question could they whisper in her ear to find out what she knew that day? And it wasn't all about simply wanting to know another's private business. Why, it was also about survival. When a man was convicted and carted off to jail, it could mean that he possibly left a job behind that needed to be filled.

It was actually quite the service that Rose provided the people of Sullivan. That was what she told herself, anyway. Each and every time she whispered into another ear.

And she never did deny a whisper. Not to anyone.

So it was that in April of 1932, when Rose showed up to the dentist's office, she had the ability to make the entire waiting room forget their own agonizing pain. They forgot that they had been filling a cavity with cloves or had delayed getting their rotten molar pulled, or that they'd chipped a front tooth in a bare-knuckle fight. Maybe even cracked one in the wrestling match trying to get their German Shepard into the bathtub. They forgot their fear, the whir of the drill and occasional groan coming from behind the closed exam room door.

They all drew their chairs closer to hers.

"Charlie Barister," one of them murmured at her. "He was scheduled to testify the other day. Wasn't he?"

Rose simply pulled her knitting out of her bag as she settled deeper into her chair.

"Yes," she said, her eyes zeroing in on her row of purl stitches. "He did."

"And?" Martin Russel pressed, leaning closer. His right cheek was swollen, though not quite as swollen as his eyes with anticipation.

"And?" Rose repeated.

"Did he lock in the case?"

"Yes. Yes he did."

"For who? How?" Ruth Latchy asked, leaning in still closer.

"Dorothy," Rose answered with assurance.

"You think so?" Martin asked. "You think his testimony will send her to jail?"

"Jail?" Rose asked. She grimaced and shook her head, her cheeks growing ever pinker. "Just the opposite. He testified that she was simply in the wrong place at the wrong time."

"He didn't," Martin pressed.

Rose nodded. "He certainly did."

"How could you *accidentally* be in a speakeasy at the wrong time?" Martin asked.

"Dorothy's husband is missing," Rose reminded them all.

"No, he's not," Martin grumbled, grimacing and touching his cheek. "Everyone knows he said he was going to find work."

"So when was the last time you saw him?" Rose asked. "Heard from him? Heard anything about him?"

Martin and Mrs. Latchy exchanged looks.

"By Christmas, Dorothy's husband was most *definitely* missing," Rose repeated.

After taking a moment to let that point sink in, she asked, "Who rents a room on the opposite side of the square?"

Rose paused to stare into their blank faces.

"Charlie," she sighed. "That's who. Charlie Barister, who was hosting a Christmas Eve party in his home. Just a small gathering. Mostly police officers and their families. Anyone not on patrol. On Christmas Eve, Dorothy was feeling lonely, it being the holiday and all. Poor little abandoned thing. Can you imagine being all alone on Christmas Eve? Your husband is gone. No word. No way of knowing where he is—if he's even okay. She had turned down Charlie's invitation weeks earlier, but when Christmas Eve found her, she changed her mind. She had to get away from the boarding house and all her empty chairs and knowing who wasn't seated in any one of them.

"Problem was, she changed her mind so last minute. She took a shortcut *behind* the speakeasy, down the alley, to get to Charlie's party before it wound down for good."

Rose's audience sighed, leaning back to fully absorb the story.

"How did Charlie know that?" Mrs. Latchy asked.

But the question was swallowed as others in the waiting room muttered, "Poor Dorothy" and "It really was a case of wrong place, wrong time" and "I always did like Dorothy."

"I always did like *Charlie*," Dr. Delmer insisted, standing in the open doorway of his examination room. "You know you can always trust Officer Barister to do the right thing. And if he says that woman was an innocent bystander, you can bet that's what she was."

Yes, Rose had believed that back then. Just as strongly as everyone else in that waiting room, including Mrs. Latchy: Charlie Barister did the right thing.

And yet, how many of them in that very waiting room had known someone who'd been caught up in the Christmas Eve raid? How many had heard the stories? *And then, right in the middle of Dorothy's song, the police showed up...*

How many of them had actually been to Frankie's speakeasy? Maybe not on Christmas Eve. But how many of them had seen Dorothy up there, gardenia tucked behind one ear, in that ivory sateen uniform of hers, belting out every song she knew?

And yet, Charlie had told a different story. On the stand, no less.

Charlie, who they could all rely on. Charlie, who would have their backs in a pinch. They all felt certain of it.

And, just as certainly, they all felt they should have his.

Rose had continued knitting that day, letting the doctor's words linger in the air. Letting everyone in that waiting room go about fixing—or reaffirming—their own easy labels to both of them: Dorothy the sweetheart, the good girl. Charlie Barister the hero.

Now, so many years later, Rose felt far less certain about what she'd done in that waiting room—or the drug store, or the newsstand, or the line outside the movie theater, or any other old place in Sullivan where she had disclosed some piece of gossip.

She felt something of a sick twist that reminded her of what it was like to have an upset stomach, wondering what hand she'd had in it all—the half-truths, the fiction that had hardened, courtesy of the frequently-repeated pieces of gossip, into fact. How many silly games of telephone she had started. How many stories she'd allowed to make the rounds, ear-to-ear, whisper-to-whisper, through Sullivan. Clearly, she'd helped to create so many of the labels that former Sullivan residents were scrambling to correct. Not just Dorothy's and Charlie's. Did they blame her for some of it? All of it?

Was that why she was here now? To right some of these wrongs?

She felt heavy and sad.

All she could do was scramble to answer the calls, one after another.

46.

~*December 16, 2019*~

Linda pulled her mug from the microwave in the history museum's break room. She breathed in the lemon-laced steam from the herbal tea before taking a first sip.

Her throat was raw from all the daily, lengthy explanations of Sullivan's secrets, given to ever-increasing crowd numbers. Even teaching hadn't worn her voice out this much.

And she had another tour in two minutes.

She took another sip, swallowing as slowly as possible, allowing the tea to linger a bit on her irritated throat.

She put her mug down, found her reflection in the side of the toaster, and slathered on a swipe of fresh lipstick just before hurrying back out into the hallway.

"Welcome!" she greeted as she began to count the faces.

And realized, somewhere around thirteen, that she did not recognize any of them.

It gave her an off-kilter feeling, frankly. Not one? Not even a *That guy seems vaguely familiar?*

Where were they coming from? Who were they? How did they know about the exhibit?

She cleared her throat. Her prepared words came easily now, having recited them more times than she could count.

"Five cent," a woman called out, interrupting Linda's speech about fifteen minutes in.

"Excuse me?" Linda asked, searching the crowd for the interrupter.

"Frankie's was home of the five-cent steak. I mean, her honest diner. Out front. Used to advertise five-cent steaks. You said ten." The voice had come from near the back of the crowd.

Linda supposed the woman was simply pointing out the discrepancy clearly visible in the photos of the speakeasy portion of the exhibit.

"Pan-fried," another voice piped up.

"Cut 'em with a fork."

A knowing murmur washed through the group.

"I—yes. Yes, I'm sure it was," Linda said, rattled, attempting to sound open to comments. "I'm sure it was very good."

"Nice that you've got a piece on Charlie—"

"Charlie?" Linda repeated.

"Quite the police officer. You know he took a bullet during a robbery?"

"T—to save the property from being stolen?"

"No—to save the life of the robber. Had a young boy at home, too. Quite the story at the time."

"He did?" Linda asked. She'd never told that story. She didn't know anything about it. How did they?

"That's—tragic," she said.

"Aw, you kidding? You got it all wrong, lady."

"Yeah—Charlie. He was rare."

"Never see another one like him."

"Had his own sense of justice—no. That's not right. He wasn't some kind of vigilante."

"He knew *everyone.* That was it."

"Didn't get swayed by a bunch of rumors."

"Something else he knew—sometimes, you do things because you have to."

"Sometimes, the outside world makes choices for you."

"He knew the world wasn't all black and white."

"You ever need somebody to stand up for you, Charlie Barister was your guy."

"Not a cruel bone in his body."

Linda's head was still spinning. Why were they talking about this Charlie Barister person? She had never mentioned him. Not once.

Murmuring amongst themselves, the group began to break up, to wander off. Distantly, Linda thought about calling back to them all. Telling them she had more to share.

But for some reason, she wound up letting them drift away.

Light streamed at her from the opposite side of the room—almost as though someone had activated the flashlight on their phone—pointing toward a nearby police display. Bouncing off a metal object on a table.

Linda glanced about, making sure she was completely alone, before leaning forward. The object wasn't handcuffs. Or an old lock from the prison.

It was a police officer's badge.

Linda immediately snatched it up, thinking to herself that the badge hadn't been there before. Not until today.

She squinted at the number on the bottom, nearly hidden by the corrosion. Turning it over, she found a piece of paper taped to the back. So old, it had turned the color of iced tea. Linda fished her reading glasses from her cardigan pocket to make out what had been written in old-fashioned, swirling cursive: C. Barister.

The sound of a phone ringing made her jump.

"Toby?" she called. "You going to get that?"

She lunged out into the hallway. "Toby?" But the ringing wasn't coming from the downstairs front desk.

It was coming from a side room. One that Toby had been using for storage.

Linda edged her way inside, where the ringing only got louder. "Hello?" she called out into the room, then felt her cheeks flame. How was someone on the phone supposed to hear that?

As she wandered deeper inside, it became clear that the ringing was coming from the back corner. From Angela's old crates.

Linda approached the crate filled with items that Toby had designated interesting but unusable—for this exhibit, at least. And found herself staring at a candlestick phone that continued to ring.

But once she touched the phone, it silenced.

Still, Linda could not shake the feeling that somehow, she had been called into the room, close enough to look inside the box.

Curious, she picked up the phone, exposing a pile of newspaper clippings. The first headline proclaimed, in bold black print: "EXONERATED."

47.

~May 3, 1932~

Dorothy staggered out of the courthouse, too relieved and confused and surprised to walk in a straight line. She gripped the handrail and lowered her backside down to the top of the stone steps. Around her, footsteps thundered, every bit as loudly as they had last Christmas Eve.

These people weren't racing for their lives, though, not like they had that brutal December night. They were simply walking home. Lawyers, reporters. Townspeople.

They seemed not to notice Dorothy sitting there shell shocked.

She had been found innocent and freed. The judge's gavel still rang in her ears.

Charlie's testimony had rescued her. Oh, so what if she maybe wasn't quite as guilty as Frankie and Edna? So what if she hadn't sold or served? She'd worked at the speakeasy—and because Frankie and Edna had gotten away, escaped town, she was the one left to prosecute. To hang out to dry, her cellmate had often said. The one to make an example of.

Robert Ludlow was already serving time. Open and shut case. A few others had been convicted as well. Disorderly conduct. Firing their weapons at officers. Dorothy had prepared herself for her own conviction.

And yet (she kept having to repeat it to herself because it was so hard to believe), Charlie had saved her. The people of Sullivan felt safe putting their trust in him. He was Good, capital G. They'd all agreed on that. Charlie was Good, so they'd nodded when he told a story many of them knew firsthand was not true. Charlie was Good, so it had to mean there was a powerful, important reason behind his testimony.

Slowly, it was all starting to soak in.

Dorothy was free.

She'd been rescued.

But for what? she suddenly wondered. What good was any of it? Her parents had stopped speaking to her when she'd chosen Chester, the musician with all those pretty, fragile promises. They had not come to see her after her arrest. She supposed the door wasn't locked forever; she could go home. But showing up would mean that she was also wordlessly agreeing to leave him.

She couldn't do that.

But where else was there? Unable to post bail, she had not worked in months, and had received word that her apartment at the boarding house had been emptied while she'd been in jail.

A jury of her peers had given her another shot at life. Partly because of Charlie, and partly because of her age. Who was ever ready to say a woman not yet twenty years old was finished?

Yes, she was young. She had erred. She deserved a second chance. But that was still not the same as actually giving her the chance itself—the kind that would come with lodging and steady income. What was Charlie going to do, follow her everywhere she went, shaking his finger at those in Sullivan, reminding them he had once vouched for her?

Besides, how many people in town knew his story wasn't a hundred percent true? How many of them had heard her sing? Twelve Sullivan residents had agreed with Charlie—but how many in town would insist on continuing to brand her a bad girl, the kind no one wanted to get all that close to? A hundred? More? How many whispers would follow her? How many would still fear guilt by association?

She was cleared, but she was not cleared. Dorothy knew that.

She also knew she had fifteen cents in her pocketbook.

She thought it again: She was free. And yet, she felt anything but free.

She lowered her head, covering her face with her fingers to hide the flood of tears trailing down her cheeks.

A pair of hands suddenly began pressing on her ribcage, under her arms. "Dear," a voice murmured softly in her ear. "Dear. I can't do this on my own. You'll have to help me. Stand up."

"Why?" Dorothy answered, choking back sobs. Maybe, she thought, if she was lucky, she could dissolve right there on the courthouse steps.

"Dear, put your feet underneath you. Come, now, help me," the voice begged.

Dorothy looked up cautiously. "Who, who—"

"It's me, dear."

"Mrs. Latchy?" Dorothy blinked, expecting her eyes to clear up. Expecting to realize it was someone else entirely standing beside her.

But Mrs. Latchy pursed her lips and announced, as if it was a foregone conclusion, "It's time to go home."

"I don't have one," Dorothy lamented.

"Yes, you do," Mrs. Latchy insisted. "You'll stay with me until you can get on your feet."

"Why?"

"You've been found innocent."

Dorothy's head spun. She looked into the woman's smiling face, unable to truly trust it. Charlie had been surprising enough. But Mrs. Latchy?

She squinted at Mrs. Latchy, thinking, *You know Charlie told a lie. A good lie, maybe. But a lie. All those nights you watched me leave. You had to know where I was going. Didn't you?*

"It's enough," Mrs. Latchy insisted. "All of it. You've been through enough. Including," she added, looking Dorothy square in the eye, "being grist for the rumor mill."

"I'll always be that," Dorothy told her. "You don't want to be sucked into it."

Mrs. Latchy sighed. "If that's true, then dear, let's get you a different story. One that you won't mind being told and told again. One that will mean you will live the rest of your life comfortably."

Dorothy stared back, not sure what to say.

"Shall we?" Mrs. Latchy asked. When she hoisted that time, Dorothy found the strength to finally push herself off the steps.

Of everything that had happened to her—Charlie's courtroom lies, Chester disappearing on her, Frankie's place being raided—Dorothy already knew she would forever find this moment to be by far the most surprising.

48.

~December 18, 2019~

Rob locked up The Page Turner, grabbed his thermos, and headed out beneath the orange-tinted twilight, across the street to Ruby's Place.

"Hey, Angela," he called out. "You got any coffee left for my thermos? Maybe a sandwich to go with it?"

"Mmmm," she murmured, picking up the phone behind the bar and holding it to her ear, listening for a moment before returning the receiver to the cradle.

"Aren't you and Geena having dinner together?" she asked.

"I just—" He shrugged.

"Still looking for him, eh? The guy you saw in front of your store?"

"I get glimpses of him all the time. On the street out here. Or even, sometimes, through the front window of Tina's flea market. Felt stupid telling Tina about him. Stopped myself mid-story before I could completely describe the guy I was looking for. After all that, I *still* went running in there the other day. And of course— nothing. No guy."

"What're you going to do if you find him?" Angela asked.

"I don't even know," Rob admitted, slumping onto a stool at the bar. "Help him—but what does that mean, right? He seemed so desperate. Like somebody who had been running for a long time. I've never had that strong a feeling—like I was supposed to help somebody."

Rob kept his head turned down, his face hidden behind the bill of his old ball cap, as Angela turned away. He wanted to redirect their conversation—toward absolutely anything else—so he quickly wound up asking, "You going to need me and Geena to work Christmas Eve again? Manage the door, take the coats, that kind of thing? We actually kind of planned our holiday around it…"

But talking about Christmas Eve only made him think of last year. How he'd sworn, for a moment, he'd seen Tom, Geena's dad. And how he'd also sworn Tom had given him the one thing he'd hungered for more than anything, back when he was a teenager: his approval.

If the depths of a young boy's affection could be measured by the strength of his desire to win a parent over, then poor Rob had once been the most in-love seventeen-year-old on the planet. Not to mention the most in-love forty-seven-year-old. Because it had flooded him with this feeling of all truly being right with the world when he'd thought it had happened last Christmas. Finally. *Tom had offered his blessing.*

Of course, in the aftermath, Rob had only wondered what he'd really seen. Tom had disappeared on him last Christmas—like the strange man had disappeared outside his shop Thanksgiving weekend. Now, he wondered if finding this missing (and possibly homeless) man would prove to him that he was not the kind of guy who went around imagining people who weren't there. If he found the man, whoever he was, maybe it would let Rob believe he really *had* seen Tom. Really had received that long-awaited thumbs-up.

He shook his head at himself. Was he that desperate?

He could hardly believe how much he still wanted Tom's approval.

When he finally glanced up, Angela was staring at the phone again, hands on her hips. She leaned in, pressing one ear closer.

"Usually you have to take it off the hook," Rob joked.

"It hums, kind of," Angela said. "You hear it?"

He shook his head.

"Ever since the other day—it sounds strange, but there's this weird clicking, too, when I place a call. Let me go check the phone in my office," she said, already moving out from behind the bar. "Help yourself to the coffee. I made a couple of sandwiches already out of lunch leftovers. On the house."

Rob nodded. But before he could slide completely off the stool, the steaming coffee pot appeared right under his nose.

"Pour it in your thermos for you?" a waitress asked.

"I didn't know Angela'd hired anyone."

"Just temporary. Like it sounds you'll be on Christmas Eve."

Rob nodded, glancing at her name tag: "Claire."

She flinched, tugging at the top button. "Uniform's getting

so thin," she murmured. "Washed it so many times now, I fig-ure my slip's showing. Then again, the whole world's been looking threadbare lately. Threadbare and left over."

Rob wasn't sure what to say to that. It was true that Sulli-van had experienced quite a few hard financial years. At one point, around the time he'd divorced, it seemed there had been plenty of chatter that the square would die off completely. But hadn't Sulli-van been making a turnaround? Wasn't his shop the lone straggler?

"Hope you haven't been sitting there too long. Just the oth-er day, I swear, had a man sitting by himself at one of my tables and I didn't notice him for I don't know how long. Felt horrible for overlooking him. My little boy had a bad cough, though. That was part of why I was so distracted. Not like I can afford the doctor. Not like anybody can, right?"

Rob frowned. Her uniform was awfully old-fashioned looking, with its dusty pink fabric and the white cuffs and lacy handkerchief square in her pocket. Nobody wore those anymore, did they?

"Poor guy just looked so *rough*. Had on this jacket that I swear reminded me of the awning over my grandmother's porch. Been out there since the Great War, all sun-bleached and covered in dirt and exhaust."

Rob perked, despite her mention of the Great War. Who referred to the first World War that way? "We might be looking for the same person. He was here? Right here, in Ruby's?"

She twisted her mouth, embarrassed maybe—or guilty.

"You know what he ordered? A bowl of hot water."

"Hot water?"

"Put ketchup in it."

"He made tomato soup," Rob muttered as Claire finally set about filling his thermos. "Used to hear about men doing that kind of thing during the Depression."

"I want you to know," Claire said, gesturing with the empty pot, "I wouldn't have done it without my boy being sick."

"Done what?"

"I didn't even notice that weird case of his until I bumped into it with my foot, bringing him his bowl of hot water. Funniest shaped box I ever saw. He was so protective of it, once I noticed it. Kind of hiding it under his legs, you know? Like it was especially valuable."

"I didn't see him with anything like that."

"You *wouldn't* have. That's what I'm trying to tell you, mister."

She was getting really worked up. Rob's eye darted for a second toward the hallway where Angela had disappeared, hoping the waitress's halfway angry voice might draw her back again.

"I found it the next day. That case. Out by the trash containers behind the building. By what was obviously a campsite. Or the remnants of one, anyway. Don't know how anybody could have stood to camp out there. Gets so cold at night. The Windy City, right?"

Rob frowned. "Isn't that Chicago?" he asked, but Claire

ignored him.

"My little boy was bad sick. Up all night. And that man had been really protective of the case. I probably wouldn't have even looked otherwise. But it had been so cold. I figured the guy— look, he couldn't have survived. Not as cold as it was. And not if all he had was some campsite. He couldn't have needed what was inside that fancy case anymore. See what I'm saying? I'm not excusing what I did. But you have to know, sometimes, there are reasons. You do what you have to. We're scraping by, just like everybody else. Bread lines getting longer every day."

"Bread lines?"

"I'm sorry, okay. You see him, you tell him I'm sorry."

"For what?"

"I stole it. I knew it had to have something good in it. I was so desperate, I didn't even look inside until I was in the pawn shop."

"What was it?"

"A trumpet, all right? A beautiful trumpet. With all kinds of vines and flowers carved into it."

"Bet you got a lot for it."

"Enough for cough syrup. And Christmas presents. For my son. You tell him I'm sorry. There was no joy for me on Christmas morning—or now, really…"

Angela's footsteps thundered into the bar. "I swear," she was saying, "the bar phone is driving me crazy…You still here?" she asked Rob.

"I was just talking to your new waitress," Rob said.

"I don't have a new waitress."

Rob snorted a chuckle, sure Angela was joking. But when he turned to point her out, all that remained was the empty coffee pot on the edge of the bar.

49.

~*December 18, 2019*~

The phone that had hung on the wall between the living room and kitchen all through Geena's childhood began to ring.

"Man," Rob grumbled into her ear. "It's almost harder to get in touch with you now that you're in town. You planning on keeping your cell off the entire time you're home?"

Geena glared at the phone she'd tossed on her coffee table two days ago. It had become a sore spot, a hindrance. Something she did not want to look at. Like a credit card bill she knew was going to be higher than usual. Or test results that were expected to contain the worst news.

Really, all that her phone would greet her with were texts from the Head of the English Department. And voicemails. Also telling her it was hard to get in touch with her.

It was bordering on unprofessional not to respond. Even at this time of year. If Geena wasn't going to sign on for another three years, he would need to start the interview process and the search for another professor.

She knew that. She also knew that, at a certain point, her silence was going to translate to a no. The offer to extend her contract would be pulled.

Still, she could not make herself turn the phone on.

"Sorry," Geena muttered. "I didn't plan on it, but it feels good to unplug. Digital detox."

"Good thing I remember the old landline number at your dad's place. Same as high school."

It was a silly thing to still have the old phone line, Geena knew. Another bill that she really shouldn't have been paying. Money wasted. But she'd called that number herself so many times—it had always been a lifeline of sorts. A safe haven as she bounced around the country, all those different cities where she'd studied and taught. Even last semester, she was calling home every once in a while. Because her father's voice was still on the ancient answering machine. It gave her comfort.

"How's the search going?" she asked.

He sighed. "This is nuts. Isn't it?"

"It's not nuts. It's the sign of a kind heart."

He laughed. "Sure."

"You'll find him. You know that, right? As hard as you're looking, you'll find him."

"I hope so," Rob sighed. "Hey—did Angela say anything to you about hiring waitstaff?"

"No. Why?"

"Never mind. Maybe I really am seeing things. Dinner tomorrow?"

"Yeah," Geena said, moving her eyes over toward her laptop, open to a blank page. "That'd be nice."

After hanging up, she was left alone again—nothing but the quiet and the empty house and the dream of writing. It only seemed to grow stronger as time went on.

"But how do you get started?" Geena grumbled.

The doorbell rang, saving her for a moment from over-thinking it all.

"Hey, Kurt," she greeted the mail carrier. Kurt, who had been a favorite of her dad's. He'd looked forward to joking with him every day—especially when Geena was away at school. "You're delivering late, aren't you?"

"Done with the regular mail route. Signed up to do additional package runs at the end of the day."

"'Tis the season," Geena said. "But I'm not expecting anything. Sure you've got the right address?"

"Yep. In fact, I've got a package you need to sign for," he announced, thrusting a cardboard box at her.

Geena frowned at her name on the label. She signed but still felt convinced it had to be a mistake.

After a few minutes of small talk—more chatter about what they'd seen happen to Angela's phone a few days back, natural disbelief that there remained no solid answer to explain it all—she thanked Kurt, and raced back inside to slice the box open with her scissors. A gift card tumbled onto the floor: "Leaky faucet in September had me looking through the closets for your dad's toolbox. Found a trove of old home movies instead. Thought you'd like to watch them again. Love you—Rob."

Geena smiled, sliding the first DVD out of its sleeve, expecting it to contain one of her many Christmases with her dad. Maybe a birthday party. Might even be footage of Rob—seventeen years old, long hair, ripped jeans. A glimpse of that old Caprice he drove when they'd been kids. She hoped so.

Instead, the images on her screen were black and white. And soundless.

A man stepped from a strange looking police car and squatted, letting a little boy run into his arms.

Geena backed up across the living room floor, coming to sit on the edge of the coffee table. She'd gotten the wrong movies back. This belonged to some other family. She wondered how she'd straighten it out with the company Rob had used to transfer the film to DVD.

Her phone rang. Again. She reached for the landline, remembering how an extra-long cord had once allowed her the ability to talk out of her dad's earshot.

"Hello?" she asked, unable to pull her eyes from the home movie still visible from her new position. "Rob? Are you there?" Where was he calling her from? All she could hear was a round of static followed by unrecognizable voices.

Then—a little boy cried out, "Dad!"

Rob was not on the line. But who was?

As Geena listened, a man's voice answered, "Hey, Tommy." The words matched up perfectly—and bizarrely—with the mouths moving on her TV screen.

Tommy? Tom was her father's name.

She edged closer to the screen, the landline continuing to provide a soundtrack for the images playing out before her. Car engines growled as they sped down the residential street. A front door creaked open. A woman's voice welcomed someone named Charlie home for the day.

The camera zigged and jiggled about. But it had no problem keeping the subjects in focus. At one point, it rested on the shield fixed to the chest of the man's uniform.

A police officer. Charlie and Tom. These *were* Geena's family movies. But not of her own childhood. This was film of her father as a child. And Officer Charlie Barister, the grandfather she'd never met.

She took a seat in her dad's favorite recliner—and gripped the receiver tighter, not questioning the how or why. Just relishing the moment.

50.

~*December 19, 2019*~

The trill of a bird turned Maxwell Ross's gaze upward, toward the cardinal preening himself on the old telephone line.

"*Rose*," he growled.

He put his hands on his hips. "She talking to you, too?" he asked the bird. "You listening to her? Huh? Christmas Eve's coming. She tell you about the one back in '31? The raid of Frankie's speakeasy? Used to be a favorite story of folks around here."

The cardinal made no attempt to fly away. If Maxwell hadn't heard the bird sing, he might not have thought it was real. Might have dismissed it as some holiday decoration, same as the aluminum stars on all the light poles around the square.

"I went to jail for it. You know that? Me. I got plenty of blame to go around for that. Top of the list is that lousy Officer Barister him*self*. Freed Dorothy with his testimony. And me? He figured I had to be the one behind that Christmas Eve call to the station, the tip that came in while his own Christmas Eve party was in full swing. You think there wasn't a drop of Ludlow's booze at that party of his?

"What a hypocrite."

The bird chirped.

"So what if I was the one behind the tip? So what if I was the one who called Ludlow to make sure he'd be there when the cops showed—*with* a whole truck full of booze? So what if I went so far as to break the lock, so I could tell the cops the back door was open? And while I'm at it, so what if I really was making hooch of my own? To come out to my place and bust me the way he did—it was nothin' but revenge. That's not what a cop's supposed to do. Is it? And yet, everybody acted like Charlie was such a great guy. A hero. And since I'm the guy the hero went after, well, I had to be the opposite of good. I had to be downright rotten, didn't I?"

Winter wind ruffled the bird's feathers.

"Look at me. Talking to some bird," Maxwell moaned. But he didn't stop. His words only grew stronger.

"I didn't have a chance after that. Charlie made sure my story got out there for busybodies to repeat in all that unending gossip, and there wasn't a thing I could do to change it. Nobody'd even let me through the front door to apply for a job. What choice did I have but to live outside the law after that? Odd jobs on the shady side for cash. The kind of jobs no one else dared to take.

"Getting caught and locked up became the pattern of the rest of my life. And part of the blame for that goes to Charlie Barister."

Maxwell shook his head.

"I've paid my dues," he said. "Far more than I should have."

The wind picked up. Maxwell reached for the brim of his hat, holding it on tight until the gust subsided. "Winter chill," he announced. "That cold only means Christmas is coming. Which makes this the perfect time for me to get even. Isn't Christmas really the holiday when you get what you've got coming? If you're good, you get shiny new trinkets, and if you aren't, you get coal. Right?" he asked the cardinal.

"Well, these people in Sullivan haven't been good. Not to me, anyway. I'm going to give them a long overdue Christmas present. Only, it's not going to be some plain old coal. It's a bit of nostalgia in a bottle, the one they once refused. A bottle that's stayed hidden until now. It brought me back. I'm going to find it. And I'm going to use what's inside to make them pay. This time, Christmas Eve will be celebrated on my terms.

"Sullivan's not heard the last of Maxwell Ross."

He nodded once at the cardinal, as though to emphasize this point before taking off down the street, under an icy sky.

51.

~December 19, 2019~

But Maxwell Ross's words had not been heard only by the cardinal.

In a forgotten corner of the square, the limbs of a half-dead tree swayed above the broken remnants of an old phone booth.

Footsteps echoed. A hand reached for the phone as a cardinal landed on the nearby remnants of a wooden fence.

A man cleared his throat, coughing and readying himself in a way that made it seem as though he had not spoken in a long time. He placed a nickel in the slot and dialed quickly and with assurance, as though that booth were new, and there was no doubt about his call going through.

"Rose!" That voice—the unmistakable blend of gruff carburetor and upset tree frog.

Yes, here he was again. Robert Ludlow. Who had once talked to Frankie on Rose's phone line about the shadier side of town. Whose voice had echoed down the alley behind the speakeasy just before that Christmas Eve disaster.

Now, his voice—which had not been heard in Sullivan in decades—was signaling another disaster could be careening for the city limits all over again.

"Don't pretend you don't know who this is. Don't pretend you didn't listen in plenty to my voice back in our day."

"Robert," Rose murmured. "Robert Ludlow. From the garage."

"*Garage.* Say it, Rose. Robert Ludlow the liquor distributor. It ain't no secret. I was taken in that Christmas Eve. I did my time."

"What—what do you—"

"You know I used to make all those deliveries to Frankie," he crowed. "Well, I'm making a new delivery now. Of news this time. But trust me, this will hit you like ten shots of whiskey to the bloodstream.

"Maxwell Ross is back. Up to no good. I've been looking for that bottle of his, the one he bragged about when we were both in the joint. But I haven't found it. You hear me, Rose? I'm afraid of what will happen if he finds that bottle before I do."

52.

~*December 19, 2019*~

"Hello?" Rose asked, turning the key. "Hello? Robert? I didn't hear that last part. Robert? You still there?"

In the Sullivan History Museum, the teapot began to rattle in the bottom of Angela's fruit crate.

And outside the city limits, another woman—the one that Rose did not know she'd connected to Robert Ludlow's call—nodded, placing the earpiece back on her own old candlestick phone.

She'd been to Sullivan recently—for a slice of a moment—staring at Angela from the sidewalk outside her business. She'd hoped the shock of being seen might be enough. But now that she'd heard from Ludlow, she knew that she'd been wrong.

She had to return to Sullivan.

53.

~*December 20, 2019*~

"Haven't seen that look on your face in ages. Not since the day we met," Ruby observed.

Dorothy jumped, pulling her eyes away from the piano keys she'd been lazily playing. Her mind spun through the decades as she tried to place the year Ruby was talking about. "1955," she finally said.

Ruby chuckled, leaning over the bar. "You looked like a woman who couldn't stand the thought of Christmas coming around again."

"I couldn't," Dorothy admitted. Mostly because that hopeful part of her—the part that had always seen rainbows in spilled puddles of oil, the part that had so thoroughly believed Chester would come home to her—was as vibrant as ever.

Perhaps, if that part of her had faded, the holidays would have gotten easier. Perhaps they would have stung less.

But she still thought, *Maybe this year.* Even if Chester himself wasn't going to come walking through her door, maybe, finally, word of him would.

Every single year, her hopes swelled. Christmas never became a holiday for others to celebrate. It never became a time to put on a smile and simply go through the motions, nothing else. Every single year, right on time, the Christmas spirit infected Dorothy. Her heart grew increasingly lighter as Christmas Eve approached.

And every single year, when nothing happened, she felt herself crash.

"I wanted a peek," Dorothy said from the piano bench, remembering the way she'd felt the day she and Ruby had met. "Wanted to see what you were doing with this place."

"What I was doing with *your* place," Ruby observed. "I could tell you had your own history with the building just from the look on your face. The way you were staring inside. It was like you were comparing what I'd done to something that had come before."

Dorothy closed her eyes a moment, replaying that day in her mind. The way Ruby had stepped outside of the bar, swinging some sort of door decoration, announcing, "I was going to hang this on the entrance here, but now I can't quite tell if I like it or not. Too much?"

It had seemed a strange thing to ask—or even be concerned about. Especially with the entire building engulfed by commotion and frenzy—construction workers and electricians scrambling to meet deadlines, furniture being delivered, the neon sign being attached to the brick over the door. Across the street, two men from the electronics store—the same that had sold Dorothy her first television—were standing on the sidewalk, smoking and grumbling about the prospects of a female business owner coming to muck up the town square.

Ruby should have had far bigger things than some silly door decoration on her mind.

But Ruby had seemed oblivious. Dorothy would later learn that Ruby had quite nearly perfected the ability to tune out the external world during her years as a performer. Back then, though, Dorothy'd marveled at the way Ruby simply held up that door decoration, asking for her opinion, like they were the only two people on the square.

"Funniest thing," Ruby'd said, still waving that decoration about. "I had some mistletoe hanging—the stuff grows naturally around here, did you know that?" When Dorothy didn't answer, she added, "Anyway, somebody took it right off my door!" She shook her head, obviously not annoyed by this at all. "Hopefully, it went to some heartsick young fellow who gets his wish on Christmas Eve."

She winked. Then asked again: "So?" as she held up her bough. "What do you think?"

Ruby didn't need an answer—Dorothy knew as much. It had been clear, from her sparkling eyes and delighted grin, that Ruby wasn't unsure about including it at all. She knew she was going to hang it. She was fishing for compliments. Ruby had eyed Dorothy in the proud way of people who believed the stars had aligned and everything was going their way.

"Told me you were a music teacher. Remember?" Ruby

asked, bringing Dorothy back to the present. "And in a way, I did think you looked like one—you were tough."

"Tough?"

Ruby shrugged. "Most teachers are. You were different, though. I knew there was something else. It was like you'd been through something. Like you'd seen something most of us don't."

Dorothy tried to picture it, the way she must have looked to Ruby that day. Whatever she'd seen, Dorothy was sure it had been the result of losing. Even though she'd maintained her hope where Chester was concerned, she wasn't quite the same girl she'd once been on a glittery New Year's Eve, certain that money and luck and easy times would always rain from the heavens.

Dorothy had learned she wasn't immune from hardship— that knowledge had left its mark.

"I thought back then that the only way you get that look was on the road," Ruby said. "Just knew there had to be something else, other than teaching."

Dorothy flinched against the idea that teaching was one of the least interesting parts of her story. "I never would have been able to teach if it weren't for my old neighbor," Dorothy reminded Ruby. "If she hadn't taken me in after—well. After the trial. Given me a place to stay. With her and her husband. While I studied. As I started teaching. People were more willing to bring me their young students at the Latchy house. She knew that, though. Yes, it was all because of her."

"Well," Ruby said. "If your abilities as a singer are any indication what kind of music teacher you were, you were the *best.* Teacher of the century. Best move I ever made, hiring you for my big opening night that year. Right there, right on the spot, out there on the sidewalk, without even auditioning you. Remember?"

Dorothy nodded listlessly.

"Didn't even know your name yet when I offered," Ruby went on. "I had this feeling about you. In my bones. And you didn't disappoint. Not just on opening night, either."

Dorothy didn't respond. What was Ruby doing? Trying to lift her spirits, get her in the Christmas mood? Show her that the sadness of the speakeasy wasn't the final word?

Dorothy knew that much was true. But she would never see her story as one of triumph, not without Chester. Or at least knowing what had happened to him. All this time she'd been coming to Ruby's as a regular, and never once had she been joined by him. Other spirits had their reunions—Elizabeth and Tom had.

Why not Dorothy and Chester?

Sometimes, it was almost like she'd dreamed him up.

Dorothy felt more down than usual because of the stories the regulars kept circulating about Frankie. *Sinister*—that was the word Angela had used after seeing Frankie outside the bar. The rest of the regulars had instantly agreed with her, even though most of what they knew was secondhand at best.

Dorothy was so confused. Had she always been wrong about people? Wrong about Chester, who'd never returned to her? Wrong about Frankie as well? Had there been this whole other side to Frankie—a vicious side—that she'd hidden from Dorothy? Perhaps because Dorothy was so young?

She had begun to stop trusting her own beliefs. It was a worse feeling than disappointment or even heartbreak. It soured everything about Christmas this year.

"You coming?" Ruby asked.

It truly was time to go. The rest of the regulars were long gone. Their glasses had been cleaned and put away. Ruby's cocktail shaker was back in its place, ready for tomorrow night.

Or maybe it was *tonight*. Maybe the date had already slipped from one number to the next.

Dorothy shook her head. She needed to be alone for a minute, in the place where it had all started. Try to make some sort of peace with everything she seemed to have gotten wrong.

"Suit yourself," Ruby said, slipping away.

Dorothy swiveled on the piano bench to face the keys again. She started plunking out an old melody line: one about taking a sentimental journey. She'd always loved that old song—but had often sung it without much attention to its meaning.

Now, though…

If only she could go back. To Chester. To Frankie. If only she could see them again with her seasoned eyes.

She wanted to know the truth. Finally. Not some pretied-up storybook version. Whatever the harsh reality was, it had to be better than this. Than being in limbo for decade after decade.

The phone behind the bar rang.

Dorothy jumped, snatching her hand away from the keys. "Ruby?" she called. "Ruby? You still there?"

No one ever called. Maybe during business hours—but never during the regulars' happy hour. Not once.

Did she answer?

If it was one of Sullivan's current residents, would they even be able to hear her? Should she ignore it, let them shrug and decide to call back again later?

Then again, what if this was someone else? One of the faces of the past?

Was this a chance she needed to take?

Dorothy pulled herself away from the piano and slowly made her way across the bar, mostly hoping that the phone would stop ringing before she got there.

No such luck.

Cautiously, she lifted the receiver.

"Dorothy. It's me. Ruth. Ruth Latchy."

Dorothy's eyes immediately began to prickle with tears. "Ruth!" The woman whose arms had lifted her up from the courthouse steps. Dorothy's heart instantly flooded at the sound of her voice. "There's so much—" Dorothy started. Had she ever properly thanked Mrs. Latchy? Told her how generous she had been opening her home to her?

Surely, she had. On graduation day. And a hundred other times. But it had never felt like enough.

It still didn't.

"There's not much time," Mrs. Latchy demanded in that familiar, stern tone she had once used on Dorothy, insisting she get up off the courthouse steps, get on with life.

"Time?"

"Don't listen to them."

"Them who?"

"*Them,* them," Mrs. Latchy snapped. "The regulars who tell stories about Frankie. Who act like they know everything about her. Remember, Dorothy, they were all wrong about me. Persnickety. Poppycock! Such a simple, dismissive title. They were wrong about you when you were arrested. How they spun you—like you were some sort of—what were the terms? Low-class canary? It just used to make me so mad. You know that better than anyone. And I'm telling you, Dorothy, they're wrong about this. They're wrong about Frankie."

"They are?"

"Of course! Have you already let them rattle you that much? Don't let them change your mind. Please, Dorothy. You know better. Don't let someone else's story change what you saw with your own eyes."

"But—I've been wrong about things before."

"Wrong about what?"

"About you! Wasn't I?" Dorothy's voice grew increasingly lower with emotion. "I dismissed you. Thought you were reveling in Chester being gone. I judged you when I shouldn't have."

"Maybe a little. But so did I. I thought I knew you, and I

didn't. The trial changed us, dear. That's what times of trials and tribulations do. They open our eyes. We see ourselves and each other in a new way. Didn't we have a different understanding, you and me? Didn't we both become better people? The kind who couldn't be swayed by gossip?"

"Most people don't change."

"They can, dear, when they are allowed to see themselves. I did. Right after I saw that newspaper article about the raid, I looked up, and I saw my reflection. Did I ever tell you that? I saw myself in some old napkin dispenser at the drug store, of all places. I was looking at myself and thinking about you. And that was the beginning of it all. The seed had been planted. How had I treated you? What had you been going through? What had you seen when you looked at me? Those were the questions that had filled my head, every single day until you were found innocent. And then, I was ready to act."

Dorothy rubbed her forehead. She didn't know what to say. But Mrs. Latchy was more than satisfied, it seemed, to fill the silence.

"Don't you know who you are, Dorothy? Do you believe that you're everything the people of Sullivan told you that you were? An old woman music teacher? A could-have-been singer who never made it past performing in her hometown? A sad and lonely lady to be pitied?

"It's wrong. It's all wrong, Dorothy. Don't let them tell you who you are. You and your warm heart and your sweet ways. I still see you, that kindhearted young woman on Christmas Eve, waiting for her Chester. That part of you is still alive. I know it."

"Chester never did come back," Dorothy argued. "Maybe I was a fool."

"Don't give up now. You're right about Frankie and you were right about Chest—"

Static exploded into Dorothy's ear. "Mrs. Latchy?" she begged, trying to bring her back.

She replaced the receiver.

Mrs. Latchy was gone, but her words stuck.

Dorothy slipped into her coat and stepped into the brisk winter night. The silver stars hanging across the square brought a smile.

Underneath it all, a tiny little light began to glow inside of her. The same light that always found her this time of year, in spite of her troubles.

Maybe, she dared to think, just as she had every single December since 1931, Christmas really would come for her after all.

54.

~December 22, 2019~

It took Chester a while to realize Maddie had stopped playing along with him. Four solo bars, to be precise.

When he did finally realize it, he lowered his trumpet to find her staring at him with her eyebrows raised.

"That was weird," she muttered.

"Just—doing a bit of improvisational work," Chester said with a shrug.

"Pretty fancy playing," Tina agreed from behind the front counter.

Chester stared down at his shoes. "I used to play professionally," he finally admitted.

"Sure am glad you worked off all the money for that trumpet," Tina announced. "I wouldn't want it to go to anyone else. Can't imagine another soul out there who could make that trumpet sing quite like you can."

"So I—it's mine?" Chester asked.

Tina smiled. "As of ten minutes ago. When the clock struck four p.m. You officially worked off the full price."

Chester rocked back slightly on his feet. He had his trumpet back permanently.

And his Dorothy was two doors down—or would be, anyway. For the after-closing happy hour.

Funny, he thought. At the end of his long journey, it all seemed so much the same. Sullivan's square was decorated as he remembered. Maybe Frankie's old place had become Ruby's—but it was the same old building. Still serving the same old cocktails. Only difference was, the bottles were now considered legal.

He felt a bit like Odysseus—a man who had traveled an unfathomable distance, all to make it back home.

With his trumpet in his hand, he felt triumphant. Weren't trumpets supposed to blare to announce a victory?

Chester chuckled to himself. "Trumpets," he muttered, too quietly for Tina or Maddie to hear.

At the back of the flea market, Rose leaned forward, reaching for one of the cords on her switchboard. "Chester!" she called out.

But he shook his head and raised a hand as if to signal for her to stop. He was communicating with her directly—one of the very few times he had.

Rose wanted to blurt it out, tell him that Mrs. Latchy had called her the night before, asking to be connected to Dorothy. She wanted to tell him all about the conversation she'd overheard. How Mrs. Latchy had primed Dorothy to be ready for Chester's return.

It was time to go to her.

What else could he possibly be waiting for?

But Chester clapped his hands and announced, "Christmas Eve!"

He was talking to Maddie, of course, but the moment he said it, he glanced back at Rose, as though to remind her it was also the date he had long ago promised Dorothy. By Christmas Eve, he'd told her, wiping a tear from her cheek before he'd left for the train station, he'd come back for her.

And Christmas Eve, he decided, it would still be.

Rose leaned away from her switchboard. Yet again.

"So," he announced, gesturing toward Maddie. "You have become quite the 'Jingle Bells' virtuoso."

Maddie stuck her chest out. "You think Mom's going to like it?"

"I have never met your mother, but I would dare say that a woman who could not appreciate such a fine rendition would surely be a woman of horrendous taste. That would not describe your mother, would it?"

"Hor-what? She likes horseradish on her sandwiches. Is that what you're talking about?"

"No, no, I mean, she's a woman who can appreciate the fine things in life. Right?"

"I don't know. She doesn't like it when I use that word."

"What word?"

"Fine. Like when she asks me how school went and I say 'fine,' that makes her sigh really long and hard like this." Maddie sucked in a breath and let out a long exasperated sigh, slumping in her seat on the piano bench.

In the back of the flea market, Rose laughed.

Not that Tina or Maddie noticed. It was inexplicable—one more thing in a long line of inexplicables.

"I think I have a much better venue in mind for your performance. But only if you let me accompany you. I'd like to play alongside you as well," he said, pointing toward his trumpet. "I would promise to stick to the main melody. And not get too fancy."

Maddie nodded.

Chester grinned, feeling happy—almost giddy. He had a plan. He'd satisfy Maddie—and see his Dorothy. Finally. All at once.

"Come with me."

Maddie followed him as he walked out of the flea market, down the street, and toward Ruby's Place.

"In *there?*" Maddie asked, jabbing her thumb toward the entrance.

Chester nodded. "Better than the flea market, don't you think?"

"I don't know. I've never been in there. I mean, Mom did promise she'd take me. On Christmas Eve. And not a minute sooner. Still, though. I don't know…Weird stuff goes on. Mrs. Merryweather said—"

"There you go again."

Maddie glanced up to find Kurt and Angela both standing

in the doorway as Kurt handed over her daily pile of mail.

"Repeating stories you overheard at the chain-link fence?" Kurt went on.

"It's not gossip," Maddie said. "It's true."

"Uh-huh," Kurt said through a grin. "Sure. Haven't been seeing you on my route lately. I've been wondering where you were."

"In the flea market."

"Bothering Tina?" Kurt snickered.

"No! Working, for your information."

"On what?"

Maddie tightened her lips. She hated the way Kurt and Angela were both looking at her. Like she was a kid. Which, she guessed, she was. But they still didn't have to look at her like she was one. When would they all stop? When did a person finally graduate from being something to put up with to being on the same eye level? Was there an announcement? Would Kurt bring her something in the mail? A graduation certificate? A congratulations card?

She tried to put on her most serious face and announced, "You have a piano!" while holding her index finger in the air.

"I do!" Angela responded in kind.

"I need one!"

"For what!"

"To give my mom her present! I learned a song! 'Jingle Bells.'"

"What a great present," Angela said, becoming suddenly serious. "She's going to love that."

"Is this a private performance?" Kurt asked.

"Is it still a present for Mom anymore if everyone comes?" Maddie wondered out loud.

"Am I everyone?" he asked.

"Do you *want* to come?" Maddie didn't really think that anyone else would even be interested.

"Of course."

Maddie cocked her head, waiting for the punchline. Or for him to crack one of those smiles that said *cute kid.*

He didn't, though. And to Maddie, that was a gift in and of itself. Was she actually making strides toward being seen as something other than an annoyance?

"*You* can come," she said. "But only if I can bring someone. To be my backup."

Angela grinned. "I didn't know you had a whole band."

Maddie frowned. "A trumpet player." Didn't they see him standing behind her?

"You and your mom can get here half an hour before we open for the Christmas Eve celebration. How's that?" Angela asked.

"And me?" Kurt asked, sounding fairly kid-like himself.

Angela laughed. "And you."

"Thanks from both of us!" Maddie shouted.

"Oh, your mom doesn't have to thank me," Angela said, flipping through her envelopes as Kurt headed off in his own direction, to the next stop on his route.

"No," Maddie tried. "I meant Chester." But Angela and Kurt had both stopped listening.

Maddie swiveled to find that she was the only person standing in front of the bar. No Chester—not anywhere on the street.

She slammed her hands on her hips. "Where'd you go—" she started, when she remembered the man she'd seen dissolve out in front of Rob's store. The same man who'd looked an awful lot like Chester.

But how could he keep disappearing? Almost like he was an imaginary friend or a...

Goosebumps danced on the back of her neck as she thought it: *a ghost.*

Was that why Angela and Kurt hadn't noticed him? Had he slipped into thin air before they'd started talking to Maddie? Could she ask one of them? Chase after Kurt, maybe, and find out what he'd seen?

She shook her head at herself. They'd never believe her if she told them.

After all, she was just a kid.

55.

~*December 23, 2019*~

Maxwell Ross pressed forward under a sunny winter sky. He had searched every inch of the square—and the alleyways that ran behind the buildings—enough times to have completely lost count. Behind Ruby's Place, his anger found him.

Well. Anger was always part of him. But this was a powerful new wave. Christmas Eve was tomorrow.

He hated being so close to his targeted deadline. Hope had dwindled. He'd come so far. But now, it felt as though his bad luck was winning out.

He kicked the old Ruby's Place dumpster. And that felt good enough that he wound up kicking the pile of half-melted snow beside it.

The snow clattered.

Maxwell squatted, eyeing the soot-stained mound. He reached in, the melting pile sloshing around him with a sound that he interpreted as a sigh of relief. Finally! He laughed as his fingers grasped what he'd spent all this time searching for.

His bottle. The one that had rolled from Angela's box as she'd wheeled her items to the history museum. The one that Maddie had tossed aside.

He inspected it, taking a whiff. Of course the liquor had aged. For decades, gaps between the wooden slats of the fruit crate had also allowed the liquor to be bathed in moonlight from a nearby window.

Did he dare? He raised the bottle to stare inside, smiling at the mistletoe he'd shoved in past the lip. Mistletoe he'd stolen from Ruby's own door back in '55. He'd always heard the stuff was poisonous. Yes, the mistletoe, the moonlight, the years: together, they had fermented to help create a cocktail that the people celebrating Christmas inside Ruby's would never forget.

Not this year. Nor any other.

He loved the fact that the mistletoe had actually belonged to Ruby herself. It was kind of ironic, wasn't it—Ruby's own mistletoe being used to destroy Ruby's Place?

The kiss of death.

His entire being filled with an excited buzz.

His plan had to work. He would make it work. His bad luck was coming to an end. All he had to do was find a way to disguise his bottle.

On Christmas Eve, everyone in Sullivan would be celebrating—never believing anything bad could happen. Much the same as they had on a Christmas Eve so long ago. Only this time, he couldn't be blamed. Why, Maxwell Ross had been gone for years. And no one had seen him. Not a single Sullivan resident or a Ruby's Place regular.

Nobody but that cardinal. And it wasn't like he could tell

anyone, could he?

Maxwell grinned. He was going to get away with it this time.

The mere idea gave him the kind of excitement he hadn't felt in ages—not since he was a kid.

He held the bottle up, staring at the vicious liquid.

No one in Ruby's would ever suspect what the moonlight—and the mistletoe—had done to it.

56.

December 24, 2019

~We Arrive in Time~

Here we are. In Sullivan. Looks exactly like I described, doesn't it? The sidewalk square with the sweethearts' graffiti, the aluminum stars on the streetlights, the red neon sign.

Everyone's heading to the square. Sullivan residents and out-of-towners both. There won't be a single space where we can park outside Ruby's Place. Don't even try.

Not to worry, though; we can head toward the bank—it'll be closed, but Scott Drummond, who works there, the one I told you about, will wave us in. It's okay to park there after-hours, he'll say, and besides, he's going to Ruby's himself.

He does not suspect that inside, his father, Walter, is making his way across the floor of the bank. He does not know that Walter was right all those years ago—and not just in a metaphorical way. The Bank of Sullivan really does deal in dreams. Hopes. Far more than it ever dealt in money.

In the darkness of the closed building, Walter crosses to a vault where he begins to turn the wheel of the large, old-fashioned combination lock: backwards twice to start, then to the three numbers that have always opened the door.

It swings open.

But no cash is inside.

It is not the vault where the Bank of Sullivan stores money.

It is the memory bank.

Why is such a thing even necessary, you ask?

Because Officer Vargas's philosophical theory regarding a town's memory—that it's really something of a tangled-up wad—is actually pretty spot-on.

Come on—you have stories you stopped telling. Don't you? You stopped relating them out loud. You stopped telling them to yourself, even. Maybe because they were painful. Because they became associated with loss. All those tidbits you tucked away and are on the verge of losing. Or think you have already forgotten.

Those memories aren't gone completely. They're still here. And they will help you connect with a long-lost loved one in a new way.

Walter pushes the vault door open as far as it will go.

He hurries back out to the main floor, past his son's desk. And he opens a window.

✳ ✳ ✳

See you there. That's what Scott will say, once we get into the parking lot. So we'll park and we'll hurry down the sidewalk, blinking the snowflakes from our eyelashes.

Our feet will touch it. Finally. The square. We'll wave back at Officer Vargas, who is walking the perimeter.

Angela will be locking the place up. Closed temporarily. Got to pull out all the right decorations for tonight's big shindig, dress the place up right. She will let only a few chosen people in to get it ready on time. We'll see Geena and Rob crossing the street from The Page Turner and heading straight for Ruby's front door.

If we time it right, we'll see Rob holding the door open for Geena. She has not told him about watching the home movies. Not yet thanked him, or even acknowledged they'd arrived. Mostly because she is unsure of what she saw. How the phone could have contained her father's and grandfather's voices.

But it is Christmas, and she tells herself that it is also time to put aside the nagging questions she cannot find answers to. Including what to do about her teaching contract. Christmas Eve is a night to exhale. A night to simply watch the world sparkle.

We'll see Tina, too. Turning the "Closed" sign and locking up the It Ain't Over Yet. Look at that giant cardboard box of hers. Just bulging with stuff. You didn't think she'd let Maddie perform without the proper decorations, did you? She has only a few minutes to spread it all—the vintage fabric, the antique metal toys, the green and red glassware—on top of the piano at Ruby's.

A performance, according to Tina, is nothing without the proper accessories.

Maddie will pop into view, though she'll no longer be skipping. Instead, she'll be walking—maybe marching is more like it—with all seriousness, wearing her very best dress. A sweet plaid number with a velvet collar and cuffs. The same dress that's been hanging on her closet door since Thanksgiving. We'll see her nails have been repainted, and she has left behind the stickers that she has often used to decorate her shoes. Her hair will have been curled over at her mother's salon. Her mother will probably even let her wear a little lip color.

She will feel like she really is becoming something more than just a kid.

We will see Chester, too. His hair combed, but his beard still obscuring his face. Trumpet case in hand.

Yes, Chester.

What, you didn't believe me? It's understandable if you're still struggling with it all. Maybe with Chester himself standing right there in front of you, you'll still wonder if the sight of him is nothing but the power of suggestion.

I mean, really. The whole thing truly is absurd, isn't it? Ruby's Place—a bar where, on Christmas, the spirits are allowed to get in touch with the living? Where hearts can mend? Where second chances can be unearthed?

Sounds too good to be true.

Listen, though. As we head over to the bank, roll down your window. I know it's cold. But turn off the radio. What do you hear?

The whiz of the car engine. The whistle of winter wind. What else? A hum? A buzz?

Maybe even, underneath it all, chatter. Voices. Stories.

No, it's not the voices of everyone rushing to the square. Quiet. Listen again.

Yes! That's it. You've got it—those voices are coming from the phone line. The same one that still stretches all the way across town. The same that connects, oddly enough, to the switchboard in the flea market. And the old crate in the history museum. And the phone in Ruby's Place. And—

Well. You can hear for yourself who it connects to, can't you?

All those voices of the past still begging to get Rose's attention.

This story of mine is riddled with so many people who have long since passed away. I know you've been thinking that. Frankie and Ruby and Chester and Charlie. Plus all those regulars who come to take part of the after-closing happy hours. It probably seems at this point that the dead outnumber the living in Sullivan.

All I can tell you for sure is that last year, it was the living who were desperate to make a connection on Christmas Eve with someone they'd lost.

This year, it's the no-longer living who are trying—with everything they have—to reconnect with each other.

Rose knows that, too. The full weight of her Christmas Eve role presses against her.

I've been thinking that maybe, in a way, gossip is nothing more than a bad connection. Misheard or misinterpreted tidbits. Overheard conversations. Sentences taken out of context.

What was it that Maddie said at the very beginning of this story? The saying of her grandfather's that she repeated? *If light bulbs could run on rumors, nobody in Sullivan would go dark for a thousand years.*

Maybe it's time for something else to power Christmas Eve—something other than gossip.

Maybe that's what this year's festivities are all about.

Hey, look. The cardinal is back. He's perched on the phone line. He's chirping away. Is his a simple Christmas song? Or is he talking to Rose, who is still hard at work? I guarantee you that right now, she's making some weird snaking time-splitting connection. She'd once done something similar when the lines were jammed, in order to make a long-distance call. Redirection. This time, it's through decades rather than miles.

She's turning the key. Opening up the line. Yes, she still knows she's doing it for Dorothy and Chester.

But she also knows her efforts are about to affect the rest of the town.

We will all be able to listen in.

Don't put all of your attention on Rose, though. Or even on that crowded phone line.

Let yourself soak it all in. When you do, you'll find that what you are struck by—the thing that will make the hairs stand on the back of your neck—will be a wildly different ingredient in the air.

You won't have to wonder what it is, though. Or where it's

coming from.

Because I'm telling you now—that ingredient will be coming straight from the open window at the bank.

It will be the memories that Walter unleashed when he opened the vault. They will belong to everyone in town. Memories of who they all once were. Their pasts. People and times that have come and gone. Questions and thoughts and what-ifs that tend to haunt us all.

Yes, if you have a past, you have your own ghosts.

It's true of everyone in Sullivan, and it's true of you, too. Think you don't have anything in the memory bank here in town? Not so. Walter has been hanging on to a few things for you. I asked him to.

I called ahead. Added you to my own reservations, remember?

Everyone knew we were coming.

Everyone, that is, but Maxwell Ross.

57.

~December 24, 2019~

Meanwhile, on the edge of town, as the snow begins to fall, a woman is stepping out into the glow of a streetlight.

She sticks her thumb out.

And a car putters to a stop.

It's an old car, the kind that should be sporting historic plates. The kind that should maybe even be on display somewhere. Some museum piece. Not driving around on the slippery winter roads where it could get totaled—it's already pretty banged up.

Seeing the old jalopy, Frankie remembers the night everything changed for her: Being guided to safety by Edna. Finding Hank racing toward the sounds of gunfire, grabbing the two women and pulling them both into this very car. She remembers the three of them driving to Edna's house. How she'd waited as the car idled in the street while Hank and Edna snuck inside. How she'd watched them carry two sleeping girls outside. She remembers riding in the center of the backseat, with two little heads on her lap. How she'd played with their hair in a soothing way to keep them asleep as Hank drove. "Shhh," she'd reassured them. "When you wake up, you'll find yourselves in the midst of a Christmas Day adventure."

They'd gone their separate ways in the earliest hours of Christmas morning, Frankie figuring the authorities would be searching for her with the most vigilance. She would be putting Edna's two little girls in danger.

But now, it seems, the car has finally turned around. Hank and Edna have come back for her.

The window rolls down—not just a bit, not just to reveal only a person's eyes, like that old speakeasy's window. It rolls down all the way. Edna smiles. "Hey, Frankie," she says.

Frankie chuckles. "Been a long time since somebody called me that."

She'd changed her name, of course. She'd always assumed Edna had as well. The girls were young enough it didn't matter. One last name was as good as another.

Now, here they are, together again, on another Christmas Eve. It feels good. Seeing Edna brings a sense of calm, even though Frankie knows it won't last. They are together again for a reason. One that could prove to be catastrophic.

They're putting themselves back in the line of fire. It's surely why Edna's girls are not in the car. It's why they're nowhere to be seen.

"Heard you might've used your old name on a letter. Say about '55 or so," Hank says, leaning forward to show Frankie his face. Assure her that he is still behind the wheel. "On a letter to Ruby, no less."

"I might've—" Frankie stops, tilts her head. There's a difference in the air between Hank and Edna. The same kind of air that had filled the spaces between Dorothy and Chester all those years ago.

"Well," Frankie says. "I always did think you were with the wrong brother, anyway."

Edna laughs.

"Come on, come on," Hank insists. "Enough with the chitchat. We don't have much time."

Frankie pops open the door and makes a motion for Edna to scoot over.

After all, the front seat is where you sit when you're on a mission to regain control.

58.

~December 24, 2019~

Back in Sullivan, Linda is finishing her final tour. The Secrets of Sullivan display is coming to a close, to be replaced in a month by The Coming of Spring—Gardens from Yesterday.

It is always bittersweet when something ends. She finds the familiar lump in her throat that had once accompanied sending her seniors out the door on their final day of class. The success of her tours has been gratifying. Surely, the history museum had racked up record numbers.

Still, she hates to see it go.

Mostly—and this is where her current bittersweet feeling is different from her old last-day feelings—she suspects the exhibit is somehow unfinished.

A big part of it has to do with that young man who'd talked to her about the vintage police items on display. She's certain she— and Toby—had gotten something about the exhibit fundamentally wrong. Why, it had been nagging at her so viciously that she'd even imagined the old fruit crate of Angela's trying to get her attention by making the candlestick phone ring.

Of course that was what had happened. She had imagined it.

Still. What had she missed? What had Toby? What was inaccurate? How could they have fixed it?

She cannot help wondering about it, even now that the exhibit is officially closed.

She wishes that Toby would extend the tour. Especially since attendance was on the rise, even on that last day. Christmas Eve, no less. It would give her a chance to figure some of this out.

"Ms. Bryant!" Toby shouts at her as he goes about turning off the computers and locking up the desk drawers. He grabs her into a bear hug. "Thanks so much for doing this. I really do appreciate it. I hope you're not disappointed with the turnout."

Linda throws her head back and laughs. "Disappointed in the turnout?" she repeats.

Toby grins at her, pleased. "Should have known. If anybody can see the good in something, it's you."

Linda's own smile falters a bit. What on earth is he talking about?

He has to be joking. That's it. Before she can think of some funny one-liner to shoot back, though, he enables the alarm and announces, "Think everything's ready for the holiday." He picks up her coat and holds it for her by the shoulders.

Linda obliges by turning around and slipping her arms into it.

"Walk you to your car?" he asks.

"Yes, that's—" Linda pats her pockets. "My phone," she says. "I left it upstairs. Those things are harder to keep track of than my glasses."

"Wait for you?"

"Oh, heavens, no," Linda insists, still feeling funny about it all—Toby's comments and the nagging suspicion that so much of what she'd said had been flawed and faulty and misleading. "I'll just run up and grab it."

"Shut the door behind you. It'll lock automatically," Toby says. "Merry Christmas, Ms. Bryant."

Linda races upstairs, where she finds her phone still on the break room table. She slips it—and her favorite mug, the one she'd been drinking her hot tea out of—into her purse before hurrying back down the hall, toward the front door.

She stops when she sees him. There he is, the young man who had talked to her about the police force in Sullivan. Leaning against the wall. Obviously waiting.

Had he been hiding? Why hadn't Toby known he was still in the building? He never would have locked her in with a stranger.

Linda gets a funny I-don't-know-about-this feeling deep in the pit of her stomach. The same any woman gets finding herself alone in an empty building with a man she does not know especially well.

"Oh, there you are," the man says, smiling at her as he pushes himself away from the wall.

"You were waiting on me?" Linda asks.

"Yes," he says matter-of-factly. "I was hoping to walk you—
"

"—to my car?" Linda finishes, borrowing Toby's line. That would get them outside. And she believes, right then, that is exactly where she needs to be. Outside.

"No. To Ruby's Place."

"Ruby's!" She laughs. How ridiculous. She is forty years older than him. At least.

"Weren't you planning on going?" he presses.

"No," she admits. "I was going home. To drink eggnog and put my feet up." *Besides,* she thinks, *you have your son. And surely some pretty young thing you want to spend Christmas Eve with.*

"I was hoping you'd come," the man tells her. "I've got some things I need to settle. I was hoping to show you."

"Me?"

"I don't want you to miss it."

Linda eyes him with complete skepticism.

The man sighs. "I regret something," he says. "Something that happened a long time ago. Trust me, you don't want to regret something. It hangs on you. Don't wake up tomorrow and regret missing this."

He opens the door.

And holds out an elbow.

This is all so strange. But there is something about him that makes Linda think, bizarrely, that the questions she has been asking herself about the exhibit will be answered. It's all there with him. She's not sure why she feels it—maybe, she thinks, she only wants it to be true. But she sighs and agrees.

"Fine," she grumbles, still not quite sure why she is getting swept up by it all. "Ten minutes."

59.

~December 24, 2019~

Maxwell Ross hurries down the alley, leaving no footprints in the gathering snow.

He carries his bottle through the doorway and down a tiny hallway, closer and closer to the sounds of clanking dishes.

Maxwell had once dreamed of what he might be able to do if no one could see him, if he could don a cape of invisibility.

Tonight, his wish has been granted.

Right then—while Geena and Rob decorate each table with pine sprigs and tea candles—Maxwell Ross is just that. Invisible.

But maybe that's when invisibility finds us all. When we are not expected. When the world rolls on, believing that we are gone for good.

He dashes behind the bar, where he slips the label off Ruby's favorite spiced rum. He places that label on his own bottle. In a rush, with a crowd waiting, Ruby will never notice the slight differences in the bottles themselves. She'll simply see the label for her own old favorite, and begin to pour, never realizing she is instead serving up Maxwell Ross's tainted liquor.

He's counting on that.

He puts his bottle on Ruby's shelf and feeds hers into his knapsack.

He slinks quickly off into the shadows of the old bar, antic-ipating glorious success.

60.

~The Door~

Back at the beginning, you heard about Angela's wish that we all had a door to our memories. One we could pass through to find ourselves not only thinking about old times but actually reliving them again.

I am here to tell you that Angela's wish is not a wish at all. Because she knows there really is such a door. It is painted green. It is adorned with a wreath. And it stands just beneath a red neon sign that reads, "Ruby's Place."

Yes, when the door to Ruby's swings open on Christmas Eve, it first welcomes the breeze carrying all those tidbits from the memory bank that Walter manages. And then it welcomes everyone else.

Come right on in, the building insists, but not to get out of the cold. Not to order a cocoa. Not to hear a few carols. When you step through that door, you step inside the past. The times you recall with fondness and the slight bitter twinge that accompanies anything that is over.

But right at the beginning, not everyone will be allowed inside. Not tonight. Only a select few. The door opens first for Maddie and her mother. Tina slips in as well. Chester. When Geena recognizes Linda, she lets her old teacher inside. While they are hugging—a warm Christmas Eve greeting—hurry! That's our chance to sneak in ourselves.

What's that? You love the smell of this place? So do I. Toasted marshmallows. Pine. Smells like all your own favorite Christmas memories.

And now, you also know why.

Because they really are here. Your own memories. Your own story. Your own loved ones.

That's the true magic of Ruby's Place.

61.

~*December 24, 2019*~

Maddie's mother is smiling and brushing her daughter's hair from her face. She is so proud, even though she has yet to hear her daughter play one note. In the ways of mothers, it won't matter to her if any of those notes are right. Maddie has worked on a song; she has spent the days leading up to Christmas practicing this special gift for her.

Maddie wiggles her fingers, warming them up, anxious to begin.

Can you feel it? That tingle in the air? It's the regulars. Trust me when I say they are on the fringes. Waiting quietly. They are giving Maddie and her mother their space. It seems a private moment that none of them want to barge in on.

It's a strange little pause, right here, before action kicks in. Ruby would tell you it's just like that moment before the curtain rises.

Here we all are, you and me and the kids. I've managed to sneak in that little dog of yours using the canvas bag I found in your backseat. He'll be fine. Ruby won't mind.

Bet she's got some roast beef he'll like.

We're here with a handful of Sullivan residents—Linda and Tina, Angela and Rob and Geena, Maddie and her mom. Kurt—

he's up there by the piano, grinning as Maddie cracks every last knuckle.

We're here with the regulars.

We're here with Ruby.

The rest of Sullivan is here, too: Scott Drummond and Kelly, who works at The Page Turner, Rob's son Justin and his girlfriend, Lou with what's left of Tina's money lining his pockets. The faces from Kurt's mail route and those that had been on the square for the lighting ceremony last Thanksgiving weekend. They're on the other side of the glass, waiting for Angela to finish decorating, finish her little private mini-party.

Waiting for the night to officially begin.

The appearance of such a crowd means Ruby's performance nerves are giving way to sheer excitement. Why had she ever doubted? Why had she feared Frankie Hall? It was all so silly. This is *Christmas*, after all. Nothing can stop Christmas.

Ruby is ready to celebrate.

She grabs her bottle of spiced rum and begins to mix cocktails, handing them off to Angela.

Maxwell sways anxiously in the shadows. He wishes the door were not still closed. Don't those standing outside deserve a dose of his revenge?

Maddie clears her throat loudly and motions for everyone to quiet down.

Chester raises his trumpet, even though he is not entirely sure who, inside the old bar, can see him. And even though he has not yet seen his Dorothy. He wonders where she could be. Does she not recognize him?

Or worse—*has* she seen him? And did seeing him only strike the fire of anger inside her? Chester did not return all those years ago with the life he'd promised. Did it matter that he had succumbed to the cold on the streets of Chicago? Or was that a failure, too? A man who did not know how to so much as protect himself from the elements. A man who had foolishly trusted a campfire in below-zero temperatures. A man who, in the end, lost his trumpet, the one thing he had that was worth some money. He would have been better off leaving the trumpet with Dorothy. At least then she could have pawned it when he didn't return. Better her than some stranger.

Is that what Dorothy thinks? Does she not want anything to do with Chester now?

Has he disappointed her that much? Hurt her that much? Is there no returning to her?

Maybe he made a mistake in not letting Rose connect him earlier. Maybe he should have let her say something. Convince Dorothy.

62.

~*December 24, 2019*~

Chester does not know that at that very moment, Rose is in the back of the It Ain't Over Yet. "Please," she's begging into the lines crowded with voices. "I need to connect to Ruby's Place. So I can help Chester. Do you hear me? Work! Just once more!"

The entirety of the board lights up again—like a Christmas tree being plugged in, the lights all flickering on at once. Has she somehow tapped into the right words? Like a magician bellowing *abracadabra?*

She hesitates. All she knows is that there is no static. No interference. No jumble of voices. Only one. Coming through loud and clear.

As clear as that particular voice had ever been, anyway. One part angry frog, one part busted car engine.

"I know danger's coming to Ruby's Place," Robert Ludlow growls. "Maybe it was foolish of me to hang on to this old phone booth. I just thought—I thought somebody might need me. Somebody might call me back. Maybe you would. I thought—oh, thunder in the winter! I'm on my way. But I still might not get there in time. Look, Rose, there's trouble coming. You have to stall.

Frankie—"

A clatter fills her ears—the sound of the phone receiver being dropped and whacking the side of the booth.

"Stall? What for? What are you saying about Frankie? Robert? Are you still there?"

Rose scrambles to connect to Ruby's Place. "Hello? Angela? Anyone? Can you hear me? Please. I have to warn you."

Silence.

And then—miraculously—it happens.

63.

~December 24, 2019~

Clear and lovely, the first notes of a solo melody begin to filter through the air. A trumpet—full of emotion—begs to be heard.

"Chester?" Rose whispers.

She touches her headset, pressing it closer to her ears, trying to pick up on any sounds in the background.

She fights a flood of tears as she hears Dorothy's voice. Because it is not her speaking voice that has suddenly exploded into her headset.

It's her singing voice.

64.

~*Timeless*~

It is no longer 1928 when Chester stretches his hand through the shadows of time, in the direction of the lovely woman's voice, to find fingers grabbing onto his own.

He finds neither a beginning nor a starting-over place.

It *is* a forever place his hand has touched. Because it is Dorothy who has grabbed on. Just as she had all those years ago, a young girl in a pretty blue gown, urged to sing at a New Year's Eve celebration. He had pulled her up onto the stage with him back then. And he has done it again by pulling her out of the past and onto the floor of Ruby's, into the pool of light near the piano.

His exterior fades—the beard, the rough clothes. His Dorothy is no longer the aging music teacher coming to Ruby's for a chance to relive the joy she'd once felt simply singing.

They are as they had once looked to each other that first night. That golden New Year's Eve.

"I promised you," he says. "I promised I'd come home."

A million dreams away, where memories begin to grow, Maddie is clunking along on the piano—yet another mistake-ridden verse. Her mother is clapping.

The clumsy song fades. Chester raises his trumpet and Dorothy warbles another line from a familiar song. The very first they had ever played together. "I Can't Give You Anything but Love, Baby." Now, here, it is true—there is nothing left. Not a single worldly possession. There is only their affection for each other.

And their music. The notes have never changed. Never gone flat or out of tune. The melody is still the same. It has held steady. Unaltered by swirling gossip.

It has never yellowed or aged.

Just like the love between Chester and Dorothy.

65.

~*December 24, 2019*~

Outside, Frankie tries to run faster. Hank takes her arm, urging her forward, begging her not to fall behind. To-night, Edna is not shielding Frankie. She is a full car length ahead and gaining speed.

Hank and Frankie have long known she is the most fearless of the three of them. And now, they are doing their best to keep up with her.

They are racing toward Ruby's, on a mission to save every-one inside.

They have been on their way ever since Rose accidentally—and, yes, providentially—connected Robert Ludlow to Frankie. Ever since Frankie heard Ludlow say her greatest fear was coming true.

Maxwell Ross is on the move. He's been on the move since Thanksgiving weekend.

Maxwell is not Dorothy. When she returned to the site of her life's greatest tragedy—the raid, the aching hole where her hus-band used to be—it was not with revenge in her heart. When she'd stared through that front window back in '55, she had not meant Ruby herself any harm.

Maxwell Ross has always been the sort who could only

think of revenge. For every slight. Every wrongdoing. Even if other actions should have convinced him there was no longer any score to settle.

Revenge is like that, though—the desire for it casts a stain, rather than a shadow. It does not drift away, given time. It remains long after it should.

Maxwell is stained. Revenge is all that he has on his mind. It's what brought him here.

Frankie, Edna, and Hank all know that.

They run, the three of them.

But Edna will get their first. Her brave heart will make sure of that.

66.

~December 24, 2019~

Inside the bar, "Jingle Bells" ends with a flourish and a final chord that includes one extra, sour-sounding low note as a kind of final punctuation. Maddie is still frowning at the keyboard, like it has somehow made a sound she never asked it to, when her mother stands and exchanges her applause for a bear hug, telling her daughter, "My best gift ever!"

It is the making of a new memory at Ruby's. Much like those old memories Angela had made as a little girl with her Aunt Elizabeth. Sweeter than the cocoa, this evening will stay with both of them. It will keep them company throughout the next year, so much so that they will want to return to Ruby's Place next Christmas Eve. This is the beginning of their own special tradition.

Maddie is busy smiling and accepting congratulations, receiving so much attention that for the first time in—well, ever—she feels no need to show off by relating some overheard tidbit.

Maybe, in a way, that's the root of all gossip. Maybe we become obsessed with others' stories during moments when there is not much happening with our own. Maybe gossip is fueled by nothing more than our need for attention—something we never really do outgrow.

Yes, in Ruby's Place, memories old and new swirl. While

Maddie and her mom hug and giggle, Chester's trumpet and Dorothy's voice begin another tune.

Not that they notice. Not even Maddie, who has been able to see and hear Chester ever since Tina held that old trumpet up to her ear. The mother and daughter are too busy solidifying their new memory, marking it with the kind of importance that means it will be carried throughout a lifetime. They fail to see anything else.

The regulars listen, though. The emotional rendition of "Sentimental Journey" has snagged their full attention. They have begun to pull themselves from the shadows. One is an older woman. With a starched collar. And two pennies in her pocket for a grasshopper. Mrs. Latchy never would have allowed Ruby to serve her a drink on the house, after all.

The long-missing twinkle in Dorothy's eyes has finally reappeared. Because it has happened. Finally. Vindication! It tastes so sweet. She was not a fool. Not ever. She was right about her Chester. He did come through on his promises.

Even if it took him more than a lifetime.

What makes one person's faith hold fast while another's crumbles beneath the slightest weight? Even now, having had all this time to think about it, Dorothy doesn't know. But maybe, in the end, it has something to do with what Ruby said when the two women had been in the bar after-hours, reminiscing about the day they'd met: Maybe Dorothy really is tough. Far more than she's ever been innocent or childlike.

Maybe Mrs. Latchy had realized it, all those years ago.

Maybe she knew Dorothy would only need support for a little while—like a wounded animal. And then she'd be as steady as ever.

And maybe Mrs. Latchy was able to recognize it because, at her heart, she was a rebel. One who could buck public opinion.

Oh, the things we get wrong about each other. But it's no matter now.

Dorothy and Chester are standing at the beginning of something new. Finally. After all this time, a wait like no other.

Ruby leans quietly against the front of the bar. Hearing Dorothy and Chester fills her with unspeakable joy. As the song ends, she rushes to greet Chester as an old friend, although they have never met.

Not face-to-face, at least. They have met in story. Sketchy bits and pieces. The small slices that Dorothy has told her.

Angela carries a plate of marshmallows to share with Maddie, telling her how much she loved them when she was her age.

Suddenly, the gooey marshmallow is smearing everywhere—and Maddie's sweet girlish laugh ripples through the air.

While Angela is busy with Maddie, Geena swivels behind the bar, picks up the tray of Ruby's rum drinks. She does not know that Ruby made them, of course. She does not see Ruby. Geena is like Maddie and her mother, in that Ruby is not really a part of her memory bank. More like an object always spied from a distance or the corner of her eye. It's Angela that Geena sees, Angela that she knows well. It's Angela that she assumes made the drinks she sets about serving.

From edge of the bar, Tom Barister watches his daughter. He can see the strain on her face. The weight of a decision she has not made. It tortures him, seeing her there. Knowing that she wants to talk to him.

Beside him, Elizabeth takes his hand. His Elizabeth, reassuring him.

On the other side of the room, Maxwell Ross steps from the shadows. His eyes are trained on the glasses Geena carries. He wants a better view of what is about to happen.

Once, he had simply placed a few phone calls to shut down a speakeasy. Tonight, he will finally get revenge using his own long ago rejected liquor, tainted by the moonlight and mistletoe and years and years of his own spite.

Maxwell's anger by itself is strong enough to poison just about anything—even without the help of the mistletoe.

67.

~December 24, 2019~

A few doors down, Rose is attempting to push her cord in further, twisting and twisting as though this will somehow better her connection. "Hello?" she tries. "Hello? Frankie is on her way. Do you hear me? Anyone?"

"What is that noise?" Linda asks the young man who has walked with her from the museum. It doesn't matter that Geena welcomed her; she feels uncomfortable being inside when the rest of Sullivan is still relegated to the sidewalk.

The young police officer is staring at the phone on the wall behind the bar.

"Ms. Bryant?" Geena asks, holding a highball glass toward her.

Linda accepts it, and Geena continues to pass the glasses around. Rob has joined her with his own tray. He weaves through the crowd, his face twisting into a strange look. He's trying to get closer to Geena.

Because he sees him. He is standing right over there, near the piano. The same man he has spent the past month searching for. The brown lump he'd discovered all crumpled up into the doorway of The Page Turner. "He found her," Rob tries to call out to Geena. The woman who had been waiting on him. The promise he had babbled about. The man is home. He didn't need Rob's help to get there. He'd transformed in the single moment of standing beside her, the singer in the long gown. He'd grown younger and stronger.

Love could always do that to a man. Rob knew that first-hand.

Did Geena see it? Rob calls out to her again. But she doesn't seem to hear over the music and the chatter and the laughter.

On the opposite side of the room, Elizabeth has taken it upon herself to help her old friend Ruby. She has her own tray and is passing drinks to the regulars.

From the alley, footsteps thunder—a storm daring to break into a cloudless day.

Rose continues to plead, her voice spilling out from the bar phone.

But no one seems to hear. No one but Linda—and perhaps the man she came with.

"That sounds—it's like this weird voice I heard on the can-dlestick phone," Linda tells him. "In the history museum. Did you ever hear it? I'm sorry—I didn't quite get your name."

The young man turns toward Linda, looking her square in the eye. "It's Charlie."

As they speak, something flutters from the pocket of his shirt down to the floor. When Linda rushes to pick it up, she finds the same piece of paper that had been taped to the back of the tar-nished badge in the museum: "C. Barister."

"A toast!" Angela cries out.

Everyone inside the bar raises their glasses.

Behind Linda, the alley door flies open.

68.

~*December 24, 2019*~

With a shout, Frankie bursts in, trailed by Edna and Hank.

"No!" they cry out. "Stop!"

But it is too late.

After all, you can't exactly stop a swallow, can you? Everyone has already knocked their rum back. Even Linda, who never would have suspected trouble would be inside her own glass.

Poison—that's what Maxwell has always intended. That's what he assumed mistletoe would do, especially now that it has had all this time to marinate. To break down in the alcohol.

Poison. Which would allow for another tragic night. Swirling lights of emergency vehicles would dance across the old aluminum stars hanging above the square.

The horror of it all would taint the building. No one would come back. Not to the reopened Ruby's Place. Especially not on Christmas. Angela would go bankrupt.

And then what? It would be too much. Maxwell was certain. The awful stories swirling around the place would be like taste aversion—everyone in town would feel an awful twist in the gut just looking at the place.

The people of Sullivan might have been able to justify the

raid on Frankie's—after all, she really had been breaking the law—but a tragedy like this? Something undeserved? On Christmas?

No one would ever want to open a business in that old building again. The town of Sullivan would be left with no other option but to knock it down. Keep the bad from happening again on the town square. Smash their rotten luck.

So much for the regulars.

So much for Christmas Eve reunions.

It's going to end here, Maxwell thinks, grinning as he watches them all take a gulp. The liquor must taste horrible, like the anger he has carried for so long.

Horrible to everyone else, anyway.

Sweet to him. Now that satisfaction will finally be his.

But as he stares, something else entirely happens.

It's Christmas, after all. And in no way would Christmas allow one of its own symbols—mistletoe—to darken the evening's festivities.

Instead, Christmas long ago settled into the bottle. And rather than turning to the deadliest of poisons, it has made sure that what is inside is actually a gift in itself.

In the brief moment of the toast, when they all swallow their drink, the entire room is bathed in light. For one flash of a moment, the regulars and the current residents of Sullivan all see each other.

Most importantly, in that flash—in that one brief moment of the drink—everything becomes clear. Everything about Ruby's

Place is understood. The full picture. Everyone inside it. In shockingly vibrant detail.

Even the regulars. They see the truth behind their own gossip—rumors that had wrongly hardened into beliefs. Stories they'd mindlessly retold about each other. About Frankie.

Mrs. Latchy smiles. And thanks her husband for insisting she share in the drink. "For *once*, Ruth," he'd grumbled. "Let someone give you something."

She has seen it all too.

Maxwell Ross's face registers the utter horror he feels. His reputation as the unluckiest man in all of Sullivan remains intact. His plan has failed, as all his plans always had.

Under his breath, he curses the sly beams of moonlight that had tricked him into believing the bottle would fulfill his need for vengeance. Or maybe he was the one who had tricked himself.

Yes, with the help of Christmas, time and moonlight had created a kind of truth serum, allowing everyone in the room one brief moment of complete clarity.

Frankie doesn't realize that, though—not yet. She only thinks everyone has gulped down Maxwell Ross's drink. The same drink that she knows was intended to do harm. She lets out a bellow, lunges for a cocktail on the edge of the bar, and throws it into Maxwell's face. She thinks, simply, that the man should drink from his own well.

Which means that Ross, in a flash, sees clearly too.

69.

~December 24, 2019~

Maxwell Ross sees Ruby's Place for everything that it truly is. He sees hopes and wishes and regret. He sees the tiniest buds of second chances. He sees one-more-last-times. He realizes, all in the single sting of liquor against his face, that Ruby's is not just a place where love is found, traditions are made.

Ruby's Place, he sees, is far more than that. It is a healer of hearts.

Maxwell dips into the crowd like a child trying to hide from punishment. He is ashamed—because with that splash of liquor, he saw himself clearly, too. He grabs his bottle and thrusts it into his jacket. Maybe he can escape with it.

Tom lunges forward, his hands gripping Maxwell's arms.

Tom's own sip of Maxwell's liquor has given him a new understanding. If there is any anger left in Maxwell's expression, Tom knows that it is directed toward himself. Remorse has seeped in along with the liquor tossed in his face.

"I felt it," Maxwell Ross murmurs. "That liquor. When it splashed on me—I felt all of it. This place. I—"

Tom glances about the bar. He sees similar expressions on all the other faces. Shock. Surprise. A strange new kind of understanding.

Frankie takes a few steps closer to the two of them. Tom can read her face, too. She—and her companions—do not need to sip Maxwell's liquor to know the truth of the building. They see it all on their own. Her face registers concern and fear. But also a steeliness—like she has come with her fists clenched. She has come to do battle.

This slowly sinks in: Frankie—and her two companions—have not arrived with the intention to do harm. Not like Ruby and so many of the other regulars had suspected.

It had all been about Maxwell. "We were trying to warn you," Frankie says. The regulars slowly move to greet her, the woman who had been coming to rescue everyone at Ruby's.

The music has stopped. It stopped with the toast, and now, Dorothy is shuddering in relief. It's so strong, she places a hand on the piano to steady herself. She'd been right about Frankie. Right about everything.

Mrs. Latchy smiles at Dorothy from the shadows.

"You going to take me away?" Maxwell asks Tom.

Tom nods once at Frankie. An *It's okay—I've got this* kind of motion.

But not because he is a police officer and Maxwell is a criminal. Not because there is a line between them—the good guy and bad guy. That's far too simplistic. He releases his grip on Maxwell's arms. "What for?" he asks. "That liquor hasn't done any damage, has it?"

Maxwell's eyes instantly sparkle, overflowing with emotion. "Is this a trick?" he whispers. He is still having a hard time believing he's been found out. He hadn't counted on Frankie showing up. Hadn't counted on Ludlow's cautions, either. Which was foolish. That awful voice—it could carry a story anywhere.

Mostly, he did not count on Christmas. He should have, though. He always should have counted on that.

"No," Tom says. "No trick. There's no danger here. That's all." He leads Maxwell down the hallway, opens the alley door.

Outside, a cardinal sits on the ledge of the building, watching.

Maxwell cannot be here, not for the Christmas Eve celebration. Not after what he has tried to do. Maxwell knows that. He has been causing too much harm to this place for too long.

If there is a kindness left to be extended, it is simply to go his own way, never to return.

Maxwell props his hat onto his head and walks from Ruby's Place into the alley.

Tom believes that he is watching the man disappear for good. Because just as gossip could reinvent or twist or distort, Tom knows, its absence could also help erase.

What story would be retold about that night? The story of Maxwell's attempt to destroy Ruby's? Or of the magical drink that had illuminated a roomful of previously unseen truths?

If Tom knows anything at all about Ruby's—or Sullivan— he knows the strange Christmas gift in a glass would outshine any other detail about that night.

What sort of fate met a man whose story ceased being told? Oblivion. To be forgotten.

Perhaps, Tom thinks, it is the worst punishment possible.

Is it too much? Especially here, at the time of year when renewals and resolutions and fresh starts should abound?

"Maxwell!" Tom shouts.

The man turns. "You know my name."

"Of course I do."

"Why? Because of the headlines, or because your dad told you about me? Big, bad Maxwell Ross?"

"He said he didn't handle the whole thing with you right. All those years ago. You and the speakeasy. He said it was the one thing he always wanted to do over again."

"He did?"

"Yeah. Said he'd lay down his life to give you another shot."

Maxwell looks shocked.

"He did, too," Tom adds, finally saying it—the one last fact that had been lingering in the air between them. "He saved you. During a robbery gone wrong. He took your bullet."

"I didn't think it was on purpose. I thought it was all an accident. I thought—"

"He saved you," Tom says.

Maxwell stuffs his hands in his pockets. "That was a mistake."

"No mistake."

"Didn't do much with that second chance."

"Can now."

Maxwell snorts a chuckle and shakes his head. "Tell Charlie…" His voice trails. "Tell him—if I could only—" Words falter and fail.

"He knows. Wherever he is," Tom says.

"I hope that's true," Maxwell says, his bottom lip wavering. He reaches into his coat and removes the old bottle, still wearing the wrong label. "Don't know why I thought I could hide this," he says, tips his hat, and slips into the dark night.

Tom steps back into the bar. As he moves through the crowd, searching for Elizabeth, a hand touches the back of his shoulder.

"There you are," Tom says, expecting to find her lovely face as he turns.

Instead, he finds himself staring into the face of another man. A police officer in uniform.

His father.

Tom's mind spins, searching. What could he say? How could he even greet him? Did Charlie know who Tom was? He'd never seen him as a grown man.

Before he can figure it out, Charlie smiles at him. As Elizabeth watches from off to the side, her own eyes sparkling, Charlie says, "That was the right thing to do. With Maxwell, son."

Tom's eyes swell.

"I thought I needed to come back to finally settle that whole thing," Charlie admits. "But I guess that wasn't right, was it?

You always had it covered."

And then it happens. Tom gets his wish. The one that had continued to take up space inside him, even after last year, when he'd talked to Geena one last time and gotten his Elizabeth back. It had all been such an embarrassment of riches: His daughter, his love, his life as a regular in Ruby's Place each night. It was too much to wish for anything beyond that. Wasn't it?

And yet, he had. Secretly. He had, throughout the last year, carried one more wish about his father. The same wish that had followed him all the years of growing up without him.

Tom has never been as proud—or grateful—as he is when Charlie reaches his hand out. It is better than any medal, any prize or commendation. Joy envelops Tom as the two men shake hands, as equals, two cops.

70.

~*December 24, 2019*~

Eight p.m., and around the square, the residents of Sullivan can hear it, finally: the front door is being unlocked.

It sends them all into something of a collective tremble. Here it is, the big moment. What they've all been waiting for. Why they have all donned their fanciest digs and have not minded standing out there on the sidewalk for a few minutes while Angela has gotten everything in place.

Excitement explodes. They shout holiday greetings at one another. They wave at Officer Vargas.

"Come with us!" a few shout at him. "Buy you a drink!"

"I'm on the clock," Vargas reminds them.

"What clock?" someone calls out, teasing him.

But Officer Vargas doesn't laugh—it really does seem that time stops on Christmas Eve. At least, it does on the Sullivan square.

The front door swings open, again and again as modern-day revelers file in.

It is not just the aroma of marshmallows and cocoa that greets them. There is something else in the air.

Expectations. Anticipation. Every bit as strong as it had

been when they were children.

A few pause to look through the front window, still thinking it doesn't seem right to leave Officer Vargas outside, where he enjoys none of this. But he waves, insisting this is his job—he wouldn't have it any other way.

He is missing so much, though. Far more than a few minutes off his beat. If he were to ever step through the door on a Christmas Eve, he'd know that.

Inside, Rob collects coats and points customers to tables. Or maybe to a few empty stools at the bar. Geena scrambles to take their orders. Angela smiles hellos. She has little time for chit-chat; she is so busy. Christmas carols and the scent of pine boughs dance across the air. There is laughter and finger pointing toward the front window, where a lone cardinal sits on the sill.

At last! their collective voices all seem to cry out. *Christmas Eve.*

71.

~*What You've Been Waiting For*~

You see him. That special someone you lost eons ago. In another lifetime.

Don't worry—I don't need all the details. I can read it in your face. He looks as you remembered. He is always on your mind this time of year.

Still, the whole scene feels wobbly to you. Like something you shouldn't trust enough to put all your weight on.

Don't second-guess it. Trust your first impression. This is your chance. Speak to him. The one you had hoped to meet up with, ever since I told you about this part of Ruby's Place. When you looked up at me in the rearview mirror, suspecting I was making it all up. And hoping, with everything you had, that I wasn't.

Go on. I'll stay here with your kids. We'll start our own tradition. Just like Maddie and her mother. We'll eat marshmallows, and they'll beg you to come again next year. Ruby's will become your place. This year will mark the first in a chain of memories.

One more thing before you go to him. This is a special year, this Christmas. Because the regulars are being joined by all those voices begging to be heard on Rose's line. I told you about some of them. But there are so many more.

Did you assume Dorothy was the only one with ties to the speakeasy and to Ruby? There are so many more. So many who frequented the speakeasy and returned for the supper club. Who maybe didn't talk about it, the old wound in their leg, part of the gunshots that had flown during Christmas Eve. Who either faded or became fodder for gossip. Twisted, mangled pieces of story.

They've come again. For the first time in ages. They've come to tell their own story.

It's such a special night; so many of them have arrived. That poor waitress from Chicago—the one who took Chester's trumpet—has come to apologize. The old Sullivan residents—those who had once listened to Rose's tales in the dentist's office. The old owners of the drug store. Even Ludlow. He has made it.

This year, there's a reset of sorts. It's going on all around us. A clearing of the air.

For the last couple of years, reunions happened between individuals who had been torn apart—Geena and her dad, Angela and her Aunt Elizabeth. This year? Reunions are happening between giant clusters of people. And between two different eras: the speakeasy and the supper club.

If you look toward the front of the room, you'll notice Frankie is leaning against the bar, narrowing her eyes at Ruby. "You really think I was coming to do you harm?" she's asking her.

"Can you blame me? Your reputation preceded you."

Frankie lets out a huff of disappointment. "My reputation,"

she repeats. "You never paid any attention. Not to the stuff I left behind. The real story was in there."

"Me?"

"Yes, you. You found stuff that belonged to me, and you just shoved it all aside. Never did bother to find out what it all amounted to. You didn't even pay attention when that bottle of Ross's showed up."

"But it didn't come until tonight. How was I supposed to—"

"No, no, no. It was 1955. That bottle has been in this very building for more than fifty years."

Ruby's face droops with shock.

"You really think this is the first time Maxwell tried to take you down? Girlie, you have so much to learn. He was obsessed with messing up your grand opening. Back in '55. He wanted to get your place closed down by the health inspectors. Used to brag about getting revenge to Ludlow while they were both in the clink. And later on, while you were in the midst of renovations, all those construction workers zipping in and out, he left a bottle right here. On your bar. Some ancient looking old bottle—"

"I never saw anything like that—"

"I *know*," Frankie sighs.

"You—?"

"Nobody answered my letter. Which I'd sent to give you a heads-up. I got to worrying about it, so I told Ludlow to do whatever he had to do to thwart Maxwell's plan. He snuck in, said he put the bottle with some trash ready to be thrown out. Guess that wasn't trash, though, was it? It was a box of my stuff, shoved in the back corner."

"I can't believe—"

"How come you never tossed my stuff, anyway?"

"It wasn't mine to throw."

Frankie wheezed a laugh. "You're a riot, chum."

"Wait. You said you wrote a letter?"

"Sure. In 1955. You shoved that in some old fruit crate, too." Frankie shakes her head.

"I gave that crate to Angela," Ruby says, looking pale and horrified. "To share with Toby. I—"

"Yeah, yeah," Frankie says. "Angela let it all out when that crate tumped over. Out there on the sidewalk."

"It wasn't her doing, though. It was me. I started this," Ruby says. "I put the whole thing in motion. Because I gave her that stuff to haul to the history museum." She looks horrified as she admits, "Everything almost fell apart because of me."

"Listen, girlie, I think we both saw that Ross's liquor didn't do anybody harm, anyway. In reality, what you did turned out to be pretty wonderful."

"Wonderful?" Ruby screeched. "How can you say—"

"Because of that," Frankie says, motioning toward Chester and Dorothy, who have launched into another carol, a newer one they've never played together before. "White Christmas." Dorothy knows the words, and Chester is improvising. Just as they used to.

"So the question remains," Frankie says, holding her hands out. "What're you gonna do with me."

Ruby chuckles. "Make you a drink, of course. Pick your poison—" she starts, but after what they've avoided with Maxwell Ross, corrects herself by saying, "What's your drink, anyway?"

"Tom Collins," Frankie barks.

As Ruby mixes it, Frankie glances around the bar. "Sure is fancy," she remarks. "My place was some old hole in the wall."

"Different times," Ruby acknowledges, sliding a glass closer to Frankie.

Frankie shrugs, takes a sip.

And spits.

"Good night, girl, what is that?"

"A Tom Collins."

"You don't know anything about cocktails. Listen, if you're going to run a respectable juice joint, you need to at least know how to make a decent drink. Ours were better, and we only had bathtub hooch to work with. Where is that Edna? Now, there's someone who can mix a cocktail."

Frankie cranes her neck, finding Edna with a group of regulars gathered around Hank, listening to his latest wild tale. She smiles, her entire body relaxing into an old memory. "You know, first time I saw that girl, I thought—what a ninny. If there's something I can't stand, it's a weak woman. But she wound up saving my life. A real lionheart. A hero—more 'n any police officer I ever met. And you know, I don't think she even realizes it, half the time."

336

"She probably only sees the times when she was scared. Or unsure. Bet she's never once felt brave a day in her life," Ruby observes. "Have you?"

Frankie snorts. "Never," she mutters. "Anyway, she's the one you want to teach you about the drink."

"And who taught her to make cocktails?" Ruby asks, raising her eyebrows in a knowing way.

Frankie curls her lips into a smile. "I can show you more than mixing drinks," she says. "If you don't mind hearing it from some old troublemaker woman on the run."

"Oh, there's a lot more to you than that," Ruby says. "You think I'm blind to the similarities between what you used to run and what I've got going here? After dark, you had a secret happy hour populated with regulars. What do I have? A secret after-dark happy hour populated by regulars." She leans closer to add, "I inherited magic in this building. Magic you left behind, every bit as much as you left some old scraps of paper and pictures that I tossed in a fruit crate."

Frankie only smirks.

"I want to hear all of it." Ruby says, raising her glass.

72.

~*December 25, 2019*~

The music of Christmas Eve slowly begins to give way to the quiet early hours of Christmas Day.

As the night slowly fades, the season's stories are being boxed and set aside, marked, "Christmas at Ruby's Place—Keep Closed Until 2020."

The interior is cordoned off into sections:

For Ruby and Frankie forging a new partnership.

Dorothy and Chester celebrating their love.

Reunions—including yours—taking place throughout the bar.

Old regulars—the ones who had frequented Frankie's place—mingling with the new, those who had known Ruby, who showed up for her after-closing happy hour. They are getting to know each other for the first time.

New traditions forming—like the ones Maddie and your own children are stitching together.

There is no place anymore in the old fruit crate for destructive figures like Maxwell Ross. There is no room for the shadows that have enveloped him.

But there might be space for a few cardinal feathers.

Such is the way of Christmas stories. The good swells until there is no room left for anything bad.

And this, as we both know, is exactly where the curtain would fall on any other Christmas story.

But this, as you also know, is not the usual Christmas story.

73.

~*December 25, 2019*~

Once the rest of Sullivan has slipped out the door, Tina stays behind with Rob and Geena, the three of them pledging to help clean up. There she is, wiping tables and tossing linen napkins into a bin to be hauled to the cleaner. As she carries the last tub of silverware toward the kitchen, she finds the phone dangling off the hook.

"Angela!" she calls. "Are you talking to someone?"

But Angela is nowhere to be seen. "Think she's in the office," comes the call from the dish sink, where water runs and plates continue to clank.

Tina shrugs, deciding to bring the phone to her ear. "Hello?"

"It's me. Rose. At the old switchboard." Static clouds the rest of her words. And then the line goes dead.

Tina replaces the receiver and begins to walk away. But she stops when the word finally sinks in: *switchboard*. She only knows of one left in town.

And it's in her own shop.

She places the tub of silverware on top of the bar and lunges toward the door, forgetting to grab her coat. She has to get back to her store. See who is sitting at that switchboard. Find out how she managed to connect to Ruby's Place.

As her platforms clomp against the sidewalk, Tina does not notice a cardinal landing beside the old liquor bottle Maxwell Ross has dropped in the snow.

74.

~December 28, 2019~

Kurt waves through the glass entrance of the Sullivan History Museum.

Linda swivels on her heel and hurries to unlock the door.

"Just happened to see you in there. Thought I'd hand these deliveries to you in person. Instead of stuffing it in the mailbox," Kurt says, placing the bundle in her arms.

"Thanks," Linda breathes, tossing her head in the attempt to shake a stray lock of hair from her eye.

"Didn't expect to see you back to work so soon," Kurt admits.

"I—uh—" Linda offers a slight grin. "Can I show you something?"

Kurt nods, allowing her to usher him inside, lock the door behind him.

Linda tosses the mail on the front counter in her race toward the exhibit room. "It's still a complete mess," she apologizes. "But I had this idea. I wanted to do an exhibit on the history of Ruby's Place. Really highlight the speakeasy days. Ran it past Toby. He said to shoot him my ideas." She points to papers near an old crate and scattered throughout the room.

In the midst of the mess, Kurt can see the beginnings of

individual displays on the police—highlighting Charlie. And the music of the era—highlighting Dorothy and Chester. Photos and headlines and antiques—including the old phone that the diner and speakeasy had once relied on, a teapot, antique glasses. The strange looking screw, which isn't a screw at all, but an extra mouthpiece for a trumpet.

And Frankie. Right there, in the center of it all. An entire display on the woman who had run the place.

"As I was doing the Secrets tour, I realized I got so much wrong," Linda explains. "The stuff Toby put aside, the stuff that seemed extraneous—that's where the real meat was. Some of the most powerful items were overlooked. I wanted to go back. Do it again. Do it justice." She pauses to turn the trumpet mouthpiece over in her hand. "Did you know that Dorothy was my own music teacher?"

"That right?"

Linda nods. "When I learned the depth of her involvement—I mean, she used to sing there! At the speakeasy!—I had to do something."

"When'd you find all this out?"

"Christmas. I saw her picture above the bar and I—" Linda catches herself. She stops short of telling Kurt something of a wild story.

"I thought, you know, people have always gravitated to that place," she says with a shrug. "To Ruby's. Even before it was Ruby's. Right?"

Kurt nods, his eyes still fixed to the image of Frankie standing outside her diner. "Home of the 5¢ steak!" painted on the plate glass.

"She was quite the character," Linda says.

Kurt nods.

"…and she could make a great Tom Collins," they both say in unison.

They turn toward each other in surprise, each wondering where the other could have possibly heard that.

Slowly, Christmas Eve comes back to them.

They smile at each other, knowingly.

It's all that needs to be said.

75.

~*December 28, 2019*~

Dressed in a pair of high-waisted '80s jeans and neon colored plastic bracelets, Tina stands in the middle of the It Ain't Over Yet, glaring at the switchboard.

"I took the price off," she grumbles at the antique. "What else do you want from me?"

She sighs, crossing her arms over her chest. "I know you have to be here somewhere. Right, *Rose*?" Her eyes bounce through the shelves. "I know about Chester. And more. I was at Ruby's on Christmas Eve. I tried to dismiss it, when I took that sip of a drink at Maddie's recital. But later on, when I heard your voice…it was all true. Wasn't it? Chester—that was him. Right here in this store. Maddie and I saw him because we listened to his trumpet. We put it to our ears. That whole thing about old items having stories locked inside of them—that's not something junk dealers like me tell each other. It's true. Isn't it? There are stories. If you listen. We heard Chester's."

She sighs with annoyance. "I know you've been sitting at that switchboard. I called Toby again. Asking him to bring me any information about the old phone company. And you." She squints at the contraption, adding, "Seems silly to have to do that, though, doesn't it? I mean, since you've been right here. Why don't you come right out with it? Tell me your story? Where'd you go? You've been here all along, just like Chester. I heard you, Rose. On the phone. Like I listened to Chester's trumpet. I would recognize you now. So why won't you show yourself to me?"

Still no answer.

"Rose, you can't be finished," she mutters.

The bells ring out as the front door swings open.

"I need to practice!" Maddie bellows, storming into the store. She holds up a hand and begins to tick off her requests on her fingers. "I need sheet music, I need a new song, and *you've got the piano*!"

Before Tina can sigh or figure out how to deal with Maddie—or even get after herself for still having all her Christmas decorations up on her door when she *should* be decked out for New Year's—the door flies open again.

"Tina!" Lou calls out. "I got something else to sell you."

"And where did you come across this little gem?" Tina asks, dragging herself toward the front of the store.

"Bet I can tell you," Maddie says, folding her arms behind her.

"Think you know everything, eh?" Lou teases.

As the back-and-forth goes on between them, Tina slips behind the counter.

A man walking down the street smiles and raises a hand in greeting. Tina waves back somewhat limply—she doesn't recognize him until he has passed her by and she can see that cardinal logo on the back of his coveralls. He's with the phone company—the same man who'd shown up to fix Angela's line.

"Here," Lou announces, clanking a bunch of new items on her front counter. "Take a look at this. It's worth something, right?"

But Tina is suddenly distracted by a twinkling light coming from the back of the store.

The switchboard.

Tina stands frozen. A young woman sits at the contraption, granite lunch pail at her feet, a knitting project draped in her lap.

Rose drops the knitting to lean forward, jam in a plug.

Even from the front counter, Tina can hear the voice coming through Rose's headset. It is a rough, low, frog croak of a voice. "Rose?" he grumbles. "It's me. Robert. Robert Ludlow."

"Where can I connect—" she starts, but is interrupted by that voice again.

"Please," he insists. "Listen. You've got to hear me. Someone else has the bottle. Maxwell Ross's. He might be gone, but that bottle of his ain't. It can't hurt anybody who drinks it—won't kill 'em, anyway. But whose hand is it in? What are they doing with it? What are they planning? I got a bad feeling. Rose? You have to help me get the word out."

76.

~*December 28, 2019*~

ob and Geena sit on the couch in her living room, separated by a bowl of popcorn, a remote, and Christmas Eve.

They have never once discussed what they saw that night when they sipped from the same cocktail. It's an odd feeling, having so much between them that remains unsaid.

It's a weight, heavier at times than all of the books in Rob's store combined. He can't even find relief in the fact that Geena does not ask why he no longer feels the need to keep driving about, searching for the man he'd run into outside of his shop.

Geena hits the remote, turning off the DVD.

"Huh," Rob says. "I'd hoped those were videos of you. I would have loved to see you as a little girl."

Geena rolls her eyes. "We *were* kids together. Most people would say sixteen still qualifies as a girl."

"Didn't seem little to me. Not then," Rob says.

"I'm glad you sent me these," Geena tells him. "It was good to see my dad. And his father." She searches his face for a sign.

Would they ever talk about what they had seen? Not just this year, but last, too? They'd both seen Tom. That had been real. Finally seeing that down-on-his-luck man again had convinced

Rob. But what about Geena?

He nods, his eyes going distant. "Did you—" he starts.

"Did I what?" she presses.

For a moment, there is only silence as they stare at each other.

He shakes his head, breaking the tension. "Nothing. Been kind of a strange holiday this year. I should go."

She nods. "See you later, then? Pick you up at the store, take you out for dinner? Maybe you can finally get that kid of yours to come along."

Rob grimaces at the mention of his store. A few small-business accounting tasks are waiting for him—as is the final tally of his holiday profit. He doesn't need to know the results down to the last dime to know it's bad. He estimates his sales are down as much as fifteen percent from last year. The store, it seems, is standing on increasingly shakier ground.

"Yeah. Sounds good," Rob says. He kisses her quickly, and she walks him out, locking the door behind him.

Geena turns back to her coffee table, presses the power button on her laptop.

While it boots, she walks into her kitchen, where she removes an old antique bottle from the cabinet. The one she found sitting in the snow, beside a cardinal, on Christmas Eve.

It is Maxwell's liquor. It had showed her everything in the bar. Would it still?

She carries it back to the living room. To tell a good story, she thinks, you need to open your mind. To remember. To see clearly.

She had never seen more clearly in her life than she had when she'd sipped from that bottle—the same she'd seen Maxwell Ross leave with on Christmas.

There wasn't much liquor left.

But, she thinks, it might be enough to allow her a chance to put the real story of Ruby's Place on paper.

Did she dare?

The liquor could provide the details she'd been looking for. It could help her write the kind of story that could turn her into an honest-to-God, money-making writer.

Maybe, she thinks, she could even make enough to help Rob.

Outside, the cardinal taps what he hopes sounds like an S.O.S. against Geena's windowpane.

She finds herself smiling, not hearing it as a warning. Hearing instead a happy rhythm, like feet skipping, or a heart beating at the sight of a loved one. It's syncopated, she thinks, like a song she might even want to dance to.

The cardinal taps harder, more insistently as she makes her way back to the living room—and her laptop.

Don't do it, Geena. Don't. Everything will fall apart if you tell our secret. Don't you know that?

He flaps his wings and chirps, trying to insist his message not get lost in translation.

77.

~The Journey Continues~

Walter has already slipped the box—the one filled with all the details from this Christmas—into the back of the Sullivan memory bank for safekeeping.

It will sit. Waiting for next year.

So are you. Already, you're thinking about going back. Oh, no—you don't have to thank me for insisting you go to Ruby's. I knew it'd be a nice fit. It always is.

As for me? Did you ever stop to wonder how I knew about the place? Did you wonder what I was doing while you were in the midst of your reunion? I didn't spend the whole night watching your kids, after all.

Oh, I see. You want to know more: Did I have a reunion of my own? Who did I meet up with? Why, those are questions that will simply need to be answered next Christmas. Along with so many others. What will happen with Maxwell's bottle, for starters.

We'll talk again. We'll meet up the next time the vault in the memory bank is unlocked and the bright red neon sign pulses against a winter sky. When the snow begins to cover the square and a lone cardinal sits atop an old phone line, watching.

See you next year.

At Ruby's Place.

Come Back to Ruby's Place

Sentimental Journey is the third installment in the
Ruby's Place Christmas Series:

Find out how it all started with **Christmas at Ruby's**.

First love takes a starring role in the second installment of the
Ruby's Place series.

In the fourth installment (and finale) to the Ruby's Place series, readers are given the ultimate Christmas gift, as they discover for themselves the truth about Christmas Eve in this special nightspot.

Look for the full series Ebook, which includes all four books in a single download.

Check
HollySchindler.com
for availability

Holly Schindler

Holly Schindler is a multi-award-winning and critically acclaimed author of books for readers of all ages. She holds a master's degree in English (creative emphasis), and has taught writing courses at the collegiate level. Schindler has also mentored extensively: honing students' creative and scholastic writing, and providing developmental edits to both published and unpublished writers for novels in a variety of genres. A firm believer that reading is as creative an activity as writing, she has worked one-on-one with students in grades K-12 to improve overall literacy skills.

Schindler insists that nothing is quite as magical as a good story or an exciting "what-if." She is currently chasing down her next "what-if" as she writes her next book. She also loves hearing from her readers. If you'd like to get in touch or subscribe to her newsletters, please visit her online at:

HollySchindler.com